- 4 MAY 2021

1 0 JUL 2021

2 2 SEP 2023

13/10/23

1 0 MAY 2024

D0531361

WITHDRAWN FROM
BROMLEY LIBRARIES

To renew, find us online at:
https://capitadiscovery.co.uk/bromley
Please note: Items from the adult library
may also accrue overdue charges when
borrowed on children's tickets.

In partnership with
 Bromley

WEST WICKHAM
020 8777 4139 2/21

BETTER
the feel good place

'A ghost story that will get under the skin of the most
hardened reader' *Starburst Magazine*

'The perfect book for cold and wintry nights, prepare to be

Bromley Libraries

30128 80446 013 0

Books by Rachel Burge

The Twisted Tree
The Crooked Mask

RACHEL BURGE

HOT
KEY
BOOKS

First published in Great Britain in ebook in 2020

This paperback edition published in 2021 by
HOT KEY BOOKS
80–81 Wimpole Street, London W1G 9RE
Owned by Bonnier Books
Sveavägen 56, Stockholm, Sweden
www.hotkeybooks.com

Text copyright © Rachel Burge, 2020
Illustrations copyright © Leo Nickolls, 2020

All rights reserved.
No part of this publication may be reproduced, stored or transmitted
in any form or by any means, electronic, mechanical, photocopying or
otherwise, without the prior written permission of the publisher.

The right of Rachel Burge and Leo Nickolls to be identified as author and
illustrator of this work has been asserted by them in accordance with the
Copyright, Designs and Patents Act 1988

This is a work of fiction. Names, places, events and incidents are either the
products of the author's imagination or used fictitiously. Any resemblance
to actual persons, living or dead, is purely coincidental.

A CIP catalogue record for this book is available from the British Library.

ISBN: 978-1-4714-0920-2
Also available as an ebook and in audio

1

Typeset by DataConnection Ltd
Printed and bound by Clays Ltd, Elcograf S.p.A

Hot Key Books is an imprint of Bonnier Books UK
www.bonnierbooks.co.uk

This book is dedicated to Loki, trickster and master manipulator, and to Odin, he who has many names: Grimnir the Masked One, Ofner (opener), the one who breathed life into the first humans, and Svafner (closer), the gatherer of lost souls.

Dear Stig,

If you're reading this I guess that means you came back to the island. I waited as long as I could, but you said you'd only be gone for a few days and it's been three weeks, so I'm not sure what to think. I tried calling, but maybe something happened to your phone.

There's no easy way to tell you this, but the day you left I saw Nina's ghost through the cabin window. I recognised her from the photo you showed me and I'm sure it was her. If you went to visit her in hospital like you said, then you will already know, but if not I'm sorry.

I tried telling you at the time, but you seemed so defensive when I asked about her. I know things ended badly between you and you don't like talking about it, but I can't help feeling there's something you're not telling me. If there is, please – I need to know.

Nina has been terrorising the cabin, slamming doors and making things fly across the room. Mum's nerves can't take it. She's in a bad way and her visions have started again. This time she's drawing pictures of me at a circus. That's how I got the idea. I have to do something to make it stop, so I'm going to the place where Nina had her accident. There must be something she wants me to do. If I can figure it out, maybe she'll leave me alone.

1

I hope you're doing OK, anyway. Some days it's hard to believe everything that happened, and I wonder if the nightmares will ever stop, but I guess it's the same for you. I realise we haven't known each other long, but after everything we went through I hoped we'd always have each other to talk to. It's OK if you've changed your mind about things. I'll understand. Just call me, please.

Martha x

P.S. Gandalf is sitting by me and keeps whining and licking my hand. He says he misses you.
P.P.S. Please take care of Mum if you can. I'm worried about leaving her alone in the cabin.

1

MORE THAN JUST STORIES

At first there are only fir trees and then the circus appears: dripping with snow and glistening in the half-light, as strange and beautiful as a newborn fairy tale. I push away a wet spruce branch and step into the clearing. The black-and-gold striped big top thrusts its way into the sky, grazing the dark clouds above and dwarfing the smaller tents that surround it. At its pinnacle a tiny black flag whips and snaps on the wind.

I check my phone and my stomach tightens with anxiety – still no message from Mum – then I trudge towards the site entrance. The archway stands alone in a field of snow, no railings or fence to either side of it, arbitrary and incongruous like a portal to another world. Carved across the top are the words 'Circus of Myth & Mayhem' in letters a metre high, the black-and-gold paint flecked and peeling as if ravaged by countless winters. A grey-chested raven swoops onto the sign, landing heavily, and my breath catches as it winks its beady eye then flaps away with a caw.

When I step beneath the wooden arch I see that the walls are etched with hundreds of runes. Running my hands over them, I walk through and take a lungful of air that is thick with silence and wood smoke. Just passing through an entrance has no real significance, I know, yet somehow it feels different on this side: the wind crueller and the sky darker.

A planked walkway leads into the site. Outside the first tent is a board announcing '*Tickets - Billetter*' in flowing gold letters. The cold bites at my cheeks as I make my way towards it and look inside. No one: just a table, a cash register and an empty chair. All around me tents billow and groan in the breeze. Tethered by dozens of ropes, the big top looks like a hot-air balloon straining to take flight. Apart from the wind and the occasional *thwump* of sliding snow, the world is eerily silent. The taxi driver warned me the performance had finished for today, but there must be *someone* here.

I walk along the path and the back of my neck prickles, telling me I'm being watched. A figure is standing in the distance – a girl. I duck down the side of a tent and hurry towards her, about to call out, when a shiver runs down my spine. It's her. Nina. She has short dark hair and wears a white shift dress, her legs bare. I stand frozen to the spot while she looks at me, her eyes two inky pools of black, her face devoid of emotion.

4

A familiar knot of anger twists inside me. After everything Mum and I have been through, we deserve to be left in peace. We should be making a new life together on the island, helping each other come to terms with our magical heritage and mending our relationship. We should be watering the tree and making sure the dead never escape again. Instead I'm here – and all because of Stig's ex. I only spent a few days with him, so why is she haunting me, a girl I've never even met? Clenching my fists, I fight the urge to yell, 'What do you want?' but I know she wouldn't answer me, she never does. Suddenly she's gone and I'm left staring into space, my breath the only ghost on the air.

A slow, steady drumbeat makes me turn my head. Faint at first and then louder, coming from inside the big top. I climb over a frayed rope and reach for the canvas door, when a deep voice sounds behind me.

'*Vi er stengt til i morgen.*'

A man on stilts towers over me, wearing a white top hat and a tailcoat. A band of blue is painted across his nose like a mask, making his eyes and pale eyelashes appear even more startling. Tiny crystals dot his eyebrows and twinkle in his pointed beard and long blond hair.

The man takes several steps one way and then the other, moving all the time, and my neck aches to look up at him. He blinks at me in surprise, no doubt taking in my weird-looking eye and the scar on my cheek. For a brief moment I want to turn and hide my face, but I've promised myself I won't do that any more. Holding his gaze, I snap my mouth shut and try to remember the Norwegian I've learned

5

recently, but the words have gone from my mind, like someone took a drawer and emptied it out.

He leans down and smiles. 'The circus is closed until tomorrow.'

I consider taking my dictionary from my rucksack, but then manage, '*Snakker du engelsk?*'

The man laughs. 'Of course.'

My cheeks burn. 'Sorry, yes, you just spoke it.' I bite my lip, realising how stupid I must sound. 'I'm looking for someone. Well, not looking for them. I'm hoping to find someone who knew them.'

The frost giant waits patiently, a bemused look on his face. He glances at my left eye, the one that's blind, and then back to the other.

'Nina. She used to work here.'

The moment I say her name his expression changes, the playful smile replaced by a frown.

'The circus is closed.'

'Yes, I know. She was a trapeze artist and –'

'Sorry, I can't help you.'

'What about someone called Stig? He was her boyfriend.'

His eyes flash with suspicion. 'He left weeks ago.' The giant takes a few steps forward and back, then bends over and puts his hand on my shoulder. As soon as his glove touches me I feel the sharp edge of his grief. An image flashes into my mind: a cold impenetrable wall, each brick made up of anger, sadness and disbelief. Every time the press or a curious visitor asks about Nina's death the wall grows higher. I'm not sure when the accident happened, but it seemed recent from the way Stig talked. Something

6

about the man's raw sadness makes me think it can only have been a few months ago at most.

He gestures towards the road and I try to hide my disappointment. I could stand here all day and ask questions, but I know he wouldn't answer them.

'OK. Thanks anyway.'

I turn and trudge back the way I came, convinced I can feel the weight of his stare. After a few minutes I glance over my shoulder and sure enough he is watching me. I lower my head and walk a little further, hoping he will forget me. I will probably have to come back several times over the next few days and try speaking to different people. I don't know what Nina wants, but if her death wasn't an accident then someone here is responsible. I don't expect it to be easy, but eventually someone will have to be willing to talk to me about her. She must be haunting me for a reason. If I can discover what happened to her, maybe it will be enough to make her leave me alone.

I go a little further then look around again. The man bends his neck and walks into the big top, his legs moving effortlessly on stilts. Once he's gone, I lift my hood and head back into the circus, this time turning right towards the vehicles.

I move quickly, only stopping to catch my breath once I get past the row of closed-up food stalls and see the first caravan. There are dozens of them, along with trucks and trailers, spread out in a semicircle around one side of the clearing. They face in all directions, making a chaotic maze. The first vehicle I come to is a huge black trailer. I turn left and the smell of fresh coffee hits me, followed by frying onions. There are more signs of life: televisions flickering, the sound of a radio, people moving around inside their homes.

A teenage girl with long blonde hair turns the corner and walks towards me. She looks about my age, and is wearing a grey cloak with an elaborate fur collar and is holding the head of a wolf under one arm. Its huge hairy snout looks alarmingly real, until I notice the cut-out eyes and realise it's a mask.

'*Har du gått deg vill?*'

'Sorry, I don't speak –'

She smiles brightly. 'Are you lost?'

'I'm looking for someone. She works . . .' I hesitate, wondering how best to ask about Nina. I don't want to be turned away again.

The girl strokes the wolf's head as if she's soothing a dangerous animal. 'Are you here about the job?' The ugly mask seems to eye me suspiciously and I'm about to say no, when something strange happens. A muscle twitches in the wolf's cheek and its snout wrinkles. I can't have seen right, it must have been the wind ruffling its fur.

'Ruth interviewed the others in her tent. I'll get her for you.'

A prickle of alarm makes my face flush. 'No, don't worry. It's OK,' I say without thinking, then glance towards the big top flapping in the breeze. I don't know what the job is for, but I have my gift, so hopefully I can find out by touching this woman's clothes. Sitting an interview could be the perfect opportunity – a chance to talk to someone about the circus and the people who work here. I turn back to the girl with a smile. 'Actually, yes. If you could just point me in the right direction.'

Her face shows a hint of confusion, but her voice is full of warmth. 'Sure. That's her place there.' She points to a tired-looking caravan with tatty pink curtains. 'Ruth is expecting you?'

I nod and consider asking her what she knows about the job, when the wolf's head turns and fixes me with an empty-eyed stare. The movement is slight and barely perceptible, yet undeniable. There's something so unsettling about it that I take a quick step back. 'Yes. Thanks for your help.'

The girl smiles and then leaves, and I go over to the caravan and raise my hand to knock when I hear voices inside. A man says something I can't quite catch and then a woman speaks in an Irish accent. 'I know you feel bad about what happened, we all do, but you can't keep blaming yourself.'

A jungle of plants fills the caravan window and it takes me a moment to make out the occupants through the mass of leaves. The man looks to be in his seventies and has a shock of white hair, but I can't see the woman. He speaks in a lilting sing-song way like all Norwegians. 'You think I'm a superstitious old fool, but they are more than just stories.' He rubs his chin. 'I should never have agreed to change things. That poor girl, I should have known something terrible would happen.'

I step to one side, out of sight, and press my back against the caravan. Could they be talking about Nina? The woman raises her voice. 'I'm the tarot reader, Karl, not you. You couldn't have known, no one could.'

The door bangs opens and my heart jumps. I duck around the side of the caravan and it shifts slightly as Karl limps down the steps. Short and slightly built, he wears a camel-coloured duffle coat with big square pockets that only accentuate his diminutive frame. He has the look of someone who's spent his entire life outdoors: his tanned and leathery skin is creviced with wrinkles and his hair is a wind-blasted bush.

The woman jumps down after him, her auburn locks flowing in the breeze. She wears a white crochet shawl around her shoulders, though she can't be much older than thirty, and she's almost a foot taller than Karl. When she lays a hand on his shoulder and smiles tenderly, I feel awkward about spying on them. 'Why not let the new manager just get on with it? You've earned a rest after all these years.'

'Oskar?' Karl snorts with derision then limps away, and the woman chases after him. 'The world doesn't stop, you know. We need to move on!'

I follow them, determined to speak to Ruth. She said she's a tarot reader. If she's looking to hire a psychic, maybe I can do more than just sit the interview: perhaps I can actually get the job. My pulse races with anxiety at the prospect. I thought I'd only need to leave Mum for a few days, but if I start working here I may have to stay longer. But then I have to do something. I can't go home and risk Nina following me. It breaks my heart to think of Mum sobbing in fear and cowering in a corner as doors slam and crockery flies at our heads. At least if Nina is here, hopefully it means she isn't at the cabin.

A harsh caw sounds nearby. A raven sitting on the roof of the caravan opposite twitches its head this way and that, then caws again, more insistent this time. It flaps to a nearby branch where it watches me intently. Can I really do this? Part of me wishes I'd never had the idea, but it will be a good way to get to know the people here. If I'm one of them, they might talk to me about Nina. I have to do something to make her leave me alone, or Mum and I aren't going to have any kind of future.

There's another reason to work here too. If I make friends with people, maybe I can find out about Stig. Mum was right. I was naive to let a runaway I know nothing about stay in my grandma's cabin, especially after he'd broken into the place. But after everything that's happened, I'm not so naive any more.

I think back to the last few conversations we had before he left, and I'm convinced he was keeping something from me. Why else would he say Nina had recovered from the accident and was fine, and then change his mind the next day? When I asked about it he got defensive and changed the subject. I don't know where he is or why he hasn't contacted me for the past three weeks – maybe he had no intention of coming back to the island – but if he's hiding something or lying about what happened to Nina, this is my chance to learn why. He's either a good person or he isn't – and I intend to find out.

2

MASKED CREATURES PARADE

I hurry after the tarot reader and call out, 'Excuse me, sorry, can I talk to you, please?'

She stops and raises her eyebrows. 'Yes?'

'I wanted to ask about the job . . . You're looking for a psychic? I'm Martha.'

'Ruth.' She extends her arm and I notice that her wrist is covered with silver bracelets. They jangle as I shake her hand. 'I don't remember that name. Did you arrange an interview?'

'No, a friend mentioned it to me. I thought I'd just come by.'

'I see.' She pulls her shawl tight then glances at the sky as if I might have blown in on the wind. 'This friend of yours, is it anyone I know?'

I swallow, my mouth suddenly dry. 'No. It was someone I met in town. I'm kind of travelling at the moment.'

She frowns. 'Is that so?'

Most people see my cloudy white eye that stares in the wrong direction and the jagged scar on my cheek and quickly glance away, or they look at me with pity. Ruth does neither. I watch her expression, hoping it might soften, but it doesn't. She has a determined face: a square jaw and lively hazel eyes, the kind that can see right into you. Something tells me this isn't going to be as easy as I hoped. I look at my feet, worried she can tell I'm lying, but then hold my chin high and remind myself that I have an advantage. I have my gift.

We're standing on the wooden walkway near the big top. Drumming sounds from inside: soft, steady and hypnotic. Two Chinese girls pass by wearing matching black ballgowns, the bottoms splattered with red as if they've been dipped in blood. One of them has red roses in her hair and the other wears a hat with a white-handled knife tucked into the band.

Behind them is a man on stilts wearing a huge raven's head with a grey beak over his nose. A plume of blue-black feathers adorns his chest and thighs, and his arms and lower legs are covered with thin scaly grey material, with claws at the end of his fingers and toes. The bird-man twitches its head in my direction as it totters by and I see that its eyes are overlaid with orange film, a black dot at the centre. The effect is so realistic it's disturbing.

'What do you do?' asks Ruth.

'Sorry?'

'What kind of psychic are you? Tarot, palmistry, objects – what do you read?'

The man in the bird costume opens his arms and two huge feathered wings unfurl on the air. I pull my gaze back to the woman.

'I read objects . . . clothes.'

'Never heard of that before.'

The drumming is louder now, two soft beats and then a stronger one, getting faster. The raven moves his feet to the rhythm, twisting his body and lifting first one wing and then the other above his head. More masked creatures parade into the tent behind him: two wolves, a falcon, a boar and two cats. A girl with pointed ears and braided white hair whirls by in a purple cloak.

Resisting the urge to watch them further, I focus on Ruth. I need to say something that will convince her to give me a chance, and for a moment I consider telling her the truth. That I inherited my gift from an ancient Norse god and a mortal weaver woman who started my family line more than a thousand years ago, and I have the power to read clothing like all the women before me. My cheeks flush just thinking about how crazy I would sound. I wouldn't believe me, so why should she? Besides, I don't know anything about her or this place. For all I know, she might not be a genuine psychic and the readings they offer are just a bit of fairground fun.

'My mum taught me. I used to do psychic shows with her in London.' I don't know where the lie comes from, but she looks impressed. I swallow hard, hoping my face isn't as red as it feels.

14

'Grand. So you have experience working with the public?'
I nod and she asks, 'How many years?'

'Oh, lots. I have lots of experience.'

She purses her lips and I immediately know I've said something wrong.

'We need someone who's done this work before, sorry.'

She walks away and panic rises inside me. I reach for Ruth's arm and grasp her shawl, and it shows me a flash of memory. She lived on the streets years ago, and then one day an old lady stopped to talk to her. She gave her a job in her shop and let her sleep in the back. Ruth's gratitude wells up inside me and brings a lump to my throat. The shawl must be part cashmere. Wool holds emotions, but cashmere makes me feel them like my own. Maybe I can appeal to Ruth's sense of charity. If she thinks I have nowhere to go, she might look kindly on me, like the lady who helped her.

'Please. I'll work for free. I just need somewhere to sleep. Give me a chance and I won't let you down.'

She tilts her head and her expression softens. 'How old are you?'

'Seventeen.'

'And you're sure you can't go home?' She searches my face and I feel the sting of a tear. I might have lied to her about some things, but not that. I can't go back to the cabin and risk Nina following me. Mum is doing her best to accept our inheritance but she still struggles to believe that magic flows in our veins; that she sees visions of the future as well as being able to read clothing like me. Her mental health is so fragile, some days it feels like she's hanging on by a single thread. I can't let her fall apart. I won't.

15

Ruth glances about her. 'You know we're leaving Velfjord and going south next week?' I take a sharp breath and nod. I had no idea they were going to be travelling on so soon. If I don't want to go with them, I'll have to find out what Nina wants – and fast. Ruth sighs and I have a horrible feeling she's going to turn me away. Desperate now, I open my mouth to blurt out what I saw in her shawl, when she smiles. 'OK. I'm not promising anything, but I'll give you a try. Come on.'

She marches away and I hurry after her, around the side of the big top and past another two tents. Her long black coat trails out behind her and skims the snow as she walks. With her tall leather boots and her red hair flowing in the wind she could be a Viking warrior.

She stops before a wooden frame as high as a single-storey house, cut into the shape of a wolf's head. The doorway is the creature's wide-open mouth, complete with two white fangs fixed overhead, threatening to graze the heads of the tallest visitors. Above the cavernous black mouth is an enormous snarling snout, two yellow eyes, and a pair of ears.

The sight of it makes me feel nervous and I'm glad when Ruth shakes her head. 'That's the hall of mirrors. We're going in here.' She gestures to the small tent opposite. Propped outside is a blackboard in an antique-looking gold frame. Flowing handwriting announces: '*Psychic readings here today - Tarot (20 minutes) 250 NOK.*' Below that are some words I can't read. I see them and my heart sinks.

'I don't speak Norwegian.'

Ruth pulls back the canvas door and a waft of incense envelops me. 'That's OK. We have artists from all over the world, so it's easier to do the performances in English. We put it on all our flyers and posters; most of our visitors speak it.' She gestures for me to go through and I duck under her arm.

I don't know what I was expecting, but it wasn't this. Inside is a proper wooden floor painted in black-and-gold checks, a rustic oak table and two red velvet armchairs. Ruth presses a switch on the floor and an elaborate chandelier lights up above our heads. We could be in a swanky city bar, not a tent in a field.

'Wow, this place is amazing.'

She grins and gestures to a chair, her bracelets jangling. I sit down, feeling at home but oddly exposed too, as if I've walked onto a stage set.

'Sorry it's chilly. We use heaters, but it's not worth putting them on just now.'

I look around, taking in the colourful rug, floor cushions and ornate metal lanterns.

'So then, clothes reading. I've heard of watches and jewellery but material is a new one on me. Can it be anything?'

I nod and Ruth takes off her shawl. 'No rush, take your time.' She watches me intently and I shift in my seat. I feel awkward demonstrating my gift in front of someone. I remember the day I tried telling Kelly, my best friend at home in London. She said she believed me, but when she hugged me her coat was practically dripping with disbelief. I soon learned to keep it secret.

17

Now that Mormor, my grandma, is dead, there are only two people in the world who know about my gift: one is Mum and the other is Stig. I think about the letter I left for him at the cabin and worry washes over me. After everything we went through, I can't believe he would ignore my texts, even if he changed his mind about coming back to the island. Maybe something happened to him?

Ruth coughs and I close my eyes and force my attention back to the thoughts and emotions in the wool. I pull at the strands of memories, searching for an image. There's a man with sunken cheeks, Ruth's father maybe? I frown and grasp harder. She had a baby when she was a teenager. She had to leave . . . Shame and guilt wrap around my heart, but they leave as quickly as they came.

I open my eyes and Ruth is looking at me. Heat creeps up my neck and into my face. I rub the shawl between my fingers, determined to make it give up its secrets. Clothes often hold recent events, but important things – moments of profound pain or joy, our deepest hopes and fears, are stained into the material. I know from touching the shawl before that it contains great sorrow, so why can't I read it now? I focus hard and glimpse the man again. This time I tug at the memory . . . and the strand snaps. There is no emotion, no image. Nothing.

'So?' Ruth smiles kindly but I shake my head. My gift has never failed me before. Not once since it started six months ago, after I fell from the tree in my grandma's garden and lost my sight in one eye. I stare at the shawl in disbelief. For months I wanted it to stop. I hated being overwhelmed by impressions from people's clothes, and now . . .

Ruth is waiting. I have to tell her something. I don't know who the man is, or if he had anything to do with the baby. Not wanting to get it wrong, I say, 'Years ago a lady showed you a great kindness. She gave you a place to stay and you've never forgotten it.'

I bite my thumbnail then glance at her, worried I might have read her shawl wrong before. Her eyes widen. 'Yes!' Emotions play across her face: shock, joy, confusion. She blows out a sigh then laughs. 'Yes, you're right. And you got that just from touching my shawl?'

My shoulders drop. I haven't failed. And then my first worry is replaced by another. Perhaps I shouldn't let her know the truth. If people realise I can tell their secrets, they might be guarded around me; it could make it harder to find out about Nina. 'I get hunches sometimes, but mainly it's just saying things and watching to see people's reactions.' Ruth doesn't look convinced.

'You have kind eyes,' I continue. 'And you were willing to give me a chance, so I guessed that someone must have done the same for you once. The rest just came to me.'

She nods. 'Yes, tarot is a bit like that. I know the meanings of the cards but a lot of it is intuition. Things just pop into my head, but I read people too.' She pauses then adds. 'So, be honest with me now, how much experience do you have with the public?'

I don't like lying, but I have to get the job. I hold her gaze and say, 'I've done five or six psychic events with Mum.'

'And you saw clients of your own?'

'Yes.'

'Grand. I will introduce you to the new manager, Oskar. I can offer you a place to stay but it won't be anything fancy.'

I nod and she stands up. 'Just to warn you, Oskar can be . . . Well, you'll see.'

Ruth leads me to a caravan that's bigger and newer-looking than the rest then tells me to wait outside. I turn my back, not wanting it to seem as if I'm spying on her and Oskar through the window. She speaks quietly and I can only make out a few words, but I can tell she's persuading him to let me stay on site. He sounds young and speaks with only a slight Norwegian accent.

After a few minutes Ruth opens the caravan door and I climb the metal steps. Oskar is sitting at a table, head bent over a laptop. He's in his late twenties, with spiky blond hair, and wears square-rimmed glasses that are too big for his face. He holds a banana with one hand and taps at the keyboard with the other. He doesn't look up, though he must have heard me enter.

Ruth smiles awkwardly. 'Oskar, this is Martha, who I was telling you about just now.'

He looks me up and down. 'Wow, what happened to you?'

'Excuse me?'

He swallows and then jabs what remains of the banana in my direction.

Shocked, I glance at Ruth. She gives me a pained smile, like a mother embarrassed by a toddler but powerless to do anything about it. I'm used to people asking about my eye, but they aren't usually this blunt. I breathe in slowly and straighten my shoulders. 'I fell from a tree last summer. The fall severed my ocular nerve.'

'Climb a lot of trees, do you?'

A tiny huff escapes me. 'No.'

'Well, that's something.'

I think about telling him how the surgeon considered operating, so that my left eye would at least face forward instead of up and to the left, but decided it would be too risky. And then I come to my senses. I don't have to explain myself to anyone.

'So you're *psychic*, are you?' He grins, and something tells me that whatever I say will be met with ridicule. Before I can reply, Ruth interrupts. 'Like I say, I've tried her out and she's good.'

Oskar finishes eating and tosses the skin at a bin. It misses and lands on the floor, where it sprawls out like a malformed starfish.

'Are you going to put her in a veil or something?' he asks.

My fingers ball into fists. How dare he talk about me like I'm not here?

I raise my voice. 'Why? Is my face a problem?'

Ruth glares at him and then gives me an apologetic smile. 'I always wear a costume. Visitors like that kind of thing. I'm sure Oskar didn't mean anything by it.'

I ignore her and keep my gaze fixed on the idiot in front of me. 'You haven't answered my question.'

Oskar pushes his glasses up his nose and peers at me, as if mildly surprised by my audacity. 'No problem, quite the opposite in fact. The eye thing could play to your advantage. I'm sure Ruth can come up with a good story for the customers.'

He holds my gaze as if daring me to answer, and the words come out before I can stop them. 'Actually, my blind eye has nothing to do with me being psychic, but it can see the dead.'

He gives me a wary look then laughs. 'So you have a sense of humour.'

Ruth grabs my arm. 'Grand. A week's trial it is.'

She leads me to the door and I jump down the steps, relieved to get away. Once we're outside, she whispers, 'Sorry about that. When God was giving out charm that fecker was last in line. I'd give him a slap but the eejit pays my wages. And don't worry – I'll see that he pays you. I'm not having you work for free.'

I smile, filled with a sudden fondness for her that surprises me. I hadn't realised how alone and in need of a friend I was; her kindness means more to me than she knows.

Just then Karl, the old man I saw talking to Ruth earlier, comes limping in our direction. He hurries straight past us without saying a word then climbs the steps to Oskar's caravan and yells in Norwegian.

We watch through the window as Oskar jumps up and closes his laptop. 'Please. We speak English here, it's so much fairer on our international staff.'

'Staff? They are not staff. They are artists!' Karl's voice is clotted with rage, his accent thicker than ever. 'The seamstress must not make that costume.' He waves a black book in the air. 'I told you before we only do the myths in here; never anything else!'

Ruth rolls her eyes as if she's heard it all before. I want to stay and listen, intrigued by the mention of myths and determined to learn as much about this place as I can, but she drags me away. 'Come on. I'll show you to your caravan. It's near the forest; I hope you like trees.'

13

You can't trust anyone

The light is fading fast as we weave our way through the maze of trucks and trailers. A group of performers in white masks comes towards us, twisting their heads to look as they pass by. One of them stares a moment too long, eyes glittering behind an expressionless face, and I find myself shivering. I can't explain it, but it feels like I'm looking at a creature from another world and not a man in a costume, as if the performer and the mask are one, or the mask is wearing the person instead of the other way around.

Ruth says something about extra rehearsals and points out the canteen tent, but I barely notice. My mind is a whirl of questions. When we were in the cabin, Stig showed me a photo of Nina on his phone and told me she'd fallen from the trapeze. Karl said he'd known something bad was going to happen. If he was talking about her, why did Ruth say he shouldn't blame himself? Maybe he was at fault.

'Why was he so angry?' I ask.

'Karl?' she laughs. 'A few sandwiches short of a picnic, that one.'

I want to ask more, but I don't like to admit I overheard their conversation earlier. I need to wait until I can bring up the subject without it seeming strange. Ruth will probably be surprised I've even heard of Nina. Part of me wishes I'd told her the truth to start with, but then she might have turned me away and not given me the job. I don't want to tell her I lied. The whole point of working here is for people to get to know me and feel comfortable talking to me, and they aren't going to do that if they regard me with mistrust.

We trudge through the snow to the edge of the clearing and I pull my coat tighter. Dark fir trees tower over us, the tallest among them leaning inwards as if suspicious of the vehicles parked beneath their boughs. Ruth stops before a small dirty caravan half hidden beneath a mass of shivering branches. Greedy vines crisscross its rounded back, from which a pair of grimy windows stares out like hopeless eyes.

She tugs open the dented door and it squeals a rusty complaint. Inside isn't much better. There's a tiny sink, an oven, and a few dilapidated cupboards to my left. Facing the kitchen are a couple of small benches with a table fixed to the wall, which I'm guessing you pull down to eat. Beyond them are two sofas which run the length of the room. I don't know when the caravan was made, but orange and brown must have been in fashion.

I peer around a concertina door and find a toilet and discoloured shower. The air is damp and smells of musty socks. Ruth switches on an electric heater fixed high on the wall then opens a cupboard and tuts at the mouldy food inside.

'We'll soon have this place sorted out. Back in a tick.'

I smile and try to hide my disappointment. Ruth said it wouldn't be much, so it's not like she didn't warn me. Once she's gone I drop onto the lumpy sofa. Dead leaves cluster in the corners of the floor and the ceiling is strung with cobwebs. Perhaps I was wrong to come here. I let out a sigh and remind myself that the sooner I find out what Nina wants, the sooner I can go home.

I check my phone but there's still nothing from Mum, then open a side pocket of my rucksack and pull out the drawings she did before I left. The first one shows a group of creatures in tattered robes with animal skulls for faces. Each one holds a long pole, decorated with feathers and topped by a ram's skull. In another picture, men wearing antlers on their heads rise up from a swirl of fog. She's drawn other, creepier things, and I put them aside, looking for the ones of Stig.

The first drawing shows him by a caravan that looks a lot like this one. In the next, he's standing outside the big top, but his face is scrubbed out with angry black lines. I think about the night she drew it and suddenly I'm back in the cabin.

My eyes snap open to darkness, the sheets drenched with sweat. I stare across the room, half expecting to see claws creep under

26

my door. It was just a nightmare . . . not real. Taking a deep breath, I get out of bed and head to the kitchen for a glass of water.

Mum is sitting at the table in her nightdress, a sketchpad before her. The pencil in her hand moves back and forth scratching at the paper, though her eyes are closed. I know she has visions of the future and has to get them out of her head, but I've never seen her do it before. Part of me feels like I shouldn't be here, that I am intruding, but she looks so cold I can't just leave her.

'Mum, are you OK?'

I will her to open her eyes and smile at me, to say that everything is fine, but she doesn't. Her hand carries on drawing, moving with a will of its own. She looks so eerie and vulnerable with her long blonde hair hanging loose about her face, and I have a sudden fear that she might be unravelling; that she might never come back to me.

I walk over, then look at the paper and gasp. She's drawn Stig outside a circus tent. 'Mum, can you hear me?' I touch her shoulder and suddenly her hand moves faster, scoring out his face.

'Mum! Stop!' I shake her and her eyes open. She looks at me in a daze and I point at the drawing. 'Do you know where Stig is? Do you know what's happened to him?' She turns away, but I have to know. 'Is he in danger? Please, you have to tell me.'

'You should never have let him stay here,' she mutters.

Ignoring her, I grab the sketchpad and flick through the drawings. Among the many pictures of circus tents are creatures wearing tatty robes with skulls for faces, and a girl with strings attached to her arms and legs like a puppet. And then I see something that makes me turn cold. Mum has drawn a close-up of my face outside a big top, a look of anguish in my eyes and tears rolling down my cheeks.

She rips it from my hand. 'Promise me you won't go there, promise you won't leave me!' I reach out my arms, about to reassure her, when Gandalf gets up from his bed and growls. His grey fur bristles and a chill runs through me. He always does that when . . .

A cup slides across the kitchen counter with a sharp scraping sound. Then a plate leaps from the wooden dresser and smashes on the floor.

Mum rushes to the open door but it slams in her face. The light above our heads begins to sway and Gandalf bares his teeth at something I can't see. A picture jerks and then bangs against the wall and Mum leaps away, her eyes wide with terror.

I glare around the room, my heart hammering in my chest. I've only seen Nina through the window before, but I know it's her. 'What do you want?' I yell. 'Stig isn't here. He's gone!' Mum covers her face with her hands and sobs as sheets of paper fly into the air. 'Please, just leave us alone!' I scream. 'Leave us alone!'

The door bangs open letting in a rush of icy air and I snap back to the present. The memory of Mum's tear-stained face brings a lump to my throat and I rub my arms, feeling helpless. I would give anything to erase her fear, to be able to protect her. Ruth walks inside, carrying a cardboard box with a pile of bedlinen folded on top. She places it on the counter then unpacks cleaning stuff, along with teabags, milk, and bread and cheese. 'The canteen tent opens at seven for breakfast and does lunch from twelve. Dinner starts at six, but if you want to eat here I've brought you a few things.' She pulls out some tins then opens a cupboard above the sink to reveal a microwave.

I take a moment to calm my thoughts and then go over to her. 'Thanks, Ruth.'

She pulls on some rubber gloves and scrubs the grubby inside of a cupboard, while I pick up a rag and go to war with the cobwebs. I expect her to ask what I'm doing here or why I left home, but she doesn't. She yawns, and I notice how tired she looks. Maybe that's why she isn't making conversation. Part of me welcomes the silence, but I need to find out about Nina.

Eventually I say, 'So how long have you worked at the circus?'

She answers without looking up, 'Longer than I should have, probably.'

'Years then?'

'Uh-huh.'

'And the acrobats, have they been here a long time?'

'Depends. We get artists from all around the world. At the moment we have performers from China, Russia, Nigeria, India and Mexico as well as various places in Europe. Some stay for six months, others have been here much longer.' Ruth wipes her forehead then adds. 'They're incredibly talented. You should go to the show tomorrow.'

I nod, thinking I'd like to see the kind of things that Nina did. And then I shiver, remembering that Stig said she fell from the trapeze. I don't know how it happened though, as he didn't go into detail. Maybe there's a way I can get Ruth to talk about the accident. I glance at her face and say, 'It always looks so dangerous, up there on the trapeze, I mean.'

Her expression darkens and she scrubs the cupboard with renewed vigour. When she doesn't say anything, I risk adding, 'I guess it's safe though?'

'Hmm.' She reaches for a bottle of cleaner, fixing me with sharp brown eyes. 'So what brings you to Norway? Are you just travelling through?'

I shake my head, disappointed at the change of subject. 'I'm staying on Skjebne in the Lofoten Islands with my mum. My grandmother was Norwegian.'

'Was?'

'She died last month.'

Ruth's gaze softens. 'Oh, I'm sorry to hear that.'

I hold back a tear and look away. It wasn't long ago that I was rushing to catch my flight at Heathrow and then boarding the ferry to the island, excited to see Mormor. I'd known something was wrong when she hadn't answered my letters, but the last thing I expected to find was a random boy living in her cabin. I was so angry at Stig for breaking in that I almost didn't believe him when he said she'd died. It might have been stupidly trusting of me to let him stay, even if he had nowhere to go and would have frozen to death otherwise, but it helped to have him there. Losing Mormor was the worst thing that ever happened to me. He was someone to talk to when I had no one.

Thinking about him makes my head pound. There must be a reason he hasn't been able to text. I hope he isn't hurt.

'So will you be going back to London soon?' asks Ruth.

'No, we're going to stay.' I don't mention that we don't have a choice. Somehow I doubt she would believe that Yggdrasil, the Norse world tree, is real and growing in my grandma's back garden and Odin has tasked my family line with watering it.

As I wipe down the walls I ask Ruth where she lived before and how she came to do tarot but she offers such meagre answers I soon give in to silence. All I learn is that she left Ireland when she was my age, and that the lady who saved her taught her to read people's fortunes. She doesn't say anything about having a baby. I'm glad she doesn't ask me any more questions. I feel bad about lying to her, especially as she's been so kind.

I know better than anyone the damage that lies can do. If Mum had told me about our gift and the fact that Mormor had died, I would have known to water the tree and the dead would never have escaped. I realise she was trying to protect me, and we're trying to put things right – we promised no more secrets – but I still can't forgive her for keeping the truth from me.

Ruth peels off her rubber gloves then drops them into the box that held the food and bedlinen. 'Now then, you'll be needing somewhere to sleep.' She pulls out one of the sofas, turning it into a bed, then wrestles a duvet into a cover and shakes out some sheets. They smell clean and homely and I fight a yawn.

She finishes and straightens up. 'You remember where I am?' I shake my head and she points to the left. 'A few minutes that way, just past the big costume trailer. The performance starts at noon tomorrow so we need to be in the psychic tent by half past one, ready for when people come out.'

I nod and she puts the cleaning stuff back into the box. 'I'm seeing a friend tonight, but come to mine for dinner tomorrow?'

I touch her hand. 'Thanks – for everything.'

She smiles then pulls me close and whispers, 'Things will get better, you'll see.' Her arms hold me tight, as if she knows how much I need a hug. Her warmth is so comforting that I want to stay there, but her shawl . . . This time it shows me the baby she left behind. Shame, regret and guilt pour out of her. I pull away, the emotions more than my heart can hold.

Ruth hoicks up the box and I open the door, the icy wind so shocking it takes my breath away. The moon is a pale silver disk, shrouded almost entirely by cloud. All around us dots of light shine in the dark, some from caravans nearby and others from far away. It makes me think of ships on the ocean. Adrift.

Ruth says, 'Sleep well,' then walks away and vanishes into the night.

As soon as she's gone the dark feels different. Like it's alive and watching me. The giant shape of the big top lurks in the distance, outlined by swaying strings of yellow lights. Beyond it, I can just make out the wolf's head that marks the entrance to the hall of mirrors. I turn away, not wanting to think about its hungry eyes and gaping mouth.

A gust of wind yanks the door from my grip. Something hits the caravan roof with a thud, a branch maybe, and the light in the kitchen area flickers. Fighting the wind, I pull the door closed and turn the flimsy lock. The hairs on my arms rise up on end and I have the feeling that someone is standing behind me.

Tap. Tap. Tap. Coming from the window opposite.

I spin around and glare at the closed curtains, my heart racing. There won't be anything out there in the dark, but what if . . . Holding my breath, I stand still and listen. Nothing. Just the lonely wail of the wind. I let out a shaky sigh and the sound comes again: three urgent taps. Steeling myself, I rip open the curtains. A mass of fir branches writhe against the glass as if the caravan is being consumed by the forest.

I go to shut the curtains, annoyed at myself for being so jumpy, and then I see her out in the darkness: a girl in a white dress, her legs bare. She reaches a hand to her throat, the whites of her eyes black. Then I notice my reflection and realise I'm wrong – she isn't outside. She's behind me. I spin around but the caravan is empty. When I look at the window again, she's gone.

My phone buzzes on the counter and my heart leaps into my throat. Six texts and nine missed calls from Mum. Reception is always bad on the island; the messages must have been stored up then sent through all at once. I phone her and she answers instantly.

'Martha, thank God. Are you at the hotel? Where have you been? I've been trying to reach you all day.'

She sounds agitated and I feel bad for making her anxious. I forgot she booked a room for me in the nearby town. I should have phoned to let them know I wouldn't be coming.

I drop onto the bench, my legs shaky. 'Please don't worry, Mum. I'm OK. I had a change of plan. I'm staying at the circus, in a caravan.' The line goes quiet and I wonder if she's annoyed with me. After she did the drawings, we went to the harbour so I could go online. A few search terms – *Nina, accident, Norway, circus* – brought it up instantly. It was the circus she had drawn. We both knew I was going to come here.

Still no answer; maybe we've been cut off. 'Mum, are you there? I'll come home as soon as I can, I promise.'

Her voice is a faint whisper. 'There's something I'm not being shown.' And then I hear the sound of a pencil scratching at paper. Perhaps I was wrong to leave her. Has she been drawing all day? What if she doesn't eat or sleep? What if she forgets to water the tree? The thought of the dead escaping again and another *draugr*, a walking corpse, attacking the cabin makes my stomach feel weak. I should be there with her.

Her breathing quickens. 'A game is in play.'

'What do you mean, a game?'

'Not everyone is who they appear to be.'

I hear the sound of frantic sketching and when she speaks again there is panic in her voice. 'You're not safe, Martha. Please, you have to be careful. You can't trust anyone.'

4

GRIMNIR THE MASKED ONE

It's been raining all morning and the sky is a strange eerie yellow. The light feels too bright, forced almost. It reflects off the gold stripes of the tents, the glare so bright it hurts. I close the caravan door behind me and rub my aching head. What with worrying about Mum and the wind and the nocturnal animal noises of the forest, I didn't sleep well.

I glance up at the giant fir trees and feel myself grow smaller. Hundreds of tall thin trunks stand in close formation, their heavy green boughs dripping with snowmelt. The forest feels darker and more foreboding than it did yesterday, the trees looming over the clearing as if they uprooted themselves and crept closer to us in the night.

I head into the site, keen to see where Nina worked and hopefully talk to someone who knew her, before I have to head for the psychic tent. The place is a buzz of activity: people chatting and laughing outside their caravans, some performers hurrying about in full costume and makeup and others in jeans and coats. A man in a dressing gown is standing on the steps of a caravan, his face coated in white paint. He sips from a mug then throws the dregs on the ground and sees me looking. With a wave of his hand, he changes his expression from a frown to a grin, and then mimes pulling off his face. He pokes out his tongue and I smile warily, unsure if he's being friendly or not.

I keep walking, past the canteen tent and on towards the row of shiny black trailers glistening with rainwater. The sugary smell of waffles drifts on the icy breeze, getting stronger with each step I take, and I feel my stomach rumble. It's strange to think that Stig was living here just weeks ago. I know he helped Nina train, but I'm guessing he had other friends at the circus too. I check my phone – no new notifications – and a familiar disappointment tugs at my heart. After everything we went through, I was sure he would come back, but maybe I didn't mean as much to him as I thought. My worry hardens into something brittle and I shove my phone into my pocket, determined not to dwell on it.

When I get near the entrance, I stop and watch people file into the circus. Parents with children, old people and couples, all bundled up in hats and coats and armed with umbrellas. They trail in through the archway, dutifully passing beneath the sign and leaving the surrounding snow untouched. Curiously, they don't queue once they get inside. Instead they mill around the ticket tent, chatting happily and somehow knowing whose turn it is next.

A girl waits by the door of the big top, taking tickets. She wears a long brown cloak with feathers around the collar and an ornate feathered mask that covers her eyes. Noises drift out from behind her: a steady rhythmic drumming accompanied by male voices singing a haunting lament. She moves to the music, hopping from foot to foot like a bird that wants to take flight. There's something hypnotic about the music and the flow of people, and I find myself walking behind them, caught up in the excitement. I want to see the kinds of things that Nina did on the trapeze. I want to see the performance that Stig would have watched.

Once the last few people have entered, I approach the girl on the door.

'I work here, with Ruth in the psychic tent. Is it OK to watch?'

She runs her tongue over her glossy red lips then says in a French accent, 'Sure. Sit anywhere you like.'

I step into a narrow tunnel lined with billowing drapes of material. Strips of white fabric hang down, obscuring my view. I push them aside and emerge to see a huge tree prop in the centre of the ring. Surrounding it are rows of wooden chairs arranged in tiers. I climb the steps of the nearest aisle then find a vacant seat and glance around.

Tall metal pillars stand about the tent like cranes, poles forming an elaborate skeleton beneath the stretched skin of the big top. Sleeping spotlights nestle in the rafters, waiting to shine on the dark ring below. I didn't notice at first, but the floor is painted with three interlocking golden triangles, the centre of the design obscured by the base of the tree. I know the symbol – it's Odin's *valknut*.

My pulse quickens and I touch my chest where my neck-lace used to be. I made the charm when I was living in London, before I even knew about my heritage. Why would it be painted on the floor? Karl said something about doing myths, so perhaps the circus performs stories from Norse mythology. Stig didn't mention it, though he didn't say much about the place at all. Maybe the tree is supposed to be Yggdrasil, which holds the realm of the gods in its branches and beneath its deepest root the underworld. The tree at my grandma's cabin. Excitement dances inside me at the thought.

A recorded announcement plays in Norwegian, followed by English. 'Ladies and gentlemen, boy and girls, giants, dwarves and elves . . . please take your seats. The show is about to begin!'

The lights dim and the last murmurs of conversation die away. Dry ice billows across the ring, a horn blasts out and suddenly the atmosphere changes, the buzz of anticipation replaced by nervous tension. The drumming slows and there's a soft rattle and jingle of bells. A surge of energy thrums through the room and I have the prickly feeling of exhilaration I always get before a storm.

A young child's voice speaks. 'There was a time long ago, a time before remembering, when the old gods walked among us. We have not forgotten their names; we have not forgotten their stories, for we are the storytellers, the dreamers of the old ways. You have stepped through our gateway and heard our calling. Now it is time to awaken. It's time to bid the gods hail and welcome!'

A spotlight comes on, highlighting an old man on a throne, seated in front of the tree with his head bowed. He has a long grey beard and wears a hooded cloak. Rolling mist obscures his legs and feet. I lean forward. There's something moving within the fog: creatures in rags wearing pale masks. They creep and crawl, half hidden within the churning smoke.

The ringmaster strides towards the audience. He wears a red cape and a top hat and carries a silver cane. His eyes are lined with black and there are runes painted on his cheeks. He opens his arms wide. 'Velkommen! Welcome to the world of myth and mayhem. Our story begins with the All-Father and it ends with him. For he is Ofner, opener, the one who breathed life into the first humans, and he is Svafner, closer, the gatherer of lost souls.'

The ringmaster points his cane to the man on the throne. 'You may know him as Odin or Wotan, but he has many names.'

A rush goes to my head, making me feel woozy. Odin started my family line with a mortal woman. Impossible as it seems, his blood runs in my veins. Being here, watching part of my own history brought to life, makes me feel humbled and a tiny bit proud.

The hooded figure bangs his walking staff ominously then looks up to reveal a white mask, the left eye painted black. He speaks slowly in a deep voice and a warm thrill of excitement swirls inside me. 'A single name have I never had since first I walked among men. Wanderer, Wayfarer, One-Eyed, the Hanged One, Grimnir the Masked One am I.'

Tiny lights flicker and explode into life on the tree behind him, starting from the roots and surging up the trunk to spark along its branches. The creatures spin away as the mist subsides and the ringmaster addresses the audience. 'He has two wolves, Freki and Geri, the ravenous ones.' Performers wearing wolf masks bound into view and prowl around Odin's feet. One of them howls and the man sitting next to me claps and cheers.

The ringmaster turns and does a little hop before bounding across the ring. 'The All-Father too is ravenous. It is not meat he craves, but knowledge. Each morning he sends his two ravens out into the world and each night they return and whisper their findings to him.'

A spotlight highlights the trapeze and I crane my neck upwards. Two performers in feathered costumes, grey beaks fixed over their noses, are poised dangerously high above the tree. The drumbeat gets faster and then one of them launches himself forward and opens his wings. He leaps into nothing and my heart falters. All around me people gasp. For a moment I think he's going to fall, but he catches hold of a second trapeze with one hand. The audience lets out a collective sigh and I want to look away, but I can't. I stare wide eyed, mesmerised by the magic of it. And then I remember that Nina fell from the trapeze in this ring. Did she slip while she was training, or did it happen during a show like this?

The ringmaster's voice booms out. 'The ravens' names are Huginn, thought, and Muninn, memory. Odin fears for the return of Huginn, yet more does he fear for Muninn.'

The second performer opens his wings and leaps into empty space. His wrists are caught by the first and I swallow, my mouth dry, as he swings to the other trapeze. The audience gasps and 'ah's as the two men take it in turns to somersault through the air.

A light picks out the ringmaster, now seated high on a platform, though I didn't see him climb the metal rigging. He points at the floor and says, 'Odin's wife Frigg sits at her spinning wheel where she spins her magic into being.' The goddess is new to me and I watch entranced, wanting to drink in every word, as if knowing her story will bring me to some new understanding of myself.

Nine women wearing silver catsuits dance into the ring. Each of them carries a strip of white gauze material, so light it floats on the air. They cartwheel in a circle, their long ribbons flowing out behind them to create a shimmering wheel. I had no idea Odin's wife was a spinner, just like the mortal woman who started my family line with him. Maybe the two things have always been connected: cloth and magic.

The ringmaster climbs down and continues, 'Though Frigg knows the fate of all beings, she tells no one.' The women exit the ring and the lights dim, leaving a single spotlight on the tree. The ringmaster drops to his knees and proffers his arms in worship. 'Odin, hungry to learn the secrets of fate, knocked upon the door of the Norns, three women who weave destiny in the mighty tree Yggdrasil.'

The sound of howling wind plays and three cloaked figures on stilts emerge from inside the trunk. They have long dark hair and wear masks covered with bits of twig and leaves. I lean closer, awed by the knowledge that the Norns are real and I have met them. When I climbed the tree last summer, it was their features I saw emerge from the bark; it was because of them that I fell and lost the sight in my eye. Later, I saw them as three women – one old, one middle-aged and one young – chanting and weaving silver threads of light, weaving fate. Reading my ancestors' journals, I realised the Norns always appear to the women in my family before we discover our gift of reading clothes. Meeting them wakes us to our destiny.

I watch with fascination as one of the women totters forward and tilts her head as if surveying the audience. The other two step out from behind her, one to the left and one to the right. They reach out their arms, their fingers splayed wide, hands dancing and twisting and feeling the air. Mirroring each other's movements, they jerk and bend their bodies like marionettes coming to life.

The lighting changes to a red glow and the wind builds to a scream. The ringmaster announces, 'When the Norns would not tell him the secrets of fate, Odin hanged himself from the tree.'

Thunder booms and the man on the throne stands up. His powerful voice commands the attention of the room. 'I know that I hung on that windy tree for nine long nights, wounded with a spear, dedicated to Odin, myself to myself.'

The ringmaster gets to his feet and adds, 'He was almost at the point of death when he looked into the well of wisdom beneath.'

Odin bends his head and intones, 'Downwards I peered; I took up the runes, screaming I took them.' He flings his arms wide and lets out a terrifying cry – a long, drawn-out shout of pure pain and passion. Gasps sound around me and a child cries. I glance along the row of faces beside me. Some look mesmerised, others shocked and slightly afraid. A shiver of wonder runs through me to realise that the myths are just stories to these people. Even those who believe in the old gods don't know the full story: that a weaver woman helped Odin after he cut himself down from the tree and they started a new family line together, women with a magical ability to read clothing, women like me.

A gurgling noise makes me glance over my shoulder. I turn and my blood runs cold. Nina is right behind me. Sitting in a chair and gazing at the ring. Her pale skin is marbled blue and her lips are dried and cracked. I jump up and the couple next to me frown and the people further along the row tut. And then I realise how crazy I must seem, staring at an empty chair.

'Sorry, I'm . . . I . . .'

I run down the steps. The girl with the feathered mask isn't there and I tug at the canvas door. Eventually I get it open. I glance behind me and Nina is in the same place, only now she's standing up, her hands desperately clawing at her neck.

5

A SEAT AT THE TABLE

I hurry away from the big top then stop and catch my breath. Nina has never got that close to me before. Doors would slam in the cabin and things would fly off shelves, but I never saw her do it. She's only ever appeared in the distance, looking in through a window or watching as I watered the tree.

I shake my head, angry at myself for getting scared and running away like that. The whole point of being here is to find out what she wants. The way she clutched her throat, it was like she was trying to tell me something. I knew she wanted me to come here. The realisation strengthens my resolve and I take out my phone to check the time. Twenty past one. I decide to go back and watch the end of the performance, then realise where I'm meant to be and my stomach drops.

By the time I get to the psychic tent my heart is racing and my hands are sweaty in my gloves. The sign outside now advertises tarot readings, along with the words: *psychic clothes reader – new. English speakers only.* The thought of having to work instead of talking to people who knew Nina is frustrating, but I can't see a way to avoid it. I run my hands over my hair, hoping I look vaguely presentable, and then step through the open door.

Ruth is inside with her back to me, lighting incense and wafting the smoke.

'Sorry I'm late.'

She turns around and for a moment I wonder if it's the same person. There are tiny plaits in her hair and a band of red is painted across her eyes and nose. She wears a long skirt and a white blouse with a brown leather corset over it. An ornate broach with two ravens is pinned on her lapel, the chain hooked to the other side. It reminds me of the jewellery I used to make and I have a sudden pang of homesickness. When our things arrive from London, my jewellery stuff is the first thing I'm going to unpack.

'Wow, you look amazing,' I tell her.

'Ah, go on with you.'

It's not just Ruth who's had a makeover; the room looks different too. The oak table is covered with a black cloth and has been moved to one side, along with the armchairs. Shiny gold material hangs to my left, creating a separate area. Ruth pulls the curtains to reveal two armchairs, a table with flickering lanterns and a vintage alarm clock.

'I've set you up in here. Don't forget to keep an eye on the time. Each reading lasts twenty minutes. Sandrine will take the money on the door and let people in, so you don't have to worry about that.' Ruth gestures to take my coat and I shrug out of it, feeling exposed. She hangs it over the back of a chair. 'Right, I think we're all set. There's water under the table. If you need anything just give me a shout. I'm not far away.'

Heat prickles up my neck. She's so close, she'll be able to hear everything I say. She'll know if I clam up or trip over my words. 'Don't people want privacy?' I ask.

Ruth frowns. 'Once we're both talking, it's easy to zone out. Customers will be too busy listening to you to notice anyone else in the room. I'm sure you've noticed that yourself at events.'

She gives me a quizzical look and I shift my weight to the other foot. The girl from the big top, who must be Sandrine, pokes her head in the door, still wearing a feathered mask over her eyes. She waves and I smile, grateful for the interruption. Lying always makes me feel uncomfortable. I've never worked with the public or done anything like this. It can only be a matter of time until I'm found out. Sandrine takes a compact mirror from her cloak pocket and applies a fresh slick of red lipstick, then blows herself a kiss. 'Ready when you are. *Bonne chance*.'

Ruth mouths *good luck*, then steps away and closes the curtains behind her.

I drop into an armchair and wipe my palms on my jeans. I don't feel ready for this. I should have asked Ruth more questions. What if I run out of things to say? What if I get people who treat it as a joke, or what if they don't like what I tell them? Worse, I realise that I don't actually *want*

46

to know strangers' secrets. I've spent months trying to avoid touching people's clothes, not wanting to get close, and now I have to use my gift to give them advice.

I reach under the table for some water and my hands shake as I unscrew the lid. I take several big gulps and nearly choke. Two shiny black shoes stand before me. I look up and see a man with shoulder-length red hair, brushed back from his forehead. A smile edges across his face, and though he's not conventionally handsome, there is something charmingly attractive about him. He must have come in while I was getting the water, though I don't know how I didn't see him.

He points at a chair. 'May I?'

I cough and splutter, then wipe my chin. 'Sorry, yes. Please do.'

He wears a long green coat, which he sweeps under him as he sits. 'Thank you. It's so nice to be offered a seat at the table. No one wants to force their way inside when they can be extended a proper invitation.'

I smile and try to place his accent. He doesn't sound English, yet I don't think he's Norwegian either. He fixes me with a lopsided grin and I notice his lips are marked with tiny scars. His amber eyes glitter with mischief as he leans forward and searches my face. 'So how does this work?' He looks over his shoulder then whispers, 'Would you like the shirt off my back, or my trousers perhaps?'

Just my luck to get a weirdo as my first client. I glance at the curtain, thankful Ruth is on the other side. I can hear her talking about the Devil card and saying to be wary of false perceptions. He nods in her direction. 'She's right, you know. Not everyone is who they appear to be.'

47

I narrow my eyes, trying to get the measure of him, when something odd happens. At first my brain can't understand what I am seeing. His appearance shifts. Almost imperceptibly, the way the sea goes light and then dark when a cloud passes overhead. His top lip becomes a little thinner, his eyes a slightly darker shade and set deeper in his skull, his hair a little more receding. Subtle differences that on their own would go unnoticed, but together are impossible to ignore.

I'm so tired I'm imagining things – either that, or the flickering lamplight is playing tricks on me. I drop my gaze and clench my jaw, determined to stay in control. 'If you can lay your hand on the table, please.'

He smiles and extends his left arm.

I touch his coat sleeve but there's nothing. It's blank. Swallowing my panic, I try again. There has to be some image or memory; some kind of impression. I tug at the material with my mind. Nothing.

He laughs and an image pops into my head. He's standing before a crowd of shadowy faces. At first I think they're sleeping with their eyes open, but then I realise that they don't have eyes. He sweeps his hand across them, bathing them in green light, then turns and grasps the head of a sleeping wolf. Green flames flicker around it and the creature howls. There is something nightmarish about it and I pull my hand away.

'You didn't hold onto it, did you? You let it go.'

His voice is low and edged with accusation. I glance at his face, realising he was projecting an image for me to catch. A flicker of panic flames inside me. Who *is* this man? It's like he's trying to provoke me or test me. Refusing to be intimidated, I touch his sleeve again. This time I close my eyes and sense shifting sands and waves on a beach, and then I see a net. It's like he wants to draw people in and catch them. Not necessarily to hurt them, just to tangle them up. It's a game he plays.

'I think you like playing tricks on people. You enjoy toying with them, sometimes a little too much.'

He thumps the table and guffaws, then wags a finger at me. 'You're good! But then I knew you would be. He wouldn't have chosen you otherwise.'

'Who's chosen me? Oskar, you mean?'

He gets up and steps towards the curtain, then glances back with a twisted grin. 'This is going to be such fun!'

I stare after him, my pulse racing. When he doesn't return, my shoulders drop and I let out a sigh. A fly buzzes around my ear – strange in winter – and I knock it away. Something the man said sounded familiar. *Not everyone is who they appear to be . . .*

I turn the conversation over in my mind but beneath every word is a crawling mass of insects. Nothing feels certain, there are only shifting sands, a sense of not being on steady ground. I frown, wary of letting my imagination run away with me. I guess there are always going to be a few odd customers, especially at a circus. I'm sure he didn't mean to frighten me. I take a sip of water and the fly buzzes around the room and lands on the bottle. It crawls across the surface and goes inside and I look away. No matter how hard I try, I can't shake the feeling that something isn't right. There was something chilling about the way the man smiled at me. Why do I have the feeling he knows something I don't?

6

IT'S NOT THE STIG I KNOW

I must have read for eight or more people. A few treated it as a joke, but most of them were desperate for advice. After the strange man was a woman with a baby. She handed me her scarf and asked if she could trust her husband. At first I couldn't get anything, and then I saw an image of her checking his phone. She knew he was having an affair; she was just afraid to confront him. The wool was sodden with pain but there was strength there too. I told her what I'd seen and said she'd get through it, whatever happened, and she wept and thanked me.

Next was a man whose grown-up son had committed suicide. I touched his gloves and described the happy memories I had seen – the summers they had spent fixing up a boat and going sailing. He blamed himself but there was nothing he could have done. I held his hand and told him so, realising that he just needed to hear it; he needed someone to say the words out loud.

After that was an elderly lady who had lost everything in a fire, including her cat Charlie Boy. Her husband had died from cancer on the same day a year previously. She grabbed my arm and sobbed. What did it mean, why did it have to happen, had she done something wrong? I tried to comfort her but I didn't know how. She left shaking her head, and I felt awful, knowing that I'd failed her.

Then there was a man with anorexia, a teenager being bullied, a woman jealous of her sister, and a man in love with his boss. Many of them walked in saying one thing, but their clothes told a different story. It was as if they had pretended to be someone else for so long, wearing a mask of respectability or playing the role of victim, they had lost all sense of themselves. As the session progressed, something unexpected happened. Once I told a customer what I had seen in their clothes, their mask slipped and I saw the real person beneath: vulnerable, hurt, and confused.

Closing my eyes, I think back over their faces. I rub my temples and let out a heavy breath. So much pain and anger, so much fear and regret and love and hope. Such raw fragility. I felt honoured and humbled to have been able to share it with them, but now I feel empty. Like a cloth wrung dry.

'How are you doing?'

I open my eyes and Ruth is peering around the curtain.

'Fine, thanks.'

'You sure? You look a bit tired.'

I nod and do my best to smile. If I've managed to offer just one person a little comfort, then feeling drained is worth it. But it's not that. Something doesn't feel right. I'm not sure I could explain, even if I tried.

'You've done great. Why don't you call it a day?'

'If you're sure.'

'Of course. See you for dinner later. Is seven OK?'

'Thanks.'

I pull on my coat then step outside. After the heaters and cloying incense, the blast of cold air is a welcome shock. The rain has stopped but the sky is pockmarked with grey, smothering what's left of the sun. I glance at the hall of mirrors opposite and zip my coat higher. Maybe it's the dark clouds, but the yellow eyes of the wolf seem almost alive, watching over the site with sinister intent. Beneath them, the creature's gaping doorway of a mouth hangs open like a dare, too black and too empty. Why do I feel like it's jeering at me?

I turn away and focus on Nina. I need to speak to people if I'm going to find out what really happened to her. I head along the walkway, determined to explore the other tents and find some of the performers. Someone must have been friends with her or have known Stig.

The big top stands to my left. I can't see it on my blind side but I can hear the billowing canvas and sense its looming presence. At first there are dozens of visitors milling about, but then I follow the walkway around to a smaller tent and suddenly there's no one. The circus feels different without crowds of people, abandoned almost. I glance over my shoulder, hoping to see someone. There's a couple with

52

a child holding a green balloon waiting by a food truck. Otherwise, the path is empty.

I turn back and gasp. The Norns are scuttling towards me on stilts, their black cloaks huddled together, their spindly stick legs moving like a spider. Their masks are crudely made and covered with clumps of leaves and twigs as if they've just crawled out from the earth.

One of them wears a large pair of rusty shears tied around her middle. She reaches a jerky, hesitant hand towards me and her mask raises its eyebrows. I step back, my heart fluttering. The wood moved, I'm sure of it. The other two women take several tiny steps to either side, their stilts tapping on the walkway, until they're surrounding me. I look from face to face, trying to understand. For a moment, I think they're going to say something, but then they point into the distance and scurry off, disappearing around the side of a tent as if they were never there.

I press my hand to my chest and try to compose myself. Watching the Norns in the ring was mesmerising, but coming face to face with them was unnerving. I know they're only women dressed up, but I don't like the sense that the actual events of my life are being mirrored around me. It feels unreal, as if I'm in a dream. It's not the performers parodying the gods that disturbs me, it's that they're too convincing. And wooden masks shouldn't *move*.

Blowing out a deep breath, I try to forget the encounter and keep walking. The first tent I come to has a chalkboard outside, propped on a wooden chair: *Knivkasteren*, and underneath, *Knife-thrower here today, 3pm-4.30pm*. I peer inside and the place is empty apart from the Chinese girls in ballgowns I saw yesterday. The one in the top hat is sitting on a chair, the other girl on her lap. She strokes her partner's hair and they laugh at some shared joke.

Not wanting to intrude, I wander towards the next tent. There's no sign but the door is open. Carnival music drifts out, slow and off key. I can't hear anyone in the tent; maybe the performers have left already. Something about the dark doorway makes me feel cold inside and I pause, unsure whether to go in, when I notice someone in the distance.

A woman with afro hair is coming out of a trailer. She wears a big pink puffer jacket and carries a pile of costumes and fabric. I smile, relieved to see someone, and step down off the walkway and head in her direction. She struggles to pull the door closed with one hand, then stumbles down the steps and drops a roll of green material. As she grabs it, another falls.

I hurry over and pick it up. 'Can I help carry something? I don't mind.'

She shakes her head, breathing fast. 'No, no. It's OK. Just pop it on top.'

I place the fabric on top of the pile under her chin and she mutters a thank-you.

'I'm Martha. I'm new. I work with Ruth in the psychic tent.'

'Ah, I thought I hadn't seen you before. That's great. Thanks again.'

She walks back towards the big top and I wonder whether to follow her. And then I notice the trailer door is open. If there are costumes in there, one of them might hold a memory of Nina.

I check no one is coming then climb the steps and slip inside. The smell of musty fabric and leather assaults my nostrils along with a more pungent odour of mothballs, reminding me of Mum's chest of clothes in the attic in London.

The trailer has two rectangular windows set high in each wall, but my nose tells me they haven't been opened in a while. Ranged down the centre are rails of clothing and beneath them sit dozens of plastic boxes overflowing with shoes, hats, belts and jewellery. The one nearest to me contains wigs and hairpieces, a long matted ponytail hanging over the side. The far wall is covered by rows and rows of masks.

I wander down the trailer, the floor bouncing slightly under my feet. There are all kinds of costumes: opulent velvet gowns, rough-looking linen shirts and leather waist-coats, feathered cloaks and bodysuits covered with sequins. A laminated name label is taped to the leg of each rail. I scan the racks, my pulse quickening when I see the word *Nina*.

Her rail is stuffed with clothes: leotards and catsuits, a black corset laced with red ribbon, lots of dresses and several coats. This could be my best chance to get to know her, maybe even to read her memories. If I could see the last moments before her accident, I would know what happened. Maybe even figure out why she's haunting me. I reach for an embroidered pink dress with layers of rainbow netting, but then I'm drawn to a velvet frock coat with gold brocade on the collar. In the end, I rest my fingers on a plain white jacket and close my eyes.

It shows me an image of Stig and my stomach somersaults. He's outside the big top, his black eyeliner smudged. He yells then jabs an accusing finger in Nina's face. I've never seen him so angry. I pull my hand away and try to make sense of the memory. The jacket must be pure cotton as the material shows facts without emotion. I can see what Nina saw, but I have no idea how she felt. It's like watching television with the sound turned off. I know what's happening, but something is missing.

Seeing Stig again is confusing, especially through someone else's eyes. It was like looking at a different person. Not the boy who juggled fruit to make me laugh when I was feeling sad, or held me close when I was scared. He was so caring and kind to me. The Stig Nina saw is not the Stig I know, but then did I ever really know him? A sudden sadness stabs my heart. Even if we didn't end up together, I thought we'd always stay in touch.

I glance along the rail of costumes, wanting to feel them but anxious about what they might reveal. I don't want to believe that Stig is a bad person. He can't be, I would have known from touching his clothes. But then so much about him doesn't make sense. Like why did he tell me Nina had recovered from the coma and was fine, only to then say he needed to visit her in hospital to check if she was OK? When I asked him about it, he claimed it was just his way of changing the subject. The first time he mentioned her accident, he said she was fine because he didn't want to keep talking about it. He made it sound so plausible, like it was nothing and I was overreacting. I tried asking more questions but he got defensive, as if I was accusing him of something. Soon after that he asked Mum for a lift to the ferry. At the harbour everything seemed fine; he kissed me and said he'd be back in a few days. He meant to return to the island and find work so we could be together.

My shoulders slump as a heavy feeling settles over me. I could accept him not wanting to see me again if he called and explained. It's the not knowing that hurts. Maybe he's lying in hospital and can't contact me. Or perhaps he had no intention of coming back.

If there's one thing I hate more than anything, it's the feeling that I've been lied to. Tricked somehow. And no matter what anyone says, you don't lie to people you care about. I try not to dwell on it, but seeing him again brings it all back. If only I could find out what happened to Nina, it might be the missing puzzle piece that completes my picture of him.

The door bangs open, startling me.

'*Hvem er du?*'

It's the girl with the wolf mask I met when I first arrived. Only now she's wearing jeans and a black bomber jacket. She strides towards me and says something else in Norwegian. Maybe she thinks I'm trying to steal stuff.

'Sorry, I didn't mean to . . .'

Her gaze flicks to my blind eye and a look of recognition crosses her face. 'Sorry, I didn't realise it was you. So you got the job.'

'Yes, I'm Martha.'

She smiles. 'That's great. I'm Ulva. Welcome to the family.'

She holds out her gloved hand and I reach out to take it. As soon as I touch the fabric, I see an image of her surrounded by a green haze. Her arms are bound and she's howling and thrashing. It doesn't feel like a memory. It feels like a nightmare.

My head pounds and I rub my temples.

'Are you OK?' she asks.

'Yes, I'm fine. I just need some fresh air.'

I hurry down the steps and lean against the side of the trailer. She starts to follow me, but then stops when Karl arrives. He calls up, 'You wanted to see me, Ulva?'

'Yes, I want to know who's going to play Baldur now that Nina –'

Karl huffs. 'No one! We're going back to the original set.'

'But Oskar said –'

'*Nei!* I've told you, we are never doing that myth again, not after that poor girl died!'

Karl walks off and Ulva chases after him.

I start to follow her, excited that she mentioned Nina by name – she seems friendly and maybe she can tell me something about the accident – when a movement catches my attention. I spin around and a little girl, no older than five, races towards me clutching a green balloon. She sees my face and stops in her tracks, her eyes wide with fear. For a moment I want to turn away, ashamed of my weird-looking eye, but I hold her gaze and smile. She's just a child, she doesn't know.

Distracted, she lets go of the string and the balloon glides away. I grab hold of it but it slips through my fingers and sails over the ground towards the big top. The girl starts to wail.

'Don't cry. It's OK, we can get it back.'

Her parents rush over and the mother smiles at me, her expression changing to one of suspicion when she sees my face. They usher the girl away and I watch them, feeling guilty. The balloon was in my grasp. I should have held onto it.

I glance back towards Ulva, but she's already disappeared. The balloon is floating and bumping along the ground; maybe I can still get it. I give chase and nearly catch it, when it blows through the doorway of a tent. It's the one playing carnival music.

Inside, the place is empty apart from a statue of a jester. It stands on a low plinth at the back, a curtain of dark netting behind it. I blink and wait for my sight to adjust to the dim light then search for the balloon. It's not exactly a big tent; the balloon has to be in here somewhere. I walk towards the statue. Maybe it blew behind there and got caught on something.

The jester stands with both arms behind its back, staring at the floor. It wears a tattered green tunic and baggy black trousers, and on its head is a grubby green-and-black striped cap with two horns hanging down at the front, each one tipped with a bell. Beneath the cap is a mane of orange hair. There is something terribly lonely about it and I wonder why it's been left here on its own.

I walk around the statue, keeping my distance. The jester's face is covered with a thick layer of flaking white paint, a smear of red over its lips. Its nose is dotted with pink and there are green diamonds painted over each eye. Its eyes are the worst thing about it. The glassy eyeballs bulge in its head, as if whoever made it used the wrong size or didn't set them in deeply enough. A fly buzzes around me then lands on the jester's face. It crawls over the statue's cheek and then walks across its eyeball, and my stomach turns.

Rasping sounds. Faint at first and then louder, coming from behind the statue. I lean forward, my face next to the jester's, and peer into the gloom. The balloon is on the ground; the string caught on the netting. I smile and reach for it when the statue blinks. I yelp and leap back, my heart banging in my chest.

The jester lifts its head with a tinkling of bells and looks at me. The paint around its mouth flakes as it speaks, its voice a gruff whisper. 'You let go of it, didn't you?'

Panic floods my body. I stare, unable to move. The jester grins, revealing two rows of uneven yellow teeth, his red lips pulled back too wide and too thin. I turn and race for the door, and he laughs and calls after me, 'Don't you want to play?'

7

BALDUR DREAMS OF HIS DEATH

I still feel queasy as I walk to Ruth's caravan two hours later. I tried to rest, but every time I closed my eyes I saw an image of the jester. I tell myself it was just one of those living statue things, a man in a costume, but I can't get his grinning face out of my mind. Something about him was disturbingly familiar, and the way he spoke to me, it was like he knew me. The more I think about it, the more uneasy I feel, my thoughts a poisonous drip in a cave so vast it could swallow me whole if I let it.

I stand outside Ruth's then quickly check my phone. I left Mum a message hoping she might have some clue as to what's happening, but there's no reply. I'm sure she's fine and has watered the tree. The alternative is too awful to think about. Straightening my shoulders, I knock on the door and force myself to smile. One way or another, I'm going to find a way to ask Ruth about Nina.

The door opens and steam billows out. 'Martha! Perfect timing!' Ruth wipes her forehead and beckons me inside. 'Make yourself comfortable, dinner won't be long.' The caravan is bigger than mine, though still old and tatty. It has the same benches and pull-down table at the front, laid for dinner, and two sofas facing each other down the sides. Unlike mine, there's a door at the back, so I'm guessing she has a separate bedroom.

The extractor fan rumbles noisily and Ruth raises her voice to be heard. 'The canteen food isn't bad, but I miss cooking. It's chicken and roast potatoes. Hope that's OK.'

'That's great, thanks.'

She waves a tea towel at the steaming oven like she's trying to tame a dragon, and I sit down and glance around the room. There's greenery everywhere: ivy trailing down from shelves, shiny-leafed yuccas and rows of cactuses in pots. Crystals clutter the window ledges and the floor is piled high with books. Even the sofas are overflowing with balls of wool and knitting needles, not to mention clothes and magazines, so that there's barely any room to sit.

Ruth places a jug of water before me then opens a bottle of wine. 'Thank God today's over. I thought it would never end. You were great by the way.' I smile, relieved to know she thinks I did well. She offers me some wine but I shake my head. After a few minutes she lays two plates of food on the table and the smell of rosemary makes my stomach rumble. Just being in the warm, surrounded by her things, makes me feel a little better.

'Thanks for this, Ruth.'

'No problem. Sorry about the noise – the fan will go off soon. So how did you find it today?'

The psychic tent feels like a distant memory, even though it was only a few hours ago. I do my best to sound positive. 'Good, thanks. I think I helped most people. There was one lady . . . she was upset about her husband and cat dying. I tried to comfort her but I think I said the wrong thing and made it worse.'

Ruth picks up a ball of wool and a half-made shawl from the bench. 'You know, in Ireland it's said that you leave a bit of your soul trapped in everything you crochet. You're meant to work in a hidden mistake so that your soul can escape.' She chucks the wool onto the sofa and sits down heavily. 'What feels like a mistake at the time doesn't always turn out that way. The lady might look back on your words and feel differently later.' She sees the look of doubt on my face and laughs. 'It will get easier, I promise.'

Ruth pours herself some wine then raises her glass. 'Here's to your new job.' I lift my water and smile, but the thought of having to work in the psychic tent tomorrow doesn't exactly fill me with joy. I don't have time to give readings, I need to speak to people if I'm going to find out anything.

Once we've finished eating, she goes to a shelf covered with a black cloth. On it are two candles, a metal dish with incense, and what looks like a small cloth figure wrapped in green thread. Arranged around the edge are sprigs of mistletoe and greenery with red berries.

She grabs a nearby pack of tarot cards. 'Want me to read for you?'

I shrug, unsure that I want to hear my future, even if it's possible. Ruth looks at me hopefully. 'I can do a general reading, or you can ask a question if you like?'

There are lots of things I want to know – like why is Nina haunting me, where is Stig, and what's happening in this weird place, but I doubt a pack of cards will give me the answers. Ruth looks disappointed. Not wanting to appear rude, I smile and say, 'A general reading is fine, thanks.'

'Grand.' She closes her eyes then shuffles the pack and places it on the table. With her left hand she cuts the deck into three and then reassembles it. The first card she pulls has a red heart with three swords buried in it. The second shows a tower being struck by lightning, and the third has a picture of a man and woman kissing.

'There's someone you're confused about, a boy.'

I sip my drink, wary of giving her anything to go on. She points at the middle card. 'Something he did made you question what you thought you knew about him.' Under the couple are the words *The Lovers*. She glances at the card at the bottom of the pack. 'You're going to be faced with a difficult decision. He's coming back.'

My heart leaps with hope and then plummets. I'm not sure I want to see him again, not unless he has a good reason for not having contacted me. 'Do you know when? Is he OK?'

Ruth grins. 'Come on then, what's his name? I want to hear all about him.' She leans forward and I realise that's why she offered to read my cards. It's a way to find out about me. As much as I want to hear about Stig, I don't want her to know why I'm really here. I'm sure she didn't have anything to do with Nina's death, but Mum said not to trust anyone.

Ruth starts to shuffle the cards and I take a deep breath, determined to turn the conversation to something useful. 'Actually, I don't want to talk about him.'

'Really?' She sounds disappointed.

'There is something I'd like to know though.'

'Oh yes?'

'I looked around the smaller tents after I finished work. I went into one with a living statue, dressed like an old-fashioned jester. I wondered if you knew him?'

Ruth lowers the cards. 'Hmm, can't think of anyone like that. There are three clowns here, but they're all French mime artists.'

My stomach lurches with unease. If he doesn't work here, then who is he? I know there's something strange about this circus – I didn't imagine seeing the performers' masks move and I didn't daydream the jester.

'Maybe it was someone who's just joined,' I suggest.

'Christ on a bike, I hope not. If Oskar's hired a new act, Karl will go mad!'

Thinking about the old circus manager gives me an idea. 'I saw Karl earlier today. He was talking to a girl called Ulva. She asked who would play Baldur now Nina's gone, and he said they were never doing that myth again. I wondered why.'

Ruth rolls her eyes. 'He has this book of stories – some can be performed and others can never be done. Honestly, the way he goes on, sometimes I think the whole superstitious thing is an act.'

Now's my chance. I sip my water then ask, 'Who's Nina?'

The extractor fan stops and the caravan is painfully quiet.

Ruth clears the plates. 'Have you had enough to eat? Can I get you another drink?'

'No, thanks. I heard Karl say she'd died?'

Ruth sighs, her face a picture of unease. 'Nina was training and she fell.'

'I'm sorry.'

She slides open a kitchen drawer then takes out a newspaper and lays it on the table. It shows a group of people posed in the big top, each one clutching a mask to their chest. I recognise the girl in the centre instantly. She holds a gold mask and has short dark hair and is strikingly beautiful. Nina shines with a light of her own, and not just because she's dressed all in gold. There is something luminous about her. She seems so happy. So alive.

Ruth pours herself another glass of wine. 'One minute we were about to open the new season, Nina was smiling and happy, the star of the show, and then suddenly she was gone. It was hard on everyone, but Karl was broken. I'll never forget his face the day he came back from the hospital, clutching a bag with her belongings in his hand.'

I look at the photo. 'She was beautiful,' I offer, realising how weak my words sound.

'Yes,' says Ruth briskly, as if trying to pull herself together. 'It was taken on the morning of the accident. Nina was going to play Baldur for the first time that afternoon.'

'I don't know the story. Is Baldur a god?'

She nods. 'He's the son of Odin and Frigg, the fairest and most beloved of the gods. When Baldur dreams of his death, Frigg makes everything in the world swear an oath not to hurt him. Convinced he's invincible, the other gods

66

throw weapons at him for sport, knowing they will bounce off him.

'One day Loki asks Frigg if there's anything that hasn't sworn an oath. She mentions that she didn't ask the mistletoe, as she thought it too small and harmless to bother with. Loki straight away makes a spear from some mistletoe and gets the blind god Hodr to throw it at Baldur. It pierces him and he falls down dead.'

'That's awful.'

Ruth stares deep into her wine glass. 'It gets worse. After that, one of Baldur's brothers journeyed to the underworld to ask Hel if she would release him. She agreed to give Baldur up, but only if every living thing shed a tear for him. The whole world wept, apart from one creature – a giantess, who was Loki in disguise. So Baldur was doomed.'

We sit in silence, the wind a low moan outside. I don't know how true the story is, but I can't imagine Hel giving up anything easily. Meeting the dark mother goddess was one of the most terrifying experiences of my life. After Stig was attacked by the *draugr*, I journeyed into the bowels of the tree to beg for his life. In return for giving him up, Hel tasked me with returning the souls that had escaped from the underworld. She gave me a cord and told me to put one end inside the tree and hold the other until all the dead had followed it back.

But I didn't. When Mormor appeared, I knew she would never leave me. She was determined to try to protect me from the *draugr*, even if it meant not returning to the underworld. I couldn't bear the idea of her soul wandering the earth, lost for eternity. I had to do something, so I dropped the rope. As I hoped, it coiled around her and dragged her into the tree. My cheeks burn with shame as guilt wraps around my heart. I didn't stop to think what would become of the poor souls I abandoned. I didn't do as Hel asked.

Ruth sighs heavily and my thoughts return to her story. She sips her wine then confides, 'The crazy thing is that Karl blames himself. The owners had been putting pressure on him to change the routines to bring in more custom. He introduced the myth against his better judgement. He's convinced the two things are connected, but it's just a tragic coincidence.'

I lean over and study the photo. 'What was she like?'

Ruth huffs and her face tells me the answer is complicated. 'Nina was an amazing flier, the best we had. She lived for the spotlight, in more ways than one.'

'How do you mean?'

'She had notions about herself; loved being the centre of attention. She was a drama queen but she could be kind when she wanted to, especially to Ulva. When Ulva's mum first took off, she was like a sister to her.' An edge of accusation sharpens her voice. 'And then she went and did *that*.'

I raise my eyebrows but she shakes her head. When she doesn't say anything, I reach for my glass and deliberately brush her arm. The sleeve of her jumper bristles with outrage. Nina did something to come between Ulva and her mum, something she had no right to do. Ruth is angry on Ulva's behalf, but there's a deeper hurt there too: a rawness that I can't quite place. Another thread of emotion tugs at my mind. Ruth feels uneasy about Nina's death. Not guilty exactly – it's as if she worries her actions contributed to what happened.

I glance at the Norwegian newspaper on the table. When I searched for the circus online, I asked Mum to translate the story that came up, but it was old and didn't say much – just that she'd fallen from the trapeze and was airlifted to hospital, where she was in a coma.

'How did it happen? Did she slip, or was her harness faulty?' I ask.

'She wasn't wearing one. At first the police were convinced she'd been wearing one due to the marks around her throat. They think it can't have been done up properly and caught around her neck before she fell through. But no harness was found.'

'Didn't she know it was dangerous?'

Ruth frowns as if I'm stating the obvious. 'No one can understand it. She was a professional; she knew the risks. Her boyfriend told the police she refused to wear it.'

My pulse quickens and I bite my thumbnail, wondering how much I can ask her. 'What was he like, her boyfriend?'

Ruth wipes her mouth as if she's already said too much. 'I'm not saying he had anything to do with her death, but not everyone believed his story, put it that way.'

I lean back and try to ignore the sinking feeling inside me. It doesn't seem right to talk about Stig when he's not here to give his side of things. 'Did the police question him?'

'Of course. They will take months to reach a final verdict, but everyone thinks it will be accidental death. We had to close during the investigation and the circus lost a lot of money. We thought we'd go bust but then the owners secured a loan and brought in Oskar. It was a relief when we could open again.'

'So what happened to Nina's neck?'

'Lots of performers get injuries from the silk ropes. The marks could have been caused by them.'

My mind clouds with questions, but at the same time I feel clearer than I have in weeks. That must be it – the police knew there was something suspicious about her accident but they weren't able to prove anything. If they pass a verdict of accidental death, the truth will never be known. Nina wants me to get justice for her.

A thud sounds behind me.

I twist in my seat and see a pot plant lying on the floor, dirt everywhere. Nina stands over it, her pale skin mottled blue and veined with purple. She sees me looking and reaches a hand to her neck. Her lips are rough and cracked, the skin flaked away. She opens and closes them like a fish, desperately trying to speak.

Ruth stands and clears up the mess and it's all I can do not to point and yell. She gives me a curious look. 'It must have been balanced on the edge, nothing to worry about.'

Nina looks at me imploringly, her empty black eyes huge. She clutches at her throat and makes a pitiful sobbing sound and my heart breaks in two.

8

AN EYE BLINKS IN THE HALF-LIGHT

Ruth opens the caravan door and the cold night air tastes dry on the back of my throat. She apologises for ending the evening early and I smile to hide my disappointment. After she cleared up the pot plant, she complained of a headache and said she needed to lie down. I'm not sure if it was the wine or talking about Nina, but her face looks blotchy and flushed.

'Are you sure you'll be OK walking home?' she asks.

'I'm fine, honestly. Thanks again for dinner.'

'You're welcome. Here, you'll need this.'

I turn and Ruth hands me a torch. She stands in the doorway and watches me go down the steps. At the bottom I glance back at her, an angel haloed in light, and she waves. And then the caravan door closes like a clam rocking shut and I am plunged into darkness. I look at the window, hoping to see Nina's face, but as always she vanished as quickly as she came.

Darkness crowds around me and I fumble with the torch then sigh with relief when it comes on. Thick grey clouds drift across the moon, smothering its light. It's only a five-minute walk, less if I hurry, but there's something about stepping into nothingness I don't like. On the way here I had the twinkling lights of the tents to see by. Now they've been switched off and blackness obliterates everything, even the big top. It's as if the circus never existed.

I wish I could have stayed and asked Ruth more questions, but at least I now know how Nina died. The fact that the police couldn't find a harness, even though they believed she was wearing one, has to be a clue. If I can find out what happened on the day of her accident, who was with her, it might lead me to the truth. And then maybe Nina will leave me alone and I can go home to Mum.

Pointing the torch down, I follow the sludge of footprints through the snow. Apart from the squelch of my boots and the distant murmur of a TV, the night is achingly quiet. A caravan looms out of the murk, its light on but the curtains selfishly drawn. Anything could be hiding in the shadows gathered around it. I long to swing the torch beam towards it, but I know the light would be swallowed up. Better to keep it fixed ahead, on the ground.

If only my attention would stay on the path. Instead it wanders the walkways between the tents, imagining all kinds of creatures in the darkness. An image of the Norns scuttles across my mind, their spider-like legs carrying them towards me. And then another image intrudes: the grinning face of the jester. My stomach churns at the thought of seeing him again. I grip the torch with both hands and walk faster.

A flash of white moves to my right. I turn and look, my heart in my mouth. It's just a plastic sheet swaying on a washing line. I lower the torch and keep going. After a minute or so the hulking shape of the costume trailer comes into view. I pause before it and something occurs to me. The photo in the newspaper . . . Ruth said it was taken on the day Nina fell. If I can find the outfit she was wearing when it happened, maybe it will show me her last memory. Karl brought Nina's belongings back from the hospital. There were lots of clothes still on her rail; perhaps he put it with the others. I don't remember seeing a gold catsuit, but it could have been there and I didn't notice.

I climb the steps and press on the door handle, expecting it to be locked, but it swings open. The smell of musty fabric mixed with the penetrating odour of mothballs is even stronger than before. Inside it's dark and I blink against the gloom. I could switch on the light, but I don't want anyone to know I'm here; better to use the torch.

I make my way towards Nina's rail when a flash of orange catches my attention. A matted wig lies sprawled across a plastic tub. It looks like the one the jester wore. I move the torch, not wanting to remember, and the beam falls on a severed arm covered in blood. I gasp and step back, then shake my head at my stupidity. It's just a model. Of course it is. Relief floods through me, quickly replaced by a stab of fear. I'm certain I'm being watched.

My skin prickles and I glance around, sweeping the torch in every direction. There's hardly going to be anyone here at this time of night, but I walk along both sides of the rails just to be sure. When I get to the masks, I stop and listen. Apart from the moan of the wind, the silence is brutal. Nothing moves, nothing makes a sound, and yet something about the trailer feels oddly alive. Even the clothes seem different in the dark: empty hanging skins waiting for a body to bring them to life.

I glance over my shoulder, unable to shake the feeling that dozens of eyes are watching me. And then I realise and a tiny laugh escapes me. It's the masks. The way they stare *is* creepy, but they're just objects. I turn to the wall and immediately recognise Hel, Queen of the Underworld. One half of her face is carved and painted white to look like a skull, and the other is a beautiful woman. The mask has been made so that she appears to be looking down, her mouth set in a grimace. Whoever made it captured her severity with frightening accuracy. Knowing I will have to face her again one day fills me with dread.

Not wanting to think about that, I scan the rest of the masks. Above Hel is a man with a wide forehead and a beard, who I'm guessing is Thor. Close by is a woman with long yellow hair, his wife maybe, but I don't know her name. The gold mask of Baldur is there, gleaming in the darkness. Next to it is a dark-green mask, the holes angled to make the wearer look as if they're laughing, which I'm guessing is Loki. The twig-covered faces of the Norns hang together in a trio. Below them is Odin, the mask crooked so that the eye painted black doesn't quite line up with the opening on the other side.

There are lots more faces, but I'm not aware of their names or their stories. Realising how little I know about the gods and my own family history makes me feel hollow inside. I haven't read all of my ancestors' journals, but Mum translated some of them before I left. They were filled with questions; the women who came before us musing about why they were chosen and their place with the gods.

Like them, all I know is that Odin tasked our family line with taking water from the well by the tree and pouring it on the tree's roots to stop it decaying. If Mum had told me everything from the start, I would have been honoured to do my duty – like all the women before me – and watered the tree after Mormor died. But she didn't, and without Mormor it began to rot and the dead escaped. That was when I turned to the Norns and Hel for help. Even though the experience was terrifying, I was privileged to meet them. But what about Odin, the god whose blood flows inside me? Is he even aware of my existence?

Bang.

I twist around, my heart racing.

The door swings open then smacks shut. I snatch my hand to my chest and let out a shuddery breath, my mind still spinning with thoughts of the gods. It's just the wind. I walk over and close the door, then turn and face the rails of clothing. The sooner I do this, the sooner I can get out of here.

Nina's section is near the end, by the masks. The wooden floor bounces under my feet as I hurry towards it. I run the torch beam along the costumes, past the dress with rainbow netting and the white jacket, then stop when I come to a collection of catsuits. Red, blue, black, green . . . something glints and hope flickers inside me. It's a catsuit, but this one is white, not gold.

A shaft of moonlight shines on the back wall and an eye blinks in the half-light.

I gasp and stare in disbelief. One of the masks *moved*. I run my gaze over the faces, my heart beating wildly. Nothing happens and I swallow, praying it was a trick of the light, even though I know it wasn't. There was Ulva's wolf mask that moved too, and the wooden faces of the Norns. The wind builds from a moan to a wail. I hold still and wait, afraid to look away in case it happens again. A mouth twitches and then, on the opposite side of the wall, nostrils flare. Here an eyebrow is arched; there a lip curls. All at once the masks blink into life.

Hel lifts her gaze and I shrink back. She sees me and a look of recognition passes over her grim countenance. I run for the door and turn back and see her single empty eye socket boring into me, her mouth open in a silent howl of rage.

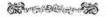

I sit in bed with the duvet bunched around me, my chest heaving. I ran back to the caravan, barely stopping to draw breath. The bars of the electric heater blaze orange but the icy feeling inside me won't go away. It's not just the masks and the jester – there's something horribly *wrong* about this place. Even the man in the psychic tent didn't seem quite of this world. Maybe it's not the circus, maybe it's me? I recoil from the thought and remind myself that the impossible is real, magic is real. I've experienced too much to doubt my own mind. The people who work here might not know what's happening, but some intuition tells me it's connected to Nina's death. I just have to figure it out.

I shuffle down the bed and check my phone. Still no message from Stig, despite Ruth's tarot reading, and no missed calls from Mum. I text her asking if she's OK, then stare at the damp-spotted ceiling. I'm sure she's been watering the tree. She wouldn't risk it rotting again, not after what happened last time.

If only I could go home. As much as I want to go back, I can't risk Nina following me. Mum was so terrified before, I can't put her through that again.

My breathing deepens and a wave of tiredness sweeps over me. A moment later I'm drifting, moving fast over the ground, caught by a sharp gust of wind . . .

The jester stands before me, holding a bunch of brightly coloured balloons. He lowers his arm and pulls them in front of me. I look, trying to decide which one to choose . . . and then the colour drains and the world becomes grey. One of the balloons rotates in the wind and I see a desperate face inside. And then another face appears – there is a person in each balloon. Mouths open and close in despair, an old woman weeps, a man covers his eyes.

The jester hands me the rope. He isn't offering me one balloon; he wants me to take the whole bunch. I shake my head but the faces are so pitiful . . . I hold the rope, somehow knowing that they are my responsibility. Suddenly it slips through my fingers and I watch powerless as the balloons separate and sail up into the sky. I know I've done a terrible thing. Something I can't take back or make right.

The jester laughs but there's no mirth in his voice, only bitter accusation. 'You were meant to hold on, but you let go, didn't you?'

TYR LOSES HIS HAND

I wake with a groan, my head littered with the debris of bad dreams. Foul unspeakable things washed up on the shore between sleep and waking, as if a trawler net has dragged through my worst fears and left them raw and bleeding for the gulls to pick. And then I remember the masks. That part wasn't a nightmare, it was real.

I check the time on my phone, surprised to see it's so late. I was awake for most of the night, tossing and turning, but I must have dropped off eventually. There's still no word from Stig, though I've pretty much given up hope, but a message from Mum flashes on the screen.

Don't worry about me. When are you coming home? x

I type a reply. *Not sure, soon I hope. Miss you x*

A lump comes to my throat as I realise it's true. We haven't always seen eye to eye, but she's all I have. The only living link to my ancestors, and I owe it to them to make sure we do our duty as they did. Mormor died of old age after a long and mostly happy life, and I hate that her last moments were spent in anguish, knowing she had failed to persuade Mum to water the tree. But I can help put things right.

My phone pings and pings again. Mum sent several texts during the night, the first at 4 a.m.

He wears a different face whenever he likes. That's why I can't draw him.

Then another just after 5 a.m.

The man I've been drawing, he's an unwelcome guest. Don't let him inside, don't bring anything of his inside. Rules mean nothing. He scares me, Martha. Please, you have to come home.

And then a few hours later.

I'm going to see the doctor today, need something to make me sleep. Reception is better at the harbour. I will call you when I come out x

My hands shake as I reread the messages. I don't know what man she's talking about. What scares me is the idea of her seeing a doctor.

The last time Mum stayed up all night sketching and painting we were living at home in London. It was before Dad left us. He called the doctor out and she gave Mum medication to stop her hallucinating; she persuaded her that her clothes-reading gift and everything Mormor had told her about the tree and the Norns was a delusion. That the visions of the future she kept painting couldn't possibly be true. Mum kept my inheritance from me because she couldn't accept that magic is real. Even now, she struggles to believe. If only she could meet the Norns herself, she would understand. Her gift, along with her duty to water the tree, is her destiny – just as it's mine.

If Mum tells this new doctor everything, he's not going to believe that Yggdrasil is in our garden. He'll put her on medication like they did before, or hospitalise her. Dad is useless; he's not going to understand that I need to stay on the island. He'll try to take me away. Or I'll be left to water the tree – living in the cabin in the middle of nowhere – alone.

I dial Mum then take several deep breaths. She always gets agitated when she's tired; if she hears panic in my voice it will only make things worse. It rings and rings. Eventually her phone beeps for me to leave a message.

'Hi, Mum, it's me. Are you still going to the doctor's today? I wouldn't tell them about the tree or, well ... anything. They wouldn't understand and they'll only ask more questions. Call me when you get this. Love you.'

I hang up, then bite my thumbnail, wondering if I should call back and leave another message. It's already gone eleven o'clock, she might be talking to the doctor right now. I shove off the covers and get out of bed, aware I have to start work in a couple of hours. I hate the idea of Mum being upset and having no one to talk to. I can't leave her for much longer, she needs me. If only I'd found Nina's gold catsuit last night. If it shows me how she died, I might be able to figure out what really happened to her. I'll look in the costume trailer again, and if it's not there I'll ask Karl.

I shower and dress, then eat some toast and go out. All around me, fir trees shake and shiver in the wind, their

81

boughs whispering conspiratorially as if they know something I don't. A sprinkling of snow covers the ground, making the caravans and trucks sparkle. Beyond them the circus tents shine like ice-encrusted jewels. Performers hurry about, and in the distance the first customers wander in through the archway.

I head to the costume trailer and pause when I see the woman from yesterday come out, her arms laden with clothes. Once she's gone, I climb the steps and open the door. The smell of mothballs makes me gag. My legs feel weak and I hesitate, and then I clench my fists and remind myself of who I am. I come from a long line of strong, magical women. I'm the descendent of a Norse god.

Ignoring the watery feeling in my gut, I approach the masks. Hel stares at the ground, her mouth frozen in a grimace. The way she glared at me last night, it was like she wanted to hurt me. I shiver and look across the rows of faces. Not a flicker of movement. Maybe they're sleeping, or waiting?

My gaze rests on Odin's mask. White with a few deeply carved wrinkles, it stops just below the nose rather than covering the whole face. There's only one opening for an eye, making the wearer partially sighted; the other side has been painted to resemble a black hole. The sides don't line up right, giving it a slightly crooked appearance.

I run my fingers over the smooth wood then lift the mask from its nail. The back is covered with soft grey felt. Something about it calls to me and I hold it close to my face. It fits perfectly: the gap for an eye on my right, the solid mask on my blind side. My head starts to move forward, but it's not me doing it. I gasp and lower my hand. When I raise it again, the same thing happens. A gentle, insistent pull. It's like the mask is drawing me closer. Like it *wants* to be worn. The feeling is alarming and yet tantalising at the same time.

'*Oskar trenger det antrekket i ettermiddag!*'

I jump at the sound of voices outside. Someone is coming . . . I return the mask and spin around, but whoever it is walks on by. If anyone comes in, they're going to wonder what I'm doing. I don't know how long I have; I should hurry.

I run my gaze over Nina's rail and then something glints inside a plastic tub. I reach past belts and shoes, but it's just a chiffon scarf. The material shows me an image of Ulva, the girl who came into the trailer yesterday. She's in a car with a blonde woman, her mother maybe. I get the sense they're driving far away from here. Chiffon holds a person's daydreams so the images it shows are usually sunlit and gentle, but this one is heavy with desperation. It's like her dream became a way to survive, something to cling to when there was nothing else.

I drop the scarf and check the surrounding rails. Maybe the catsuit got put back somewhere else? After half an hour, I stop and rest my hands on my hips. Just because it isn't in the trailer, doesn't mean it's not in the circus somewhere. The woman I saw earlier had clothes over her arm and yesterday she was carrying fabric. If she's in charge of making the costumes, she might know where to find it.

I leave the trailer and head in the direction she went. The ticket tent is empty; the show must have already started.

Her footprints lead to the rear of the big top, where a doorway is hooked partially open. I put my head inside and smell talcum powder and hairspray. There are ten or so people, some sitting at tables applying their makeup and others dressing in front of standing mirrors. They move swiftly and talk quietly, all seemingly focused on their tasks.

Eventually I spot the costume woman's afro hair behind a rack of clothes, where she's working at a sewing machine. I take a hesitant step inside, expecting someone to challenge me, but no one glances my way. The woman looks busy, but she was friendly when I spoke to her yesterday.

I walk over. 'Hi. Ruth sent me to look for something. Is that OK?'

The sewing machine judders and stops. 'Damn it.' She snaps a thread with her teeth and looks up. 'What? Hmm, yes. Help yourself.'

'Thanks.'

There are lots of catsuits on the rails, but none are gold. I start to ask if she's seen it, when the voice of the ring-master booms out from behind a canvas wall. 'The Sly One sired three monstrous children: Hel, half living and half dead; the sea serpent, Jormungand; and the giant wolf, Fenrir. The Norns, who decide the fate of all beings, warned that this terrible brood would destroy the gods.'

The sound is coming from the other side of a curved black screen. I'm well acquainted with Hel, but I've never heard of the Sly One or the other creatures the ringmaster mentioned. I glance over my shoulder. No one is looking.

Intrigued to learn more about Hel and her family, I edge along the wall then peek through a narrow opening. The spotlights momentarily blind me and I blink against the glare. The ring looks much bigger from down here, the trapeze higher and more forbidding. The huge tree has gone. In its place is a long strip of white material hanging from the centre of the ceiling.

I watch the ringmaster's back as he approaches the sea of faces before him. 'Odin cast Hel down to the underworld. The sea serpent he threw into the ocean of men. But Fenrir was different, for the Norns had foretold that he would devour Odin at Ragnarok. The wolf was so dangerous it was decided he should be raised in Asgard under the watchful eye of the gods.'

A performer wearing a long fur cloak and a ferocious-looking wolf mask rushes towards the audience and snarls. I'm not surprised when a child screams; the mask's huge snout looks frighteningly real.

Someone coughs behind me. Startled, I turn and see a burly man dressed for battle, a rune in the shape of an arrow painted on his cheek. That's one of the worst things about being blind in one eye; people can sneak up on you. Mumbling an apology, I move out of his way and he bounds onto the stage.

The ringmaster continues, 'None of the gods dared go near the monstrous wolf, except for Tyr, god of truth and justice.' The man takes a bow and the ringmaster adds, 'Fenrir grew bigger and more powerful by the day. Fearful, the gods attempted to bind him. They told the wolf the chains were a test of his might and cheered when he broke free.'

I know I should be looking for Nina's catsuit, but there's something so mesmerising about the lights and actors.

Seeing the myths brought to life, realising that the gods are real, fills me with awe. The more I know about their stories, the more I feel I know about myself. But it's not just that. The performance has a magic all of its own. The masked actors are brimming with so much energy that in this moment it feels as if they're more than human.

'Dismayed at the creature's strength, the gods asked the dwarves to forge a chain that would be unbreakable.' At the ringmaster's words, a male acrobat tumbles down the silk rope, the material twisting and turning around his body, before he drops and lands with a bow. Another man follows him, and another, all wearing leather tunics and belts.

The acrobats take it in turns to jump over one another, leapfrogging faster and higher. One of them clambers onto the other's shoulders and pulls up the third. They raise their arms, encouraging people to clap as they march around the ring. After a few moments they drop down and then stand in a circle with their backs to the audience. The lighting changes, bathing them in a flickering orange glow, and they swing their arms in time to the sound of metal being struck in a forge.

The ringmaster raises his voice. 'This the dwarves did, using five things that don't exist and against which it is therefore useless to struggle: the sound of a cat's footsteps, the beard of a woman, the roots of mountains, the breath of a fish and the spittle of a bird.'

The dwarves lift up an invisible chain and the ringmaster tells the audience, 'Gleipnir, or Open, was its name.' He points his cane at the wolf and a single green spotlight comes on. 'When the gods tried to lay the curiously light chain on him, Fenrir sensed a trick. Before he would allow himself to be bound, he demanded that one of the gods put their hand in his jaws as an act of good faith. No one agreed, knowing it would mean the loss of a hand. And then one god came forward . . . Yes, the noble Tyr!'

The actor steps up and extends his arm. At the same time, the dwarves lower the chain onto Fenrir. The wolf writhes then throws back its head as a sound of howling plays.

The ringmaster raises his cane. 'Unable to break free, the wolf bit down!'

Tyr shouts and something thuds and bounces across the ring. Cries and whoops go up from the audience as the ringmaster bends to the floor. I move to get a better view, and then I see what he's holding. It's the severed arm from the trailer.

I wonder why the god of truth was the one to deceive Fenrir? I suppose the wolf trusted him above all others. Perhaps Tyr felt guilty about lying, and that's why he willingly sacrificed his hand. Even though the lie was a noble one, done to protect the gods, he knew it was wrong.

The wolf charges towards me. Realising this part of the show must be over, I hurry into the changing area and stand to one side as performers enter and throw off their costumes. The actor playing Fenrir yanks down the mask. It's Ulva. Of course, I saw her holding the wolf's head the day I arrived. She takes a gulp of air and her eyes burn with ferocity as she strides across the room, the creature's furry snout hanging grotesque around her slim neck. I think about saying hello, but she disappears into the changing area.

Instead I head over to the seamstress. She has her head bent, focused on her work, and I cough, hoping she might look up. She doesn't.

'Hi, sorry . . . me again. I wondered if you'd seen a gold catsuit anywhere?'

She frowns. 'Look, I'm kind of busy right now. Did Ruth say why she wanted it?'

I mumble a reply just as Karl enters the tent. If I can get him talking, maybe I can ask him if he has Nina's catsuit. He walks over, a tiny figure in his oversized duffle coat, and snatches the green material from the sewing machine. The seamstress jumps up. 'What are you doing? Oskar wants that for tomorrow's dress rehearsal!'

Karl huffs. 'We've never had an actor play the Sly One and we're not starting now.' He walks off and she shakes her head. 'Afraid of change, that's what he is. The performers are sick of doing the same routines. Ulva's been here since she was a child and she's only ever been a wolf. It's ridiculous!'

'Who's the Sly One?' I ask.

She grabs some green fabric from a plastic tub behind her. 'Loki, but Karl won't let anyone say his name.' I wish I had read the myths growing up. All I know is what Ruth told me, about him causing the death of Baldur, and his three monstrous children that the ringmaster just mentioned.

'Why doesn't Karl want anyone to play him or say his name?'

She rolls her eyes. 'Who knows? Anyone would think the gods were real, the way he carries on.'

I nod sympathetically and say a hasty goodbye. Maybe Karl isn't as crazy as everyone thinks.

For an older person he walks surprisingly quickly, despite the limp. I hurry after him, aware I have to start work in the psychic tent in a few minutes. By the time I catch up with him, he's almost at the hall of mirrors.

'Karl! Wait, I need to talk to you.'

He turns and there's a weary look in his eye, like a wounded general who knows the enemy could reappear at any time.

'Yes, what is it?'

I hesitate, realising how strange it will sound if I ask him what he did with Nina's belongings. Instead I find myself pointing at the material in his hand. 'The costume – why don't you want the seamstress to make it?'

The furrow in his brow deepens. 'When did you start working here? Yesterday, wasn't it?'

He makes it sound like an accusation. I hold his gaze and force a smile. 'I just want to understand.'

He turns to leave and I call out, 'Wait! Please, Karl. I know something strange is happening. I've seen things and –'

'You work with Ruth, don't you?'

I nod. For a moment I expect him to joke about me being psychic but he doesn't.

'What have you seen?'

I swallow hard, unsure how much to tell him. He hasn't done anything to make me suspicious, but Mum said not to trust anyone.

'There was an old-fashioned clown in one of the smaller tents. Something about him wasn't right, he was threatening.'

Karl frowns, the lines on his forehead deepening. 'He threatened you? What did this man look like?'

'He had long orange hair, though I think it was a wig. He was about your height, and he had thin lips and a husky voice.'

Karl shakes his head. 'There is no one here like that.'

'And the masks are . . . strange.'

'Strange how?'

If he hasn't seen them move then he probably wouldn't believe me. I decide to take a different line.

'Nina, the girl who died – do you still have her belongings?'

His bushy white eyebrows jump in surprise.

'Why?'

'Ruth mentioned you brought them back from the hospital. Could I see them, please, just for a moment?'

He narrows his eyes. 'Who are you?' When I don't answer he lets out a sigh. 'They are no longer in my possession. Not that it's any of your business.'

'The gold catsuit she was wearing . . .'

His expression darkens, telling me the conversation is over. He turns to walk away and I grab his arm, hoping to find some clue in the material. His duffle coat is riddled with resentfulness and apprehension; half-formed fears that have eaten into the fibres of the wool. He knows the circus

90

is in danger. There's a monster at the gates he has to keep out, but he doesn't know how to fight it. The realisation makes me shiver. I knew there was something wrong about the circus, but I hadn't considered it might be in danger.

He gives me a wary look, and I release his arm and lower my voice to a whisper. 'I know there was more to her death.'

Harsh caws sound from the edge of the clearing. Dozens of ravens sweep the sky and blacken the treetops, calling a warning to each other.

'Please, Karl. Something isn't right. I just want to know what's going on.'

His face pales. 'I should never have let them perform the myth of Baldur.'

'Why? Because of Loki?'

'Never say that name. We call him the Sly One. I wouldn't let an actor play him, but yes, I allowed his story to be told.'

A tiny pulse of excitement beats in my throat. Could he know that the gods are real too? But his coat revealed only vague fears. I watch his expression, unable to decide if his apprehension is based on mere superstition, or if he believes that Loki had something to do with Nina's death. 'So you think it was Lo— the Sly One's doing?'

Karl sniffs. 'I am not a child. I know the gods are not real. They are not here, walking among us.'

I frown, confused. 'But you think it brought bad luck somehow?'

'Stories change over time but the myths are different. No matter how much they change on the outside, their meaning inside stays true.' He taps out a rhythm – one-two, one-two – on his chest and adds, 'You can feel it between the words like a heartbeat. My father used to say the myths are a vessel of truth.' He studies my face for a reaction then shakes his head, seemingly frustrated. 'Some things are not meant to be changed.'

He turns to leave and an angry gust of wind shakes the treetops, making the firs tremble. Dozens of ravens line their branches, watching the circus with dark intent. I'm sure there weren't that many before. A sudden foreboding grips me, and I have the feeling that things are spiralling out of control in a way I can't understand.

Karl turns his watery eyes to the sky. 'A storm is coming.' I glance at the slate-grey clouds and shiver. He speaks so ominously I can't help wonder if he's the one who's brought bad fortune on this place. He gazes into the distance and continues without looking at me. 'I've lived and worked here all my life. My father managed the circus before me. I belong to these tents and these people; it's in my blood.'

He falls silent, and I consider what strange coincidence brought me to this place. I may not belong to the circus in the way that he does, but I have a place with the gods, and like my ancestors I am part of their stories. And yet I know so little. Perhaps I am in over my head.

As if he knows what I'm thinking, Karl turns to me, his face stony. 'Whatever happens, my place is here. But not yours. You should leave while you still can.'

STIG ISN'T HERE BECAUSE HE MISSES ME

Ruth lied. It doesn't get any easier. The seventh customer eases herself up from the chair opposite and I sniff back a tear as she exits through the curtain. Her husband used to beat her. It started on their wedding day and lasted for five years, until she called the police last week. She left with nothing, just a body covered in bruises, a suitcase and her two children. She's staying with a friend in town, who paid for her to have the reading with me. How will she feed the children, where will they go? What if he comes after them? She wanted so much to know what her future holds. I couldn't give her any answers so I gave her a hug.

As the pain flowed out of her coat, I whispered what it was like for her living in fear all those years. There was such relief on her face. Maybe it was realising that someone believed her, or having someone put into words what she had kept hidden for so long. She didn't have to tell me the awful things he'd done, because I saw them. Part of me wishes I hadn't, but it's over now. And I will gladly carry it with me if it helps her the tiniest bit.

Sandrine's feathered face appears around the curtain and I lean back in my chair, relieved the session is over. 'There's one more, sorry.' From the strange expression on her face, I'm guessing it's not going to be an easy customer. She goes and I rub my pounding head, not helped by the fog of incense. I sigh, desperately wanting to be alone. I've barely had a moment to think about my conversation with Karl.

The curtain draws back and I stand up to welcome my last client.

Stig.

My heart roller-coaster dips. I don't know whether to feel angry, relieved or happy. I blink at him, my emotions tumbling inside me. His dark hair is pulled back into a ponytail and he wears his usual black eyeliner. He smiles, revealing two perfect dimples, and I jump up.

'You're OK!'

'Yes, I'm fine,' he laughs.

'So you went back to the island, you got my letter?'

He frowns. 'No, I haven't been there. Sorry I didn't reply to your texts. I've been busy and . . .' He opens his arms as if to hug me. 'It's so good to see you, Martha! I've missed you.'

He's been busy?

The words are a cold fist, reaching into my chest and stopping my heart. I step back and glare at him, unable to

94

hide my hurt. Do I mean so little to him that he could just disappear without a word? I was convinced that something must have happened to him, that he would have got in touch if there was any way he could. And now here he is, larger than life and not a trace of worry on his face.

He looks at me expectantly but I have no idea what to say. In the end, I manage a terse, 'I'm glad you're OK.' There is something different about him, and now I realise what it is. His clothes are still black, but his battered leather trench coat is gone. In its place is a military-style jacket that looks brand new. Even his jeans are clean and less ripped.

'How did you know I was here?' I ask. And then it occurs to me that maybe he didn't. 'Presuming you came to see me.'

'Of course I came to see you!' He gestures to the armchairs. 'Can we sit?'

'Actually I've just finished for the day.'

He smiles. 'I've paid for twenty minutes.'

I frown, wondering if he's joking, and he looks slightly bewildered. What was he expecting – that I would throw myself into his arms? I grab my coat and he touches my arm.

'Can I walk with you then? Please?'

'If you want, but it's not far to my caravan.'

'I know.' I throw him a sideways glance and he adds, 'Ulva told me where you're staying. We're friends – that's how I knew you were here. She called me yesterday and mentioned someone new called Martha had started; a psychic who reads clothes.'

95

We step through the curtains and Ruth looks up from reading for a client, her smile faltering when she sees who's with me. Stig nods in her direction then quickly drops his gaze, and I realise they probably know each other. He must know a lot of people here. I hope Ruth didn't overhear our conversation. If she knows I've met Stig before, she'll realise I didn't come here by chance. She'll know I lied. She's been so kind I don't want her to think badly of me – or make me leave.

Outside, the sky is heavy with snow and the cold is more ferocious than ever. Stig pulls up his collar and we walk in uncomfortable silence, the wind ringing in our ears. All around us tents suck and billow in the breeze. I look at the frayed ropes, wondering how many storms they've weathered, and how many more it will take until they snap.

An icy gust pushes us back and Stig grins at me. For a moment it's like before, us battling together. I frown, confused by how I can feel so many things at once – angry and upset and yet relieved to see him at the same time. Part of me wants to turn on him and demand the truth. Did he ever have any intention of coming back to the island? Could he really not have found the time to send *one* text? Pretending not to notice the hope in his eyes, I drop my head and keep walking. I like the chill of the wind. Numbness is a relief from the tug-of-war emotions inside me.

At the caravan I fumble with my key and open the door. Inside it's freezing. The tiny sink is full of dirty cups and plates and I didn't convert the bed back to a sofa this morning. It has that same smell of damp socks. I take in the squalid-looking sheets and feel my cheeks burn, but then why should I feel embarrassed? I wasn't exactly expecting company.

Stig picks up the kettle. 'I'll make us a drink.'

I give him a tiny smile, thankful he's busying himself in the kitchen so I can at least straighten the duvet and hide my dirty clothes. Once I'm done, I switch on the electric heater then pull down the table from the wall.

'Tea or coffee?' he asks.

'There's only tea.'

I sit on one of the benches and watch him slide open a drawer and take out a teaspoon. It was the same in the cabin; he always knew where to find things. How does he do that – just seem to *belong* wherever he goes? He's so relaxed in himself that he takes up all the space around him, while mine shrinks.

He puts two steaming mugs on the table then sits opposite me. Most people glance at my blind eye, distracted by the way it faces the wrong direction, but Stig holds my gaze as if he doesn't notice it. He was that way from the start; I'd forgotten how accepted he made me feel. He leans forward with a smile. 'So how are you? How's your mum doing?'

The question catches me off guard. He knows we haven't always got on well, but that's not why I feel uncomfortable. And then I realise. I liked the fact that no one here knows me. It meant I could be free of the past, free to be someone else.

'She didn't make you return to London and live with your dad then. I'm guessing you signed up to the school on the mainland?'

I wrap my hands around my mug and mutter, 'I'm starting in a couple of months.'

'Great. What are you doing?'

'Norwegian Language with Tourism Studies.'

He grins. 'Cool. That way you'll be able to read your ancestors' journals for yourself, and tourism studies will help when you open the guesthouse.'

I chew the inside of my cheek. I'd forgotten I'd mentioned the idea in front of him. After he left, Mum and I talked about it a lot. How we could sell the house in England and turn the warehouse by the harbour into an artists' retreat. I even phoned my friend Kelly and told her about it. She said she couldn't wait to visit and we talked about her coming to the island next summer.

Stig looks at me for a long moment. 'You know, I still can't believe you're here. So are you just earning money before school starts?'

I sip my tea and it tastes funny, the milk sour. 'Yeah, something like that.' He's the one who disappeared, so how come it's me answering all the questions? I think about asking where he's been, but I don't want to appear desperate. If I really mean nothing to him, then why should I give him the satisfaction of opening my heart? Better to let him think I'm not bothered than reveal how much I care. Biting back the urge to ask what's really on my mind, I find myself saying, 'What about you? Are you working or studying?' The fact that I have no idea what he does, never mind where he's been for the past three weeks, makes me realise how little I actually know about him.

'Mum wants me to apply to university but I haven't decided yet.'

'Oh?'

'I always thought I'd be a mechanic like Dad.' His eyes light up as he talks. 'I used to help him restore vintage motorbikes. There's something about bringing an old bike back to life and seeing it run again.' He laughs and adds, 'I had this crazy idea I'd fix up an old classic, and then go touring around Europe for six months.'

'So why can't you?'

He opens his mouth to say something and then closes it again, a coy smile on his lips. When he finally speaks, I have a feeling it's a different answer to the one that came to mind. 'Dad's bike business went bust and that's when he started drinking and things went wrong between them. I don't want it to be a painful reminder for Mum. She thinks I like fixing up and riding old bikes in memory of him, but it's not that. It's what I enjoy.'

He goes quiet for a while then glances around the room. 'I like this caravan.'

I purse my lips, presuming he's trying to be funny. Or is he skirting around the issue, hoping that I'll break down and ask where he's been? He can't have come all this way just to make small talk.

'It's cosy. I used to stay here sometimes,' he adds.

'How come?'

'If Nina threw me out, I'd sleep here.'

'Oh.' I squirm in my seat, wondering what other revelations he might have. I want to ask why he argued with

Nina. I want to know everything there is to know about his ex-girlfriend, but not for the reason he might think.

He takes a deep breath. 'You must be wondering why I didn't come back to the island.'

I shrug, determined to keep my face blank.

'If I'm honest, I left because . . .'

My phone vibrates.

I grab it from my pocket, relieved to see Mum's name. 'Sorry, I have to take this. Do you mind?'

I glance at the door and Stig reluctantly gets up. 'Sure, sure. Of course.' He pulls his coat tighter and goes outside.

I smile, a tiny bit pleased that he's the one being kept waiting for a change. Once he's gone, I swipe to answer. 'Yes, I'm here, Mum. Did you see the doctor?' There's so much interference on the line I can barely hear. 'Say that again?'

'I said he's given me some sleeping tablets, and no, before you ask, I didn't say anything about the tree. Please tell me you're on your way home.'

'Not yet.'

Mum sighs. 'I know you had to go to the circus, I felt it when I drew the pictures, but I want you to come back now.'

When I don't say anything, she whispers, 'Please, Martha. I don't like being on my own. When I water the tree I can feel someone watching me.'

My chest twinges as if a hand is squeezing my heart. I hate hearing her sound afraid. 'Don't worry, Mum. If you can sense something, it will be the Norns. They won't hurt you.'

'Please, you have to leave that place. He scares me. You mustn't invite him inside.'

I look out of the window. It's blowing a gale and Stig is pacing up and down, his chin to his chest.

'Who are you talking about, Mum? Who scares you?'

The line goes dead. I call back but all I get is a recorded voice telling me to leave a message. Maybe I should go home. What if there really is someone watching her and it's not the Norns? I sigh and return my phone to my pocket, then open the door.

Stig hurries up the steps and huddles under the electric fire. Whatever his story is, I hope it's good. 'You were about to tell me something?' I say.

He shoves his gloves in his pockets then worships his hands to the heater. 'Yes. The reason why I left . . . It was because of Nina.'

'I know. You told me you were going to visit her in hospital.'

'No, you don't understand. I mean I saw her in the cabin. You remember how you helped me inside after the *draugr* attacked me?' Thinking about the corpse that clawed its way out of the tree makes my stomach shrink. Stig touches his neck, revealing a glimpse of pale pink scar, and I nod, the image of his frozen face clear in my mind. Mum helped me get him to the sofa and I covered him with blankets. We didn't know if he was going to make it.

I sit down and Stig slides into the bench opposite. 'When I opened my eyes, I saw Nina.'

A shiver runs through me. I remember him saying her name when he came around. I wondered why he was talking about her, and Mum said it was the cold; he was confused.

'What did she look like?'

Stig's eyes flash with alarm. 'Dead. She looked dead!'

The anguish in his voice surprises me, and then I remember what he was like in the cabin. I was fearful of the ghostly faces in the shadows, but he seemed terrified.

I soften my voice a little. 'I know. But what was she wearing?'

He pinches the bridge of his nose as if he doesn't like remembering. 'A short white dress, nothing on her legs and feet.'

'Have you seen anything else, things moving in the shadows?' I ask.

'No, and I don't want to. I only saw her that once.'

He rubs his arms and glances at the window. It's snowing thick and fast, great eddies of white swirling to the ground. Perhaps it was his brush with death that allowed him to glimpse Nina. If Hel hadn't released him, he would have died from his injuries that day, and it seems a coincidence that he saw her just as he came around. He wasn't able to see the other shadowy dead, so perhaps it was a one-off. If he's lucky, he'll never see her again.

He doesn't say anything for a while, and when he does, his voice sounds far away. 'None of it feels real. The last I heard, Nina had recovered from the coma. I couldn't believe it when I saw her. I tried telling you about it when we were at the tree.'

I recall standing under its branches with him. He asked what the dead looked like and I told him that I didn't want to talk about it. It was just after we had kissed. A prickle of heat creeps into my face, remembering about how much I liked him. I've had crushes on boys before, but not like that. When we kissed it felt so right, like it was the start of something. Needing something to do, I sip my tea but it's so disgusting I spit it back out. I thought it was a weird thing to ask me about at the time, but I never imagined that's why he wanted to know. Not that I could have told him anything. Nina looks nothing like the restless souls I helped get back into the tree. She seems more solid and real somehow.

Stig speaks quietly, almost to himself. 'I had to go home. I had to know if she was dead or I was going mad.'

He looks so stricken I feel sorry for him. I guess that explains why he said Nina had woken from the coma and was fine one day and then seemed to change his mind the next.

'Why didn't you just tell me though? At the time, I mean.'

'I'm not like you.' I narrow my eyes and he adds, 'You could cope with seeing the dead. Part of me couldn't believe what was happening. I needed to be surrounded by ordinary things. I needed to go home – to be normal.'

I start to speak but the words turn to stone in my mouth. What exactly does he think I am? I didn't ask to see the dead. And I certainly didn't ask to be haunted by his ex-girlfriend. I should be at home with Mum building a new life; one that doesn't involve her screaming as crockery flies at our heads.

'Why didn't you answer my messages?' I ask.

'No, you're right. And I'm sorry. When I found out that Nina had died I couldn't face anyone. It brought it all back – losing Dad.' He draws a quick breath. 'I should never have walked away from her. If I hadn't left that day, then maybe . . .' His voice wavers and I wish I could say something to help. I know how much his dad meant to him; I can't imagine what it must have been like to lose his girlfriend too.

Seeing him upset brings a lump to my throat. Those first few days after Mormor died were so hard, and listening to him talk about his own grief made me feel a little less alone. I'll always be grateful he was there for me. I squeeze his arm, wanting to reassure him, and his coat sleeve buzzes with remorse. The energy is weak and stretched thin, making me think he can't have worn it many times.

The material starts to show me something else but he pulls away. I take back my hand, suddenly self-conscious. He knows about my gift; I don't want him to think I'm prying. But it's not suspicion I see on his face; it's sadness and loss and a flicker of hope.

'I really am sorry. I thought about coming back lots of times, but if I'm honest I couldn't face it. I didn't want to think about the dead and the idea of being in the cabin surrounded by ghosts, I just couldn't do it. You're so brave, Martha.' I raise my eyebrows and he peers into my good eye. 'Seriously, not everyone could have killed that creature. It's not just your ancestors that make you special. You're smart and kind – and you know how to swing an axe.' A smile comes to my face and he grins. 'I've missed you. Did you miss me, even a bit?'

He touches my arm and I shake my head, trying to make sense of things. I understand why he'd be anxious about going back to the island – you don't get over being attacked by a walking corpse that easily. And he came to the circus the moment he heard I was here, so maybe he really did miss me. But none of that explains why he ghosted me.

'You could have replied to my texts, Stig. Even if you didn't want to call, you could have messaged to let me know you were OK.'

'You're right and I'm sorry.' He looks down, then steals a glance at my face. 'I wondered if you'd come to the circus to find me?'

I cross my arms, unsure how to answer. It occurred to me that I might find out more about him if I came here, but I wasn't exactly scouring the country searching for him.

'Actually, I came because Nina is haunting me. It started the day you left.'

His eyes widen. 'What? Why?'

'I wish I knew.'

'What do you mean, haunting you?'

'Doors banging, things falling off shelves.'

His gaze darts around the caravan. I don't have to touch his clothes to know what he's thinking. If Nina is haunting me that means she's here; maybe in the room with us right now.

He swallows hard. 'But why would she? Nina didn't even know you.'

I look at the window. It's something I've wondered about myself. Nina is nothing like the dead I helped return to the tree. They were shadowy and only able to form in darkness or low light, yet Nina looks almost solid. If she isn't one of the souls I abandoned when I dropped the rope, where did she come from? All I can think is that she came to the cabin looking for Stig and then realised that I could see her. But if Stig saw her too, why not haunt him? For some reason, she chose me. 'I think she wants me to find out what happened to her.'

'Nothing *happened* to her. She was training and she fell.'

I lean back, shocked by how defensive he sounds. I watch his face and say, 'Ruth told me the police think she was wearing a harness and it caught around her neck, but no harness was found. Doesn't that sound odd to you?'

'I've been over this with the police already. When I saw her, she wasn't wearing a harness.' He blows out an angry sigh. 'God knows I begged her to wear one.'

'So why didn't she?'

A thud sounds above and Stig startles and stares upwards. Another clump of snow lands on the roof, then another.

'Stig? Why didn't she wear it?'

He pulls his gaze from the ceiling. 'She did it to get a reaction from me, because she knew it would upset me. Everything had to be a drama with her.'

I glance out of the window and the snow has started to settle, an insidious white blanket hiding what went before.

'Has Nina spoken to you?' Stig's voice brings me back to the room and I shake my head. 'Then how do you know what she wants? Maybe there's another reason she's haunting you.'

'Like what?'

The wind howls around the caravan, rattling the windows. And then the electric heater fizzes and goes out. Stig shivers and I feel it too, the sense that we're being watched. A cupboard door in the kitchen creaks open. It moves painfully slowly, centimetre by centimetre. Stig glares at it and back to me.

Clink.

We turn and stare at the sink. Something fell – a knife.

I survey the empty kitchen, my heart racing. 'Nina, is that you?'

Stig jumps up, his eyes wide. 'Martha, don't!'

I know he's scared, but if Nina is here, I have to find out what she wants.

Stig reaches for the door, a spooked look on his face. 'I'm staying with Ulva. I need to spend time with her, but can we meet later?'

I frown, wondering if they're more than just friends.

'I don't know, Stig. I'm pretty tired.'

'Tomorrow then?'

'I guess.'

He opens the door then pauses. 'Have you thought that perhaps Nina doesn't *want* anything? Maybe she came looking for me and attached herself to you because she was jealous or something.' He must be able to see the disbelief on my face as he adds, 'Just be careful, Martha, you don't know what she's like. She plays with people.' He gives me a pained smile then leaves, and I think back to something Mum said. She talked about a game being in play. Is Nina toying with me?

I wipe my breath from the cold window and disappointment settles over me like an overcoat as I watch him trudge away. Maybe I should have told him that I missed him, but then I can't let myself be hurt again. I have enough to think about with looking after Mum and the tree. I need to focus on finding out why Nina is haunting me. As soon as I figure that out, I can go home.

Stig is nearing a line of caravans, almost out of sight, when two boys step into his path. I can't hear what they're saying, but I can tell they're arguing from their body language. A guy with tattoos on his neck shoves Stig, who shouts at him. I open the narrow window and a blast of cold air hits my face, but I can't hear anything. A moment later it's all over, and Stig walks away. The boys head in my direction and I strain to hear their words.

'He needs dealing with.'

'Let's get everyone together tonight. Then we'll decide.'

The boy with tattoos glances over and sees me looking. I duck away then slump onto the bench. If the people here don't like Stig, would he really risk coming back? And then it occurs to me. Maybe he isn't here because he misses me. Maybe he's come to stop me finding out what happened to Nina.

AN AUDIENCE OF THE DEAD

After I've eaten dinner and taken a shower, I send Mum a text to say goodnight, even though the reception's so bad she probably won't receive it until the morning. Pulling the duvet over me, I open the book I bought at the ferry terminal. I read the same paragraph three times, my mind unable to settle. There's something *unreal* about this place. I understand why Karl feels the way he does. It's like there's something bad at the circus, but it's just outside – waiting. I don't know if Nina's death is connected to whatever strange thing is happening here, but some instinct tells me it must be.

The wind screams and howls like a banshee. I know the caravan is too heavy to be blown away, but I don't like the way I can feel it rocking beneath me, or the way the air whistles and whines through the cracks of the windows looking for a weakness in the structure, testing the metal, trying to get in.

The overhead light flickers and threatens to go out, and I close my book and shiver. The caravan feels colder than usual, the shadows darker. I pull on another jumper and stare around the room, checking the gloomy corners of the kitchen. Even with the heater on, I can see my breath. Water drips from the tap, landing in the sink with a rhythmic plop. The sound makes me feel lonely and I shuffle down the bed and close my eyes. A moment later, I'm drifting towards sleep when a knock at the door startles me awake.

'Who is it?' My voice sounds small and unsure, and I clear my throat then call again, louder this time. 'Who's there?'

I hold still and listen, but the only answer is the low moan of the wind.

I get out of bed and cross the room, then take a deep breath and turn the lock. A rush of icy wind spits in my face as I scan the dark caravans in the distance. Whoever it was didn't wait around. I turn to go inside when I spot something on the step: a cardboard box. I peer in every direction, half expecting someone to appear, but the night is empty.

I stare at the box, unease stirring within me, and then tell myself not to worry. I'm sure it's nothing untoward. Stig probably left it, or Ruth. I pick up the box and take it indoors. It can't contain tins of food, it's much too light. I place it on the table and turn it around but there's no label on it. No writing at all. The top is open and I reach inside and feel straw. There has to be something . . . I dig deeper and my fingers touch string. I remove a chunk of packing and a fly buzzes out. I bat it away then look in the box. Under a pile of cord is a slender wooden arm.

I lift out the puppet and it dangles to one side, a mass of long blond hair hanging down. The head is smooth wood – no face at all. It's dressed in jeans and a jumper, its hands and feet on crude lengths of string. Wedged between its arms is a crisp white envelope.

I drop the puppet on the table and it lies in a jumble of limbs and strings, its blank face watching me as I open the envelope and take out a piece of card. Written in neat black handwriting are the words: *The big top – tonight.*

The tattooed guy who was arguing with Stig said something about a meeting. Maybe he saw Stig leaving my caravan earlier and decided I should know what they're saying. I pull back the curtain and wipe the cold glass. The tents rise from the darkness like snow-capped mountains, the circus lights trembling on the wind, their yellow glow blurred and hazy as if I'm looking at them through tears. An eerie light emanates from the big top, shadows dancing against the canvas walls like flickering flames. Something about it makes me uneasy.

Ignoring the anxiety rising inside me, I get dressed then grab the torch. Judging by the lights in the big top, the meeting must have already started. If they're discussing Stig, I have to be there. I open the door and the wind is so fierce it nearly blows me back inside. I jump down and my boots sink into snow half a metre deep. The quickest way to the big top is past the costume trailer, but I can't face going near it in the dark. Instead I turn right and head towards the trees at the edge of the clearing.

The forest is a wavering mass of black. Tall slender trees knock together in the wind, their branches creaking and groaning under the weight of ice. The lower parts of their trunks are covered with short spiky branches that stick out like daggers, making the dim light even murkier. I walk quickly, keeping my head down.

A twig snaps and then another, as if something is moving through the trees. I stop and stare into the gloom, my heart racing.

White fingers creep around the edge of a trunk.

I hold my breath and wait. A moment later a pale face emerges. Nina looks at me imploringly, her eyes filled to the brim with emotion – with fear.

I step closer and call, 'Please! If you can talk to me . . .'

She shakes her head and it feels like a warning. I will her to speak but she just stares at me, and then she's gone.

I scan the trees, desperately searching for a glimpse of white. Maybe she wants me to follow her into the forest. I push away a snowy branch and step into the woods. It's so dark; what if she doesn't reappear? I glance over my shoulder towards the big top. I have to know what they're saying about Stig.

I turn away from the forest and hurry across the site. The ground before the big top is pristine white without a single footprint. Yet there are lots of people inside. I can see their silhouettes against the walls of the tent. They must have entered at the rear, via the costume-change area. Aside from the wind, the only sound is the angry slap of canvas.

The door is hooked partially open, snapping in the breeze like it wants to bite me. I duck under it and enter the fabric tunnel, relieved to escape the wind. There's no murmur of voices, not even a whisper. I point my torch at the ground and something brushes my face. I gasp and reach up, but it's just strips of fabric. I push them aside and enter the shadowy ring.

Inside is empty, the seats of the auditorium dark. It's freezing without the heaters on and I stamp my feet, my teeth chattering. A movement makes me glance upwards. The trapeze is gently swinging – with no one on it. I glance around, but there's no girl in a white dress. There's no one here at all. How can that be?

Something moves in the corner of my eye. I turn to my left and scan the rows of vacant chairs. It's hard to see in the dim light, but I'm sure I glimpsed someone at the top of an aisle. I sweep the torch up the steps and, sure enough, there is the figure of a man. More shadows flicker at the back of the tent. I peer into the gloom and the top section is full of people, some seated and others milling about.

Grasping the torch with both hands, I climb higher. A man is sitting at the end of the row to my left. I can't make out his features, but he seems to be watching the empty ring. Maybe he's waiting for someone to start the meeting.

'Hello?'

He swivels towards me and I stifle a sob.

The top part of his face is missing; his dented skull a gleam of white. He looks through me with empty black eyes. I sweep the beam of the torch along the row behind, my hands shaking. The circus is full of ghosts: an audience of the dead.

A tall thin woman with wild hair stumbles down the steps and my heart skitters. Like the others, her eyes are two inky pools. I turn to run, but the man is standing right behind me. Holding my breath, I move to one side, hoping the woman will walk by.

She passes me and I sigh with relief. And then she pauses and takes a slow step backwards. Her head twists towards me and a look of recognition flickers across her pinched face. Panic rises inside me, every muscle in my body tense. *Please don't see me.* I say it in my head, over and over again, but it's useless.

She reaches out to grab my throat and I turn and hurl myself down the steps. The man moves in front of me and bares his teeth. His fingers swipe through my body and it feels like a knife has cut into my flesh. Iciness burns where he touched me, and I cry out and clasp my hand to my middle. I race for the door, the beam of the torch swinging wildly as I run through the tunnel and into the night.

I curse my feet, willing them to move faster, but the snow is so deep. My lungs burn in my chest, but I don't stop. I keep running, not daring to look back. I can sense them behind me, gaining on me. At last I see my caravan and tears of relief sting my eyes. The shadowy dead only form in the darkness. Once I'm inside I can put on the lights.

Hundreds of grey figures fill the night in a vast writhing fog. Men, women and children: their mouths opening and closing, pleading with me. I scream as hands reach out to grab me. I race for the caravan; fumble with my keys, bite off my glove. A mass of cold air presses against my back. I shove the key in the lock, my fingers trembling.

114

Slamming the door shut, I lunge for the light switch then rush to the window. The light forms a yellow pool of safety, keeping the dead away. Beyond it are masses of shadowy figures, all jumping and snatching. They remind me of the restless dead at the tree, but I haven't seen anything like that for weeks. Not since I dropped the rope to save Mormor. If these are the dead I didn't return, why are they here now – at the circus?

The fly buzzes around me and I knock it away then stare at the puppet on the table. It's wearing the same clothes as me. Why didn't I notice that before? I nudge it and it turns over, its face smothered by hair. Taking a deep breath, I lift up the handle and its body twists and turns. A bitter taste comes to my mouth. The face is no longer smooth wood, but has features.

It looks like me.

I drop the puppet and its handles clatter to the table.

Before I can decide what to do with it, a hideous face appears at the window. The jester. I scream and jump back.

He moves his hand as if working the handles of an invisible puppet. I stare at the thing on the table, afraid it will come to life.

Suddenly my right arm jerks into the air. I yelp and try to lower it, but it won't budge. I stare at my fingers and watch in horror as they wave. The jester grins and waggles his fingers in reply. I desperately try to move but I can't.

'What do you want from me?' I shout.

He shakes his head in admonishment, as if I've done something wrong. *You dropped the rope*, he mouths.

Confusion gives way to panic. He left the card because he wanted me to go to the big top; he wanted me to find the dead. But why? Has he brought them here to punish me?

A moment later my arm drops heavily to my side and I clutch it close, my heart pounding. A jangle of bells fills the air and I stare at the window, but he's gone. A bang sounds on one side of the caravan and then another, and then I hear laughter outside. I spin around staring, terrified the jester will get in.

12

I COULD REALLY USE A FRIEND

Tapping sounds at the door, quiet and insistent.

'Martha, are you there?'

It sounds like Stig . . . I pull the duvet tighter and roll over, convinced I'm dreaming.

A knock at the window jolts me awake. I sit up and yesterday crashes over me like icy water. The jester tormented me for only a few minutes, banging on the caravan walls and laughing, but I lay awake for hours afraid he would return.

'Martha?'

'I'm coming!' I stagger out of bed, then open the door and blink in the light.

Stig frowns. 'You OK? It's late.'

I smile, relieved to see a familiar face. And then a shadow of anxiety slants across my thoughts as I wonder what made him come back to the circus.

'I'm fine. I just didn't sleep very well. What time is it?'

'Eleven.'

I look along the side of the caravan, afraid of what I might see, but there is only a bank of white. After the jester didn't reappear, I threw the puppet out of the window. There's no sign of it now; the snow must have covered it in the night.

'I'd better get ready for work, I guess.'

Stig smiles as if he's got a secret. 'A tree came down in the storm and the road won't be cleared until later. If it snows again they might not be able to move it until tomorrow.' When I don't say anything he adds, 'No one can get into the circus. You've got the day off.'

'Oh. Thanks for telling me.'

I glance at the pale swollen sky and shiver. If no one can get in, that means no one can get out either. I start to shut the door, but Stig steps closer. 'I wondered if you wanted to go for a walk. There's a frozen lake on the other side of the forest. Or we could watch the rehearsal? Oskar is getting everyone to practise for the show, assuming it goes ahead tomorrow.'

A group of performers walk by wearing tattered rags and horned headdresses. The top parts of their faces and the ends of their fingers are painted black, their mouths and jaws white. Each of them carries a pole decorated with feathers and topped with a ram's skull. It reminds me of the drawings Mum did before I left. On the back of the paper was a girl with strings attached to her arms and legs. Thinking about it, she had short dark hair, just like Nina.

Something seemed different about her last night, and then I realise. Her eyes were always black and empty before, but this time there was real emotion behind them. She was afraid. Did she know the dead were waiting for me in the big top? Was she warning me, because she knew what the jester was doing? Is she afraid of him too?

The jester left me the puppet, and if Mum drew Nina with strings, then perhaps the two of them are connected somehow. I still don't know if I can trust Stig, but going for a walk with him has to be better than mulling it over on my own, and maybe there's something he can tell me.

'OK, I'll come. I just need to get ready.'

'I'll wait here for you, Miss Martha.'

I close the door, stung by the casual affection of his words. He used to call me that in the cabin. At the time it made me feel special, as if he really cared for me. A tiny thread of hope pulls at my heart. How does he do that – yank on my strings and make me feel things I don't want to feel?

I throw on some clothes then clean my teeth and brush my hair. It needs washing, but I can have a shower when I get back. I go out and Stig smiles to see me, no doubt relieved that I didn't keep him waiting for long.

We turn right, away from the caravans, and head towards the edge of the clearing. The site is bustling with activity. Workers hurry about carrying wood and calling to one another, and men with spades clear the walkways while others hammer and pull on ropes. Oskar stands in the centre of it all, waving his arms and shouting.

Stig notices me looking. 'They're doing Ragnarok for the closing night. There are posters for it everywhere in town. I've never seen them do a fire show before. It should be amazing.'

I nod, remembering how the seamstress said she had to make new costumes. Whatever Oskar has planned, something tells me that Karl won't be happy about it.

Stig leads us away from the circus and it's a relief to turn my back on it. The treetops are thick with ravens, calling to one another with caws and gurgling croaks. The sound sends a chill through me and I scan the trees nervously. I don't think I've ever seen so many birds in one place. It feels like an omen.

He points into the forest. 'The trail starts over there.' I follow in his footsteps, my feet sinking into each ice-crusted crater like it was made for me. Watching him trudge through the trees, his hair hanging over his shoulders, reminds me of another time. We didn't exactly have fun at the cabin, but I'm glad he was there to help me, to hold me when I was scared. Sadness tightens my throat. I could really use a friend right now. I wish things were how they were before, when I still trusted him.

Stig turns and smiles awkwardly. 'The path will open up soon.' He seems apologetic about us having to walk in single file, but I'm relieved we can't talk for a while. It gives me a chance to organise my thoughts. The last few days have felt so unreal, I don't know how to begin to tell him about any of it, or even if I should. He was freaked out by

Nina, so how will he react if I tell him about the masks and the horde of dead and the jester?

Just thinking about the dead in the big top makes me shudder. The shadowy figures looked like the souls I abandoned at the tree. Whoever or whatever the jester is, he knew about me dropping the rope. He left the card because he wanted me to find them. But why?

I walk faster and a hideous thought creeps up and taps me on the shoulder. Now the dead know I'm here, what if they come after me again? I remind myself that they only manifest at night or in dim light. I need to stay focused on finding out about Nina – and this is my chance to ask Stig about her.

We climb higher, the path falling away beneath us. The forest feels ancient compared to the one on the island. Here the trees are taller and the ground uneven, great hollows and dips in the earth making it look primeval. Among the pines are thicker tree trunks and patches of green moss peeking through the snow.

After five minutes or so the trail widens and we walk side by side. Stig glances at me then coughs and looks away. Silence grows between us with each step, taking on a shape of its own like a third person on the path. Eventually the trees thin and I see a flash of sparkling white. He pushes away a snowy branch and my breath catches.

The lake is much bigger than I expected. It looks more than a mile wide. Beyond the expanse of glittering ice is a huge steep-sided valley, covered by an army of fir trees. Fog hangs over the hillside, obscuring the tops of the trees in a swirling shroud of white. It is breathtaking, but there is savagery in its beauty.

'Wow. I had no idea this was here.'

Stig grins. 'I knew you'd love it. We can walk on it if you like.'

I nod and follow him to the shore, my boots sliding on snowy gravel. He steps onto the lake and offers me his hand. I don't take it, but then my foot slips and I grab his arm.

The impressions from his coat are sketchy, I guess because he hasn't worn it very much yet. Even if I tried to read it, I doubt it would hold many memories. All I can sense are passing emotions. Right now, there's a faint buzz of anxiety mixed with happiness. The idea of seeing Nina again scares him, but it's a risk he's willing to take to spend time with me. I pull away, surprised by the tenderness of his emotion, then look at the hard ice and remind myself that he could have something to hide. I don't want to get hurt again.

'We need skates,' I mutter.

'What, you didn't bring any?' he laughs.

I smile and keep walking. The lake appeared smooth from a distance but peering down I see the pale and bumpy ice is pockmarked with blue-grey bubbles and scored with lines. We venture further out, both of us treading carefully. Stig's phone rings. He pulls it from his pocket then blows out an angry sigh.

'Your mum?' I ask.

'She won't leave me alone. When are you coming back, you can't keep running from your problems, we need to talk . . .'

'What does she want to talk about?' I ask.

'She's selling the house I grew up in and moving to the suburbs with my stepfather. She wants me to live with them and take a job in his factory. Erik is dependable and hardworking, he eats herring on Tuesday and tacos on a Friday –'

'So?'

'So he's boring. Dad wasn't perfect but at least he knew how to have fun. If I had a bad day at school he'd let me stay off and we'd go camping, or he'd take me for a ride on his motorbike. Dad was a free spirit. He always had a bag waiting by the door.'

I think back to the first time I met Stig. When I touched his leather trench coat, I felt two distinct types of emotion – love and kindness, and then a deeper feeling of bitterness, jealousy and hate. I didn't understand it at first, until he told me that the coat used to belong to his father. Stig is fooling himself. His dad crashed his car and died because he'd been drinking. He wasn't some free spirit; he was irresponsible and angry at the world.

Neither of us speaks for a while and somehow the silence makes the air seem colder. The sky weighs heavy above our heads and the wind has dropped for once. There is something oddly still about the place, oppressive almost. This whole time I've been telling myself I can go home whenever I like, all I have to do is call a taxi, but now the road is closed. I know they'll probably clear it, but what if Karl is right and a storm is on the way? If more snow comes, I could be trapped here, like a horrible dream I can't wake up from.

Stig turns to me, his eyes piercingly blue. 'You know, I wasn't sure how I'd feel about coming back, but I'm glad I did.'

He smiles at me expectantly but all I can think about is the boy with tattoos.

'When you left yesterday, I saw you arguing with that guy.'

I expect his expression to darken, but his smile barely wavers.

'He thought I took something of his, but I didn't. It was nothing.'

I hold his gaze, unconvinced, and he sighs. 'Nina dated him before me, but she ended it. He's hated me ever since.'

It starts to snow, huge white flakes swirling around us, and Stig throws his arms wide and grins at the sky. I imagine how we must look from above: two tiny figures in the middle of a vast icy wasteland. The sense of insignificance is so strong I can feel it in my body: a shrinking, gnawing emptiness in the pit of my belly. It's like we're trapped in a snow globe – specks of nothing for the gods to look down on, to shake whenever they like.

Stig steals a hopeful glance at me and I do my best to smile, but my mind is a blizzard of questions. He was the last person to see Nina alive; there must be something he knows. I think back to what Ruth told me. She said the police were convinced Nina was wearing a harness and it got caught around her neck, yet they were unable to find one at the scene. When I mentioned it to Stig, he got defensive. If he has something to hide, then asking him outright isn't going to work. I need to take a subtle approach.

'When did you say you first came here?' I ask.

He smiles hesitantly, revealing two tiny dimples. 'The circus travelled up from Oslo a few months ago. I wanted to get away and Nina suggested I come with her.'

'Did you get on well together, you and Nina?'

'Sure.'

'You didn't argue?'

He gives me a strange look. 'Why do you ask?'

'You said you stayed in my caravan after she threw you out. I'm just trying to understand.' I don't mention that I touched Nina's jacket and saw him yelling in her face.

He blows out a sigh, his breath like smoke on the air. 'You still think there's some big mystery to be solved, don't you?'

'I think Nina got me here for a reason, yes.'

Great flurries of white float down and for a moment I can't see across the lake. Suddenly it feels dangerous to be out in the middle of nowhere. Stig starts to walk away but I step in front of him.

'When we were in the cabin, you told me Nina had met someone new. I remember you joking about her leaving you for a lion tamer. Is that what you argued about, the fact that she was seeing someone else?'

Stig chews his lip and looks away. I know I'm prying, but I can't stop. 'Or did you just say that, and you hadn't really split up?'

He glares at me. 'No. Nina did finish with me. The day she fell, she told me she was seeing someone else.'

I start to ask another question but he speaks first. 'Seriously, Martha, we need to get back.' He's right – the snow is coming down so fast I can barely see the trees ahead of us. We keep our heads down and hurry over the gravel, only pausing once we reach the forest.

He pulls away a branch for me to step onto the trail and we walk side by side, our shoulders almost touching.

'So did you find out who she was seeing?' I ask.

'No. I believed her at the time, but I never found out about anyone else. I think she just said it to upset me.'

'You told me before that she refused to wear a harness to get a reaction from you. Why did she want to make you angry all the time?'

An edge of bitterness creeps into his voice. 'Nina was good at finding my weak spots and poking her fingers in them.'

'You haven't answered my question.'

He pauses and turns to me, snowflakes glistening on his hair. 'I wish I had told you everything in the cabin, about seeing Nina's ghost. I wish I had returned to the island, I wish I had replied to your messages. I want to be honest with you, and I am trying, but sometimes the truth is complicated.' He holds my gaze, his expression open. There is such kindness in his eyes. I can tell he's trying to put things right.

'I know you're angry with me for disappearing like that, and you have a right to be, but please, can we start over? I'll tell you everything from now on. You can trust me, I promise. It's just, I know you want things to be black and white, but sometimes they're not.'

'OK, I'm listening. Explain it to me.'

He starts walking again then says, 'Nina saw life as one big party. Everything was an adventure, an event. She was exciting to be with, one of the most exciting people I've ever met, but after Dad died I wasn't much fun to be around. He always used to say that women are fine when you're being who they want you to be, but show any weakness and they don't want to know. It was like that with Nina. After he died, I had no energy for anything and she took it personally. She was talented and beautiful, the star of the show, but she was insecure too. If I'm honest, I was tired of pretending to be someone I wasn't. I was tired of being her audience.'

I nod, unsure what to say. One thing I do know, the more I hear about his dad the less I like him.

Stig adds quickly, 'I don't mean to say she was a bad person. She wasn't. She was kind and fun and generous. She just didn't know how to help me, and I . . .' His voice cracks. 'In the end it was me who let her down.'

I hate seeing him upset, but at the same time I'm relieved he's telling me all this. It feels like I'm finally getting somewhere. He seemed so earnest about wanting me to trust him – and I want to, but something doesn't add up. I get that Nina craved attention, but I still don't understand why she'd want to provoke him.

'So what did you two argue about, when she threw you out?'

Stig pushes away a branch. 'She didn't like me spending time with Ulva.'

A clump of ice falls down my neck, making me cringe. 'So you're seeing Ulva?'

'No. We're just friends. Ulva is easy to talk to. She didn't expect me to be happy, or make jokes, or entertain her. We just sat in her caravan talking and watching movies. Nina

127

knew there was nothing between us – she just wanted me to spend all my time with her.'

I remember the chiffon scarf in the costume trailer and how Ulva desperately wants to leave the circus. I'm sure Ruth said something about her mum taking off.

'What happened to Ulva's mother?' I ask.

Stig gives me a sideways glance, as if surprised by the question.

'I touched her clothes,' I explain.

He pushes a strand of hair behind his ears. 'Her mum was an acrobat here. She was an alcoholic and had a lot of issues. She left when Ulva was twelve. She's been brought up by the circus since – by Karl and Ruth and Nina and the others.'

'But she wishes her mum would come back and take her away?'

'She did come back. It was just after we arrived here. She asked Ulva to leave with her, but Nina stopped it from happening.'

'How?'

'Ulva's mum left a note in her caravan telling her to meet by the entrance that night. If she wasn't there, she'd know she didn't want to go with her. Nina saw the note before Ulva did, and she took it. Later, she admitted what she'd done and tried to explain that she did it to protect her, but Ulva wouldn't forgive her. Nina did everything she could to make it up to her. She even promised she could take the lead role and play Baldur.'

I think about the image I saw of Ulva bound and thrashing to get free. I guess that explains why she feels trapped here.

Stig shakes his head. 'Ulva was really upset. Most of the others stayed out if it, but Ruth went crazy – screaming and shouting at Nina, saying it wasn't her decision to make.'

I remember when I brushed Ruth's sleeve. She was outraged on Ulva's behalf, but there was more to it than that. The baby she left behind in Ireland must be a teenager now. I know she wants to go back and see her. Maybe she got angry because it triggered a fear in her, imagining how she would feel if someone stopped them being together. I still don't understand why she'd feel guilty or worry that she'd contributed to Nina's death though.

We walk the rest of the way in single file. This time the silence wraps around us like a blanket, allowing us to take refuge in our thoughts. The snowfall has eased and a murky gloom settles over the forest, wisps of fog circling the trunks like lost spirits. The world seems oddly quiet and then I realise why. When we passed this way before, the trees were full of noisy ravens. Now there's not a single bird. It's as if something frightened them away.

We're almost back when we hear a shout. It's a woman's voice, high pitched and panicked. She's saying something in Norwegian. I look to Stig but he shakes his head, as if her words don't make sense. We walk faster and then a man who sounds as if he could be Nigerian yells, 'She's right. Look! It's been carved into all the trunks!'

13

THE CIRCUS IS CURSED

A dozen performers invade the forest, their horned head-dresses advancing through the trees like mythical beasts. I shrink back as a huge man crashes towards us, shoving away snow-covered branches and grunting. Like the others, he wears a costume made from strips of rough hessian sacking. Antlers are fixed to his head; long tatty ropes hang down his back in a parody of hair. His forehead, eyes, nose and cheeks are completely covered by black paint, his jaw and bushy beard coated in white. He pauses a little way ahead of me and yells, 'It's the same here!' At his words, ragged horned creatures approach from every direction.

Stig hurries over to the group and I follow him and push my way to the front. Four runes have been carved into a trunk, one below the other. I glance to either side of me and see that dozens of trees have the same symbols. There's something chilling about seeing them repeated over and over. A man calls in the distance, 'Here too!' Another cries from the opposite direction, 'And here! They're all around the clearing!' People speak over each other, some in Norwegian and others in English, their voices taut with worry.

Karl limps through the crowd and shouts above the din. '*Hva skjer her?*' Everyone falls quiet and moves aside to let him pass. He touches the carved symbols with trembling fingers, his face pale. Suddenly the atmosphere changes, loud surprised voices replaced with hushed fear. Karl pulls a notebook from his jacket pocket, and still no one speaks. The only sound is the stirring of the wind in the treetops, as if the forest is whispering dark curses.

Oskar arrives sweaty and out of breath. He glances at the circle of faces then pushes his glasses up and peers at the trunk. 'A few marks on a tree! Come on, back to work.'

The bearded man grunts, 'It's hundreds of trees, a whole ring of them right around the clearing.' A performer wearing sackcloth with holes cut out for eyes shakes his head, his long straw-hair rustling. Next to him, a man with an animal skull fastened over his face murmurs in agreement. 'The way they appeared from nowhere, it would have taken dozens of people working together.' People turn and glance around, and I feel it too. There's something out there in the gloom, something bad. A woman puts her hands on her hips. White streaks are painted on her cheeks and down her chin and she wears a string of bones around her neck. 'It's not natural.'

Oskar gives a nervous laugh. 'It's a prank. Someone will have done it during the night.' The performers look to one another, unsure. When no one contradicts him, I step forward. 'We walked this trail an hour ago. They weren't here then – we would have noticed.'

Stig speaks up behind me. 'Martha's right. They weren't there just now.' He gives me a reassuring nod and a warm glow spreads in my belly. It feels like how it was before, the two of us facing the world together. A woman notices and tuts, a look of suspicion in her eyes. I glance at the faces around me, and the way they stare at Stig makes me uneasy. I don't have to touch their clothes to know he isn't welcome here.

Oskar turns on him. 'You were Nina's boyfriend, weren't you?' Stig drops his gaze and the circus manager continues, 'I thought you'd run off weeks ago, and yet here you are . . . and trouble right behind you.'

Karl waves the notebook at Oskar like a preacher damning a sinner. 'You are the one bringing trouble. Tell me, which myth were you doing just now?'

Oskar blows out a sigh. 'You know very well, Karl.'

'I do know. And I warned you against it. Again and again I warned you.'

Oskar raises his voice. 'I'm sure your book of fiction is all very interesting, but the fact remains we need to rehearse.' He turns and addresses the crowd. 'We've invested a lot of money in tomorrow night, not just props and costumes but hiring extra crew and security. I'm assured that the road will open in time. If the show is a failure, we're ruined. The circus will close. Everyone will lose their jobs. Those are the facts.'

Performers look at one another, anxiety written on their faces. Oskar smiles as if pleased his words are having the desired effect. 'You can either stand here and listen to superstitious nonsense, or you can get back to work.'

A few people at the back of the group walk away. The huge man with the beard sees them leave and turns to Karl. There is kindness in his voice, as if he's trying to understand. 'Why shouldn't we do this show tomorrow? What will happen if we do?'

Karl clears his throat then says in a loud voice, 'Many years ago, before I was born, the circus was nearly destroyed. It happened shortly after my father became manager. There was a fire that destroyed the big top; nine performers lost their lives.'

Oskar tuts. 'A terrible tragedy, yes, but what does that have to do with anything?'

Karl glares at him and continues, 'It happened the first time they performed a myth with the Sly One. My father ruled that the circus would never perform his stories again and it's been that way for ninety years. I've seen to it that nothing has changed.' He jabs his black book in the air. 'Until the owners demanded I introduce a new routine. *Everyone* loves the Sly One, they said, and so we did the myth of Baldur, and poor Nina . . .'

A ripple of unease goes through the crowd. Oskar snorts incredulously. 'Because you did one of Loki's stories, you think the circus is cursed?'

A German woman speaks up. 'The day we began practising the myth of Baldur, people became different, their personalities changed. I'm not the only one to notice it.'

The crowd murmurs in agreement and Karl smiles with relief. 'Yes! Klara is right, we shouldn't have changed things.'

'*Dummkopf*!' shouts Oskar. 'The myths are just stories – they don't have some special power!' He points at Karl. 'You can't keep doing the same old routines and expect visitors to come back year after year. If you don't change, you die. Admit it, you hate change. You're scared of it. You've been against this new performance from the start. How do we know *you* didn't carve the marks in those trees?' He sighs and addresses the crowd. 'If you want to keep your jobs, then get back to work!' He turns and strides towards the circus and half of the performers follow him. The rest watch him go, then trail after him reluctantly.

Standing alone, Karl makes such a dejected figure that my heart aches for him. What if he's right and acting out Loki's stories really has brought bad luck? Maybe Loki *did* have something to do with Nina's death. All I know is that he sired three children – Hel, the wolf Fenrir and a sea serpent – and that they're meant to destroy the gods at Ragnarok, the end of the world. Ruth told me that Loki caused the death of Baldur, but she didn't say *why* he did it. I wish I knew more about the gods. I wish I knew more about everything.

I go over to Karl and ask, 'Can I see your book, please?'

He hands it to me and I flick through pages of scrawled handwriting along with rune symbols and drawings of set layouts.

'It lists the myths that can be performed and those which shouldn't be done?' I ask.

Karl nods then adds, 'It was my father's. He ran this place before me.'

Stig follows me and peers over my shoulder as I read a section entitled 'Loki – Master of Manipulation'. At the top of the page is a black cross. Lots of myths are described: Loki Mothers Odin's Horse Sleipnir, Loki Cuts off Sif's Hair, Loki Invents the Fishing Net, Loki and the Kidnapping of Idun, Loki Is Refused an Invitation, Loki Bets His Head. I skim-read the stories. In many of them Loki appears to get the gods into trouble, then saves the day with his cunning.

I go back and read the last one, Loki Bets His Head.

No one loves a wager more than the Trickster. Having persuaded a pair of dwarves to create three fine treasures, Loki bets two others that they can't make anything as good. If they can, he tells them, they are welcome to his head.

The dwarves set to work and create the boar Gullinbursti, the golden ring Draupnir and the hammer Mjolnir. Never one to play fair, Loki shapeshifts into a fly and repeatedly bites the dwarf manning the forge-bellows. Despite Loki's best efforts to cheat, Freyr, Odin and Thor are so impressed with the dwarves' craftsmanship they declare them the winners.

When the dwarves attempt to cut off Loki's head, he tells them that they are welcome to it, as long as they don't damage his neck in the process. Frustrated at being tricked, one of the dwarves sews Loki's mouth shut.

I reread the last sentence and shiver. The man in the psychic tent . . . A sudden gust of wind turns the pages and I gasp to see a picture of an old-fashioned jester holding a net.

I hold out the book to Karl, my hand shaking. 'Who's that?'

He tuts as if the answer is obvious. 'The Trickster. He can take any form, but that is one of his oldest guises.'

A cold feeling crawls across my skin as I realise that he's here, at the circus. I've been so stupid! Of course the jester is Loki! And the man in the psychic tent, that was him too.

I look back at the book and there are four runes, the same ones carved into the trees. Next to each symbol is a letter. L-O-K-I.

'Why didn't you tell everyone what the runes mean?' I ask.

'They wouldn't believe me.' He glances about him and I have the feeling he's just as afraid as the others, maybe even more. 'Oskar is right; people will think I did this.'

'I believe you, Karl. The old-fashioned clown I told you about, it was a jester. I've seen him – the Trickster. He's here at the circus.'

Karl looks at me with disbelief.

'What? You have to be joking.' Stig laughs nervously.

Ignoring him, I point to the rune markings in the book. Beneath are written the words: *If you want change, you have to invite chaos*.

'Wasn't one of the myths called Loki Is Refused an Invitation?' I ask.

Karl nods and I turn back a few pages and read aloud. 'After he caused the death of Baldur, Loki was turned away from the hall of the gods. Angry, he forced his way inside, demanding a seat at the table as was his right as Odin's blood brother.'

I glance at the old circus manager and he explains. 'Odin mixed blood with him in a gesture of friendship – they aren't related.'

'So what does the Trickster do once he gets into the hall?' asks Stig.

Karl sniffs. 'He insults all the gods. After that he takes off and shapeshifts into a salmon, but Thor catches him. The gods later chain him to a rock where a snake drips venom on him. It's foretold that he will stay there until he breaks free at Ragnarok, where he will cause chaos and carnage.'

Something shifts in the cave of my mind and bile floods my throat as the realisation hits me. The circus kept Loki out by not doing his stories. As soon as they performed one of his myths, Nina died. She was going to play Baldur, the god that Loki killed in the myth. It can't be a coincidence; he must have had something to do with her death. And now the circus is going to do one of his biggest stories – Ragnarok, the end of the world.

Karl mutters in Norwegian then says, 'They have to cancel the performance.'

He strides towards the clearing and I chase after him, with Stig following behind.

'Martha, wait!' Stig catches up with me. 'What did you mean about Loki being here?'

I don't answer and he grabs my arm and spins me around. 'Tell me.'

I sigh heavily. 'He came to see me in the psychic tent as a man and then I saw him again, only as a jester.'

He looks at me unsure. 'Faen. You're serious, aren't you?'

'I didn't want to tell you, but it's not just Nina here. I saw dozens of dead in the big top last night. I don't know why or how they're here, but Loki wanted me to find them.' Stig's eyes dart in the direction of the road and a huff of disappointment escapes me. Of course he won't want to stay now. 'Don't worry. I'm sure they'll open the road soon.'

'What?' He shakes his head as if I've misunderstood him completely. 'I'm not going anywhere, not if you're in danger. I'm staying with you, if you'll let me.' I give a tight smile then look away, knowing that words are easy.

He takes a deep breath. 'Look, I've promised to be honest with you, Martha, and there's something I should say.' My body tenses and I search his eyes, afraid of what I might see. 'I told you before that I was nervous about going back to the cabin after everything that happened, and it's true. But there's another reason I didn't reply to your messages. I needed time to think about what I really wanted. I've fallen into relationships before and they didn't go well, and I wanted things to be different with you.'

I raise my eyebrows and he talks quickly. 'I know you can't leave your mum, not with how she is, and you have to water the tree. Moving to the island meant giving up my dreams – of biking around Europe and seeing all the places Dad talked about. I wanted to be sure, because the last thing I want is to let you down, and if I messaged you

I knew we'd start talking and I wouldn't be able to keep away from you.' He pauses and then adds weakly, 'I guess I was worried things were happening too fast.'

'You should have told me.'

He nods, a tentative smile on his face, and I find myself feeling sad instead of angry. He's right. Things did happen fast between us. But then everything was so intense, seeing the dead and the *draugr* attacking the cabin. At one point, we weren't sure if we were going to survive the night. I spent so much time worrying about the way I look and wondering if he liked me. Perhaps I focused on him so much because I didn't want to face the awful things that were happening. He was something to cling to when everything felt hopeless.

Though it doesn't excuse his behaviour, I understand why he needed time alone to come to a decision. If he's been impulsive and rushed into relationships before, it makes sense to want to be sure.

'So what made you change your mind?' I ask.

'Nothing. I just needed to figure things out, and I have. I want to be with you.'

He squeezes my shoulder and then glances at his glove as if inviting me to read the material, but I don't need my gift to know that he means every word. A familiar fondness spreads in my chest, along with relief. If Loki was involved in Nina's death then Stig didn't have anything to do with it. Whatever happens in the future, right now I'm glad to have a friend.

I glance in the direction of the clearing, torn between talking to Stig and going after Karl. Stig notices me looking and gives me a pained smile. 'I know now isn't the time to be saying all this, but I'd already decided to go back to the island when I heard you were at the circus. I realise I have to make things up to you, but I want you to know you can rely on me. Please can we start again?'

I pull his hand from my shoulder and his expression changes from anxiety to relief as I squeeze his palm and smile. 'OK, but you're right, now isn't the time. Come on, I want to see what Karl does.'

14

HER DEATH WAS NO ACCIDENT

After a few minutes, we emerge from the forest. The performers are in the field gathered around the ringmaster, who stands on a high metal platform. He raises a fist to the sky and booms in a deep voice. 'At Ragnarok, all chains will be loosened, freeing those that are bound. The wolf Fenrir will escape his shackles and Loki himself will ferry the dead to fight the gods.' Horned figures thrust their skull poles in the air and scream a war cry. So that's what the performers are meant to be: a horde of the dead brought by Loki.

A group of wild-looking Viking women stride to the front, some carrying shields painted with rune signs and others beating animal-skin drums. They wear armoured leather breastplates with winged shoulders and their hair is braided into tiny plaits. Most have metal chains stretched across their foreheads with elaborate silver centrepieces – a raven, a wolf, a *valknut*. Their makeup is simple but stunning. A band of black covers their eyes; some with vertical lines on each cheek, others a feathered network of branches reaching to their hairline.

Performers file in behind them: the Norns and ravens on stilts and various gods and goddesses. I recognise Sandrine in her bird outfit, but otherwise it could be anyone behind the masks. The drumbeat quickens and the warrior women move their tongues fast, yelling an ululation – a wavering, high-pitched sound somewhere between a screech and a howl.

Karl stands to one side, talking animatedly to Ruth and the seamstress. He shouts for them to stop the performance, but his voice is no match for the ringmaster's. Refusing to be beaten, the old man hurries across the field and climbs the rigging of the platform. He yanks the loudspeaker from the ringmaster's hands and dozens of people below pause and stare in bewilderment. Eventually Oskar appears and waves his arms, signalling for them to break. A few drift away, but most of the performers crowd around him and demand answers, their voices full of fear.

'How do you know Loki wanted you to find the dead?' Stig asks me.

I tell him about the puppet and invitation and his eyes grow large.

'Can I see it?'

'The card?'

He nods and I shrug. 'Sure, it's in my caravan.' I don't know what Stig thinks he can do to help, but it's a relief to have someone to talk to about it. As we near my door, I see something that makes my throat close. The puppet is sitting on the step, back straight and head tilted to one side, its red slash of a mouth twisted in a smile as if happy to see us. I turn away, not wanting to think about how it got there. Maybe it crawled out of the snow. Thinking about the jester makes me feel weak. I don't know if my life is in danger, but I know that he can control me, that I am completely powerless against him.

Stig sees my face and frowns, his jaw set with determination. 'I'll get rid of it.'

'Be careful, Stig.'

He strides to the door. 'I think there's some matches and lighter fluid under the sink.'

I hand him my key, careful not to go near the thing, and a moment later he emerges with his pockets bulging. He lifts the puppet by its foot and it hangs limply from his hand. 'I'll take it to the far side of the site. I'll be as quick as I can. Will you be OK on your own?'

'Yes. Thanks.'

He hesitates, his eyes full of concern. 'Are you sure?'

'I'll be fine, really.'

He gives me an uncertain smile and then takes off. I watch him hurry across the field and let out a shaky breath, grateful that I won't have to deal with it. Dozens of performers are walking back across the site, so presumably Karl managed to stop the rehearsal.

I spot Ulva heading towards her caravan and walk in her direction. I don't know what Loki wants with me or what kind of perverse game he's playing, but I won't let him distract me. I need to find out what happened to Nina, and Ruth said that she and Ulva were like sisters. She must know *something*.

❦

I reach Ulva's caravan just before she does. She's wearing the same costume as before, a grey cloak with a lavish fur-lined collar, the wolf mask tucked under her arm.

She greets me warmly. 'Hi, are you looking for Stig?'

'Actually, I was hoping to talk to you.'

'Oh.'

'Is it OK to come in?'

'Sure.'

She looks a little confused, but takes out her key and opens the door with a tentative smile. Her place is bigger than mine but just as shabby. Everything is pale and faded, from the floral sofas and curtains to the laminate wood-flooring and cupboards. Dirty plates clutter the counter and it smells of cooking: mashed potatoes and the tang of pickled fish.

She places the mask on the table, and the wolf leers as if daring me, its empty eyes seeing both nothing and too much.

'Do you want a drink or something to eat?'

'No, I'm fine, thanks.'

She gestures for me to sit then goes to the counter and says over her shoulder, 'Sorry, I'll be with you soon. Work always makes me hungry.' While she fixes a sandwich, I slide onto the bench and then look around the room. The flowery wallpaper is peeling and in places it's been picked off, or 'Ulva' is scrawled over it in green crayon. There are no pictures, just a few flimsy magazine posters stuck to the wall: one of a snowy mountain scene and one of a snake. A pile of children's picture books lies abandoned on a dusty corner unit. Stig said that Ulva was raised by the circus. I can't imagine what it must have been like for her. No wonder her daydream felt desperate when I touched her chiffon scarf. She must miss her mum so much.

She puts a glass of water and a plate on the table then sits opposite me. For a moment neither of us says anything, then she smiles nervously. 'You do know Stig and I are just friends, don't you?'

'Yes, Stig said.'

I watch her eat and wonder what he's told her about me. Presumably she knows I didn't get a job here by chance. Does that mean others know too? Would she have told Ruth?

'Good.' She swallows another bite of her sandwich and looks at me kindly, her voice sincere. 'Only you seem nice and Stig deserves to be happy, especially after Nina.'

I take a deep breath and keep my voice level. 'I heard about the accident.'

Ulva raises her eyebrows and I have a feeling I need to tread carefully.

'Ruth told me about it,' I explain. 'She said you and Nina were like sisters. You must miss her.' I wait a moment then add, 'I hope you don't mind me asking, but Ruth sounded like she was upset with Nina about something. She mentioned they had some kind of argument and I wondered if you knew –'

Ulva tears off some sandwich and barely chews before swallowing and taking another bite. She wipes her mouth with the back of her hand, then reaches towards the mask on the table and strokes the wolf's fur, her eyes burning with quiet intensity.

'Ruth is a good person. She was just looking out for me.'

'How do you mean?'

She glances at me as if suddenly aware of my presence. 'Nothing, sorry. I shouldn't have said anything.'

'Please, go on.'

'I was planning to leave the circus with Mum, but Nina tricked me into staying.' She looks away and her face darkens as if she doesn't like remembering. 'When Ruth found out she got angry, *really* angry. She even put a binding spell on her.'

'A spell?'

Ulva shrugs. 'She's into magic and things. She wanted to stop Nina from doing anything like that again.'

I remember the evening I had dinner in Ruth's caravan. There was a shelf with some candles and a figure wrapped in green thread. I didn't think much about it at the time, but maybe it was an altar.

146

Ulva adds quickly, 'Please don't mention it to anyone. Ruth didn't have anything to do with Nina's accident, but I can tell she worries about it, and I don't want her to feel bad.'

I nod and Ulva forces a smile then changes the subject. 'I wanted Nina and Stig to be happy, I really did, but they weren't good for each other. They made one another miserable, arguing all the time. Anyway, he has you now. I guess you'll be going home together soon.'

She sees my expression and adds, 'Sorry, did I get it wrong? Stig said something about going to the island with you. I forget the name of the place . . .'

I smile in surprise, realising that Stig must have told Ulva he wants to move to Skjebne. He seemed so different in the forest, honest and open in a way he hasn't been before. Maybe we *could* have a future.

A noise makes me startle – a swish, snap and thud.

We turn and look together.

'What was that?' I ask.

Ulva meets my gaze, her face pale.

She stands up and walks across the room and I follow her, the skin on my arms prickling. It sounded like it came from inside. There are two closed doors at the rear of the caravan. She pauses before one of them and I hold my breath. I can't hear anything now, but I have a bad feeling about what might be behind the door.

Ulva pushes it open and Nina is swaying from the ceiling, scrabbling at a seemingly invisible rope around her neck, her eyes bulging. I cover my mouth and swallow a scream.

Her skin is grey, the veins on her forehead protruding as if they might burst. She struggles, gasping for breath, then her body goes limp and her head drops. 'Weird, must have been something outside.' Ulva carries on talking but I barely hear her. I want to shout and point at the dead girl hanging from her bedroom ceiling, but I don't. I want to look away, but I can't. How horrific it must have been to fall from the trapeze. Nina has put me and Mum through so much, but there's no anger inside me now. All I feel is a gnawing sense of pity. If only there were something I could do, some way I could help her.

'You OK? Martha?' Ulva touches my arm and I nod without turning my head.

Nina's eyes snap open. She looks at me pleadingly, as if I'm the only one who can save her, and I hold her gaze, silently promising to get justice for her. And then she vanishes. I rest a hand on my chest and try to calm my nerves, and that's when I notice it. Under Ulva's bed is an open shoebox, with a gold catsuit inside it.

Coldness blooms in the pit of my stomach. I *know* it's hers. Nina wanted me to find it, that's why she appeared. I turn to Ulva, my heart racing.

'Actually, could I use your toilet, please?'

She points to her right. 'Sure, it's just there.'

I watch as she walks into the kitchen and turns on the tap. Now's my chance. I slip into her bedroom and pull the door closed. My blood pounds in my ears. I don't stop to catch my breath or ready myself. I drop to my knees and pull out the box. Ignoring the photos, letters and jewellery, I grab the catsuit.

148

Impressions slam into me. Snatches of images and feelings jumbled up together. Nina is screaming at Stig outside the big top. Betrayal, jealousy, anger ... each emotion stronger than the last.

I take my hand away and catch my breath. The mix of materials is confusing. I'm seeing facts, so the catsuit contains cotton. But the way it hurls emotions at me, it must contain polyester too.

I clutch the fabric and demand to see a memory. This time I see the world through Nina's eyes. She's climbing the metal rigging in the big top, rage pumping her legs ever faster. The higher she goes, the more powerful she feels. Stig is far below, a small figure in the middle of the ring. She wants him to shout her name; she wants to make him care.

Stig calls up, 'You're being stupid!' He paces and flaps his arms. 'Just wear your harness, Nina. Please!'

'It's over, Stig! I mean it this time. I'm seeing someone else.'

She peers down, sure that he'll say something. She wants him to fight for her but he just stands there, saying nothing. She grabs hold of the nearby trapeze and sways her body outwards. Her hands are sweating. She knows she should be wearing a harness, but she's done the movement a thousand times before. Her muscles have a memory; her body carries a confidence of its own.

Why doesn't he say something? She swings back the other way, changing her grip. His silence makes her reckless. She spins and turns, snatching the bar of the trapeze. If she carries on like this, he'll be forced to climb up.

'You OK in there, Martha?'

Ulva's voice jolts me back to the present. I drop the material and swallow, my mouth dry. What do I do? Should I steal it? I hold still and listen, but I can't hear footsteps. After a moment, I open the door. She's wiping down the kitchen counter, her back to me.

'Yeah, I'm OK. I'll be out soon.'

She starts to turn around and I dip back inside, praying she doesn't see the door move. I have to be quick. I pick up the catsuit and shut my eyes.

Nina is now standing on a high metal platform; the ring empty below. She gasps as two strong hands tug at her harness from behind. *Stig*, she thinks, his name like a kiss on her lips. She wants to take him in her arms, but the harness is holding her so tight she can't turn around.

I drop the material, my heart racing. So she *was* wearing a harness; Stig fastened it for her. The police were right . . . they said she was wearing one and it must have caught around her neck. Of course. That's why Nina kept clutching her throat; why she appeared to me hanging. I can't believe I didn't figure it out before. She's been trying to show me how she died. She wanted me to know that Stig lied. He must have hidden the harness or the police would have found it, which means her death was no accident. I thought Loki was behind it somehow and it couldn't be Stig, but now . . .

I stare into space, my chest heaving. Did he do it up wrong on purpose? Did he push her? I grasp the catsuit and knead the material, demanding to see. The thread of memory snaps and suddenly there's nothing. No image, no emotion. It's like before, when I tried to read Ruth's shawl. Tears sting my eyes. My gift can't fail me now.

15

An Unwelcome Guest

I burst out of the bedroom, my head throbbing. Stig isn't a murderer, he can't be! There must be an explanation. Something I'm not seeing. Ulva jumps up and gives me a strange look but I don't stop to explain. I rush to the door, desperate to get away.

She follows me outside. 'Are you going? What's wrong?'

I mumble an apology and stumble down the steps. As I hurry to my caravan, I check all around me, hoping I don't see Stig. A lump comes to my throat and tears prick my eyes. He said he would be honest with me; he said I could trust him.

I head in the direction of the big top, deciding to cut through the circus. The workers and performers have gone

152

and a cold grey mist hangs over the ground, giving the site an unearthly feel. I pick up my pace, grateful the walkways have been cleared. They wouldn't have done that if more snow was forecast. Maybe that means the road's been opened now.

I follow the path around the side of the big top then stop dead. A huge wooden Viking ship stands in the field to my right. The thin wooden frame has a dragonhead at each end and a row of circular shields pinned to the side, painted with rune markings. There's something unnerving about the way it's suddenly appeared, as if it was left there by unnatural forces, not constructed by men working hard with hammers and ropes.

Something out in the fog catches my attention. At first I think a group of performers are gathered in a circle, but then I realise that they aren't people. Around twenty poles have been driven into the ground. Fixed to the top of each one is an animal skull: a ram's head, one with antlers, another that looks like a dog.

A woman is coming along the path, half hidden in the shadow of a tent. Maybe she can tell me if the road's been opened. I walk faster, relieved to see someone, when she steps into the light. Where it touches her, she all but vanishes. Part of her lower arm fades and then she turns and the side of her face disappears, her leg disintegrating in a swirl of mist.

My heart bangs against my ribcage. If one ghost has formed, it won't be long until there are more. I clasp my hand to my middle, remembering the icy pain I felt when one of them swiped its fingers through me.

Beneath the big top is a patch of deep shadow. Something about it doesn't look right. It pulsates, but the movement isn't swirling fog; something is taking shape. A grey arm reaches out, fingers curling under the edge of the tent. More arms appear, grabbing and struggling, as if dozens of people are trapped under the canvas, trying to get out.

I run to the end of the walkway, then jump down and race to my caravan. It's darker in the forest. Shadowy faces peer from between the trees, all of them pained and despairing. A young boy, no older than six, sobs and reaches out to me. What do they want from me? Why are they here?

I fumble with my keys and dart inside, then lock the door and switch on the lights. Exhausted, I drop onto the sofa and wipe the window. There's no crowd of dead outside, but it won't be long until it's dark enough for more of them to form. The town isn't far. If the road is open it should only take a taxi twenty minutes to get here. My heart sinks. I still need to walk across the site to get to the entrance and then cut through the forest to reach the road. When I was in the big top, the man's hand cut through me like a shard of ice. Who knows how many of them are out in the darkness? I can't risk it.

Tapping sounds at the door and I stare at it, not moving. *Please don't let it be the jester.* I wait and it comes again, louder this time.

'Martha! Are you OK?'

I pull the curtain back a fraction and Stig is outside. He kicks at the snow. 'I burned the puppet. Ulva said you left in a hurry. Are you OK? Did something happen?'

I keep quiet, hoping he hasn't seen me. I feel bad for not answering, especially after he got rid of the puppet for me, but I can't face talking to him right now.

'I know you're in there,' he shouts. 'I can see the lights on. Please, Martha, I'm worried about you!'

The door handle rattles, then goes quiet and I hold my breath. After a few moments my shoulders drop with relief. He's gone.

But then a loud knock sounds at the door, followed by another. 'Martha, please!'

I bite my thumbnail, my mind racing. If I don't answer him, he might try to break in. I steady my nerves and call, 'Sorry, but I don't feel well. I just want to sleep.'

His voice softens. 'Can I come in? Please, I just want to make sure you're OK.'

Mum said something about a man who shouldn't be invited inside. She called him an *unwelcome guest*. Stig broke into Mormor's cabin and I let him stay, even though I didn't really want him there.

Bang.

Something hits the side of the caravan and I scrabble away, my heart pounding. What will Stig do once he realises I know? I saw how angry he can get when I touched Nina's jacket in the costume trailer. He came all this way to stop me finding out the truth, so how far will he go to keep me quiet? He's silent for a moment then says, 'If someone's said something, you can tell me. You can tell me anything.' When I don't reply, he sighs. 'OK. I'll see you in the morning, I guess.'

I pull back the curtain and see him walking away, his shoulders slumped. Above him, the pale moon hangs lonely in the starless sky, its scarred face veiled with cloud. I watch him disappear from sight and then rest my arms on the table and lower my head. My brain aches from trying to make sense of it all. I don't want to believe that Stig is a murderer, but then why did he tell the police that Nina wasn't wearing a harness? I think back to what Ruth told me. She said they looked for a harness but couldn't find one. If he did it up wrong on purpose, maybe he took it to hide the evidence. And what about everything else that's been happening: the masks and Loki and the horde of dead? I was sure Nina's death must be caught up in it somehow. Maybe Stig killed her but he was made to do it. Maybe it wasn't his fault?

I sit going over it all until my arms are numb from the cold. Shivering here won't help. I may as well try to sleep. I glance outside and the sky is darker now, the tiny lights of the tents glowing bright in the distance. The wind has dropped and a heavy mist rolls across the site, and then I realise why the fog seems to be moving. It's writhing with the dead, heading this way. There are twice as many as when they followed me back from the big top.

I snatch open the curtains and the light from the kitchen spills onto the snow, forming a ring of protection. The dead rush closer and a moment later they're surrounding the caravan. Masses of shadowy arms form a circle, all reaching and snatching as if desperate to grab me. Loki has brought them here. Does he mean to punish me for dropping the rope? One touch from the man in the big top felt like a knife in my side. I don't want to think what will happen if more catch hold of me. They must be out there now because they want revenge after I abandoned them. What other reason can there be?

16

I'M DONE HIDING FROM HIM

My sleep was thin and frayed by strange dreams, and now my head aches with tiredness. It's early but the site is already busy: workmen unravelling cables, climbing metal rigging and fixing outdoor lights into place. As soon as it got light I went to Ruth's caravan, desperate to see a friendly face. When I knocked on her door she didn't answer, so I came here, to the psychic tent.

I pause outside it now, hoping she hasn't figured out that I know Stig and didn't apply for the job by chance. I'm not sure what I'm going to say, or how much to tell her, I just need to be with someone I trust. The door is hooked partially open. I step inside and Ruth is on her hands and knees under the table; a black tablecloth draped over her shoulders so it looks as if she's been beheaded. The table is covered with animal bones, arranged in the shape of various runes. In the centre sits a human skull, a spread of tarot cards beneath. I think back to the reading she gave me and realise she was right. Stig did come back. Ruth drags out a large woven basket, cursing under her breath, then straightens up – and yelps when she sees me. 'Christ! You nearly sent me to my maker!'

'Sorry.'

In her hand is a white latex mask, its ghoulish face hanging to the floor. She notices me looking and explains, 'A little jump scare for the clients. Oskar says people will love it.' I frown, thinking it looks like a cheap fairground trick, and she rolls her eyes. 'It's a shite idea, but what can you do.' She tosses it in the basket and sighs. 'Karl is right – Oskar will be the death of this place. All these changes he's making, it's chaos.'

My stomach tightens to a hard knot. *If you want change, you have to invite chaos.* I bite my thumbnail, wondering what will happen if they go ahead with the new performance. 'Karl hasn't persuaded Oskar to reconsider then?' I ask.

Ruth huffs. 'No. Ragnarok is right on schedule, despite his best efforts. You heard about the carvings they found on the trees? Apparently they spell "Loki". Karl insists he didn't make them, but I'm not falling for it. I've always thought his whole superstitious thing is an act. He hates Oskar taking over. I bet you any money he carved them himself, hoping to scare the others and make them cancel tonight.'

I shrug, deciding to keep quiet. Karl was right not to show people the runes in his book. They would think he was responsible for the ones on the trees. Karl has managed to keep Loki out for years, just as the gods banished him after he caused the death of Baldur. But now Oskar is making him the star of the show. If rehearsing this new myth has invited him here, does that mean other gods are at the circus too? Odin features in all the performances.

I lean forward and chew my thumbnail harder, wishing I could make sense of things.

Ruth gives me a worried look. 'Is everything all right? If something is wrong you can tell me, you know. I'm a good listener.'

I want to tell her about the jester but if she doesn't believe Karl, someone she's worked with for years, she isn't going to believe me.

'Is it Stig? I take it you have some history with him.'

I look at her in surprise. I desperately want to ask about him but I'm not sure how much to tell her. She shrugs, not pressing the matter further, and gestures for me to take a seat. I sit down heavily and watch as she rummages through the basket and tuts at a jumble of fairy lights. She lifts out a ball of cord with tiny wooden skulls attached.

'Are you any good at unpicking knots?' she asks.

I nod and she drops the string into my lap. As she leans close, her shawl brushes me, showing me the man I saw before. Suddenly I know who he is. It's her older sister's husband; he's the father of her baby. He forced himself on her, but Ruth was too scared to tell anyone. She was terrified of what he might do, so she left the baby with her parents and ran away.

The feeling of shame and guilt is overwhelming. She thinks about her daughter every day. She longs to go back to Ireland, but her little girl is a teenager now. What if she can't forgive her? I glance at Ruth, wishing I could tell her that the shame she feels isn't hers to carry. I know she's scared, but she can't keep running from the past. She has to see her daughter again, or she'll never find peace. The bitterness of Ruth's regret makes me think about Mum, and a sudden pang of love fills my chest. I'm lucky I have a chance to put things right between us. Not everyone has that.

Sandrine appears in the doorway and it takes me a moment to recognise her without the bird mask. A pile of costumes hangs over her arm. 'Brand new off the sewing machine!' she trills.

Ruth gives a weak smile then glances back to me, and I get the feeling she was hoping to speak to me alone. She nods towards a chair. 'Grand. Leave them on there, would you?'

Sandrine puts down the clothes. 'I can't believe it's the end-of-season show already.'

'Personally I'll be glad to move on,' says Ruth and sighs sadly. I wonder if she's thinking about Nina. She turns to me and asks, 'Shall I find you a costume, Martha? You don't have to take part in the show, but I could do your hair and makeup if you like?'

I hesitate, and Sandrine squawks, 'Oh, do me!' She pulls a black toolbox from under the table and opens it to reveal tubes of face paint. 'I saw Ulva last night. She didn't seem herself at all. I'm worried about her.'

Ruth shrugs. 'You know how close she and Nina were. It's going to take time. She'll pull through.'

Sandrine sighs. 'I know, but she's been acting strangely for weeks now. She needs to stop playing that ugly wolf if you ask me.'

Ruth scoffs. 'I don't see what that has to do with anything.'

Sandrine rummages through the box of makeup and speaks without looking up. 'Ulva's always had a temper, but lately she snaps at the smallest thing. I told you about my weird dreams.' Ruth rolls her eyes and Sandrine turns to me and explains. 'Freya had a cloak made from feathers and when she wore it she could change into a falcon. I've been playing her falcon for ages, but a couple of months ago I starting having dreams that I can fly.'

She picks up a pot of black glitter then shoots me a look before saying, 'That boy Stig was in Ulva's caravan. Do you think Karl has called the police?'

Ruth frowns. 'I doubt it. Karl thinks they'll pass a verdict of accidental death. I imagine he wants to put the whole thing behind him, like everyone else.'

I tug at the cord on my lap, my fingers throbbing. 'Why would Karl call the police?'

Ruth opens her mouth to answer me, but then Sandrine delves into the box. 'Oh, look, they're just like talons. I've got to use these!' She lifts up a packet containing black false nails and Ruth laughs. 'You want to be careful with those; you'll have your eye out.' Suddenly the two of them are busy looking for nail glue. Something tells me I'm not going to find out anything with Sandrine here. I need a way to get Ruth's attention.

'Actually, Ruth, would you do my makeup?'

'Of course!'

She pulls her chair closer and I smile and try to relax. It's been so long since I put on makeup. I never wore it much anyway, and after the accident I didn't want to draw attention to my face. Ruth swirls foundation onto a brush. I wait a couple of minutes then ask, 'What did you mean before, about Karl calling the police?'

The two women share a furtive glance, then Ruth selects some eyeliner from the box and turns to me. 'I noticed you and Stig left here together the other day. And a little bird tells me you went for a walk in the forest. I take it you know him?'

Sandrine's face flushes and I can guess who the little bird might be. She flaps over and starts to braid my hair. I speak cautiously, unsure how much to tell them. 'We only met recently . . . We spent a few days together but then he left.'

Ruth paints my cheeks. 'From what Nina told me, Stig tends to move on whenever there's a problem.' She gestures for me to look up and then applies eyeliner. 'He took off straight after giving a statement to the police. They wanted to speak to him again but they couldn't trace him. Karl agreed to call them if he ever came back.'

An icy feeling spreads in my chest. So Stig *was* on the run. He broke into Mormor's cabin because he needed somewhere to hide. I clench my jaw, anger building inside me. If only I'd been able to read Nina's catsuit properly. I don't want to believe he hurt her on purpose, but maybe he fastened her harness wrong by mistake and she fell by accident.

Ruth finishes my face then picks out some clothes from the pile Sandrine brought. She holds them out to me, but

I shake my head. All I can think about is Stig and the lies he's told. I feel like such an idiot. I should never have let him stay in the cabin.

'I want to see how it looks with the makeup. Please, for me?' Ruth grins hopefully and Sandrine screeches, 'Yes, you have to be a Valkyrie! Please, we need to see!' She points a long black talon towards the curtain where I do my readings. 'You can get changed in there.'

I hesitate and she grins. 'Come on, who doesn't want to be one of Odin's shield maidens? You get to choose who lives and dies on the battlefield. The Valkyries have the best makeup and costumes.'

'She isn't going to stop until you agree,' laughs Ruth.

'OK then.' I pick up the pile of new clothes and take them through. There's a pair of black leather trousers, a tight tunic with hardened breastplates and winged shoulders, and some arm shields. It takes a while to get everything on, but it fits perfectly. It's only dressing up, make-believe, but the thought of being one of Odin's chosen ones sends a shiver of excitement through me. I've no doubt that being a Valkyrie would be dangerous, but I would love to stand at Odin's side, to know that I have a place with him, to belong. I sweep a black cloak over my shoulders and do up the fastening at my neck. When I pull the curtain back, both women beam at me. Sandrine reaches for a mirror and I'm about to look when there's shouting outside.

The huge bearded man from the forest thrusts his head into the tent, his massive antlers snagging on the canvas doorway. He sounds out of breath. 'Ruth, come quick! It's

Karl. He's dismantling everything. We tried to stop him, but he won't listen.'

Ruth grabs her coat and rushes out, and I follow behind her. There are lots of people, some yelling in Norwegian, others in English. From their snatches of conversation it sounds as if Karl is trying to sabotage the floodlights in the field. A woman yells and someone else lurches as if they've been shoved. A group of masked gods joins the crowd and jostling breaks out.

I spin around and search for Ruth, but I can't see her. And then I spot Stig on the walkway up ahead. He dashes into the hall of mirrors and I push my way through the crowd. I'm done hiding from him. I want answers.

A PUPPET OF THE GODS

I pause before the gaping hole of the wolf's mouth. Its sinister yellow eyes unblinkingly watch over the site and I shrink beneath its stare. The thought of entering its throat makes me cringe and I nearly turn away, but then I see the back of Stig's head disappear down the passageway. Taking a deep breath, I step inside and blink in the dim light. The floor and ceiling are checked with black and gold, as are the walls. The effect is disorientating.

I hurry to the end of the corridor then stop and shiver. Grey faces stare down at me, caught in a swathe of netting. I survey each of the masks in turn, my heart thumping. The unblinking eyes of men, women and children watch me with perverse interest, as if they know I'm walking into a trap. I wait a moment longer, checking for signs of life.

166

When none of them move, I glance at the open doors to either side of me.

Turning right, I find a narrow space with floor-length mirrors on either wall. Dozens of wooden puppets hang from the ceiling in a jumble of strings, their arms and legs at awkward angles. Gaudy fat-faced trolls with snub noses and matted hair, pale pointy-faced elves with grotesquely long fingernails, and a tatty thing with a horse's skull for a head and too many legs. The overhead light flashes and I rub my temples. I don't know if it's an effect done for the customers or because it's about to stop working, but it makes me feel nauseous.

I peer into the room then quickly check to my left. There's no one here, but I hate feeling that someone could creep up on my blind side. Stig must have gone the other way. I retrace my steps and cross the hall. It leads to an identical-looking area. The same black walls and mirrors; even the puppets are exact copies. I frown, a gnawing sense of unease in my belly. Maybe I'm looking at a mirrored wall? But I can't be, as I don't see my reflection.

'Stig, are you in here?'

My words come back to me in a faint mocking echo. I swallow, my mouth dry, and call again. Nothing. The only sound is my own ragged breathing. There are only two ways he could have gone, so where is he? I clench my fists and spin around. Did he lead me here on purpose? Is this some kind of trick?

'Stig, this isn't funny.'

I start to leave when a thought occurs to me. Maybe one of the mirrors is fixed to a door and that's where he went. I walk into the first room and a warrior with plaits in her hair strides towards me, a lightning-bolt painted on her cheek. I startle then glance down at my costume – the hardened leather breastplate and winged shoulders. The girl is me.

I touch an unsteady hand to my cheek and my reflection does the same. Ruth hasn't tried to hide my scar or blind eye; she's accentuated them. The unflinching woman who stands before me doesn't just accept the way she looks; she is daringly unafraid, proud even. I take in the fierce black eyeliner and the jagged scar on her cheek that she wears like a war trophy, and I want to be her. More than anything, I want to be that girl.

I look in the second mirror and I am bizarrely elongated, my face and torso stretched out and concave. In the next my body is short and stumpy. I lean closer and my face widens until it's barely recognisable. After the accident I hated looking at my reflection. I saw a monster, a distorted version of myself. I return to the first mirror and I'm grinning so hard I can feel the warrior girl's confidence radiate from the glass.

I see something move out of the corner of my eye and I glance up. A troll hangs lifeless above me, its apple-red cheeks bulging in a manic grin. Something about it seems different. The swollen black tongue that lolls from its mouth ... I'm sure it wasn't there before. I watch for movement but the puppets are still.

I take a moment to steady my nerves then turn to my reflection. What I see makes me gasp. My face has gone, replaced by the back of my head. Cold dread creeps across my skin. I'm looking in the same mirror as before, so how can . . . ? The head slowly revolves even though I'm not moving. The girl is me, but tearful and afraid, mascara running down her cheeks. She looks at me pleadingly, her eyes full of panic. My legs tremble like I'm standing on the edge of a precipice. I stare at her – at *me*, unable to accept what I see.

The girl coughs and starts to choke. She touches a finger to her lips and her eyes widen as a fly crawls out. Insects swarm from her mouth – more and more, until there are hundreds, thousands of them. They circle around her, buzzing upwards in a swirling vortex. The drone of wings reverberates in my head, the noise so loud it hurts.

I want to run, but I can't pull my gaze away from the mirror. I watch in sick fascination as the girl disintegrates and a new image forms: the shape of a man. It reminds me of a beekeeper I once saw, covered head to toe in bees. Only the insects aren't covering him, they *are* him. The buzzing subsides as the flies congeal and the face becomes solid: first his forehead, then nose and mouth.

The man throws back his head and laughs; a harsh unnatural sound that makes me shudder. He holds out his arm with the flourish of a stage magician, then grabs his chin and peels up his skin to reveal a familiar face beneath. 'Stig. How can . . . ?' And then I realise – it wasn't him I followed in here.

Shock gives way to fear as Stig's face vanishes and new ones appear: men, women and children of all nationalities; a giantess with a bulbous nose, a horse, a salmon, a falcon, a fly. Quicker and quicker they change, until only one remains. The jester.

I race for the door but it slams shut. I pull and pull but it won't open. The idea of him controlling my limbs, of being his puppet, fills me with terror.

'Not to your liking? Perhaps this will prove more congenial.'

I return to the mirror and the image changes to a man with long red hair brushed back from his forehead. His amber eyes flicker with mischief and I catch my breath, disturbed by the wildfire that rages behind them, thrillingly alive yet devastating at the same time. His mouth twists to one side in a smile, his lips edged with tiny scars. I want to look away but I can't. He is utterly mesmerising, like a snake.

The man in the psychic tent ... When I touched his coat I sensed shifting sands, someone who couldn't be trusted, someone who enjoys tangling people up in cruel games. That's why Mum couldn't draw him; he can change his face whenever he likes. Loki – *shapeshifter and master manipulator*. He's the uninvited guest.

I clench my fists. 'What do you want with me?'

'Come now. You could at least *try* to enter into the spirit of things. Besides, it's Odin who brought you here. He's the one who chose you.'

'Chose me for what?'

'As his player, of course.' Loki pulls a mock shocked face. 'What, he didn't tell you? It must have slipped his mind, but then he is rather busy and I suppose you don't feature that highly in his priorities.'

The words burrow under my skin, even though I know not to believe a thing he says. After the sacrifices I've made to water the tree, the sacrifices my ancestors have made, I can't bear to think that I mean nothing to Odin. But if he really did bring me here, why isn't he the one talking to me?

Loki grins, as if pleased to see the confusion on my face. I clench my jaw and stare at him. 'A player to do what exactly?'

'Oh, I do love a wager!' He pauses for dramatic effect then frowns. 'He really hasn't told you any of this, has he? Strange, I thought you would have meant more to him. In that case, allow me to enlighten you.'

He turns to his right and walks out of the mirror, reappearing in the next a moment later, his long green coat and head bizarrely elongated. 'You know, it was Odin who first came across this place. He found it on one of his little wanders.' He laughs and adds, 'Now I think about it, I suppose he would be taken with a *travelling* circus.' He paces back and his image returns to normal. 'I couldn't understand the appeal at first. Mortals play-acting at being gods!' He leans towards the glass, his face earnest. 'But the more I came here, the more I felt its pull. Yes, it's just a few tatty tents in a field, but there is magic in the old myths. Who among us doesn't want our name to be remembered, our stories to live on?'

I hate agreeing with him, but I know exactly what he means. I've felt the same magic too. There was something wonderful about seeing my ancestors' history brought to life. I couldn't have looked away from the performance, even if I'd tried.

He moves again, his coat gliding across several mirrors. I spin around and he appears in the glass behind me. 'One day I noticed that I didn't feature in their performances. There was a Loki mask but no one wore it. Why? Because years ago they did one of my stories and there happened to be a fire. Odin nearly laughed his beard off when he told me. He said I am usually to blame when things go wrong, so I shouldn't hold it against them for holding me responsible.' He presses his lips together and they turn as pale as the scars around them. 'Yes, Odin found it most amusing.'

He forces a smile. 'So when the circus *finally* performed one of my myths, the story of Baldur no less . . . Well, let's just say I got a little excited. Odin thought it best I leave, no doubt jealous I had been included for once. I refused and he offered me a wager, and here we both are.'

I blink at him, trying to make sense of things. Karl said a fire burned down the big top years ago. His father thought Loki was behind it, but he was wrong. It wasn't doing performances with the Trickster that brought bad luck, it was keeping him out.

Loki's image fills the glass as he leans close and whispers. 'Odin bets that a mere mortal can unmask Nina's killer by the time the last visitor leaves tonight.'

A lump lodges in my throat. I've been dragged here to take part in some *game*? I don't want to believe it, and yet something in the pit of my belly tells me it's true.

When I don't say anything, he whispers, 'Haven't you wondered why Nina appears different to the rest of the dead?'

I stare at him, afraid of the answer.

'Odin sent her to the cabin to haunt you. And in case that wasn't enough to get you here, he gave your mum visions of the circus.'

If Loki is telling the truth, then Odin must have a good reason for wanting me here. He must need my help. I don't like the idea of being manipulated, but at the same time I feel a flicker of pride at the thought of being chosen.

'What do you mean, I have to unmask Nina's killer?'

Loki grins. 'Get her killer to confess to the old circus manager Karl, and I will go.'

Anxiety crashes over me. 'And what happens if I fail?'

He ignores my question and says, 'Do you know that an actor is finally going to play me? Now that I've been given a proper invitation, there's so much fun to be had!' He claps his hands and something jangles overhead. The troll twists and jumps on its strings, the horse rears and snaps its skeletal jaws, and the long-fingered creatures convulse.

Loki laughs and I recoil, knowing that fun for him means suffering for others. He clicks his fingers and the puppets collapse, their limp bodies swaying above me.

His voice deepens. 'Lose the wager and I will destroy the circus. And if they cancel and refuse to tell my story, then no one's shall be heard.' Yellow flames flicker around the edge of the glass and consume his face as a new image appears: the big top on fire. Smoke fills the sky, dozens of masked performers lie face down in the mud, and the charred puppet that Stig destroyed crawls over them. And then I see a girl with blonde hair in the dirt, her lifeless eyes staring open. One of them is milky white and looks in the wrong direction.

Fear and adrenaline turn to rage. 'You're going to kill everyone at the circus, just because they didn't include you?'

He yells at me. 'Do you know how it feels to be kept out? To be the outsider? To have your lips sewn shut?'

'That was a punishment for your own trickery!'

'Was it? Or was it because I'm not afraid to speak the truth? Because I alone am willing to expose the hypocrisy of the gods?'

I bite back my arguments. I don't know enough of his stories to judge. Perhaps his cruel games *are* motivated by something more than just mischief.

His eyes glisten as he rants. 'I've given the gods so many gifts. If it weren't for me, Thor wouldn't have his hammer, Freyr would be missing his beloved boar and Odin would be without his spear. I've got them out of more scrapes than I care to count, and what thanks do I get? I am vilified, made the scapegoat – kept out.'

He speaks with the conviction of righteous anger, his eyes overflowing with hurt, and he's right. I have no idea how it feels to be kept out by those who are meant to love you. But according to the stories in Karl's book, it was Loki who got the gods into their various 'scrapes' in the first place.

'What about Baldur?'

He narrows his gaze and the emotion I saw in his eyes a moment ago is gone, replaced with stony coldness. 'Now why would you want to bring that up?'

He vanishes from the mirror and someone taps me on the shoulder. I spin around and scream. The jester is in the room behind me.

'It's always *my* failings told in the stories, have you noticed that? The others are no better than me . . . Luckily

I am here to expose them for what they really are.' He looks at my blank face and laughs. 'You think you have it all worked out, don't you? Everything black and white. Odin is good and I am bad.'

He circles me, the bells on his cap jingling. 'You are nothing but a puppet to him, a player in a game. He started a whole ancestral line to task them with watering a tree. If he's so powerful, why doesn't he do it himself? He doesn't care for mortals any more than I do.'

A gaping hole opens up inside me and dark thoughts rush inside. All the sacrifices my ancestors have made – surely they weren't just being used? The women who went before me had such strength and resilience; they were given magic in exchange for watering the tree. If they mean nothing to Odin, where does that leave me?

Loki sneers. 'The fruit doesn't fall far from the twisted tree. You too serve only yourself.'

I drop my head, knowing what he is going to say. I've done something terrible, something I can't take back or make right.

'Hel tasked you with saving the dead. She told you to hold the rope until *every* soul had returned to the under-world. But you let go. You sacrificed hundreds of souls to save one.'

Shame burns inside me. He's right. I didn't stop to think what would happen to the others when I dropped the rope. I thought only of making sure Mormor would be safe. I thought only of myself.

He leans into my face, his bright red mouth a parody of sadness. 'Don't cry. I've rounded them up for you.' I shake my head, even though I know it's true.

'No? Then how else do you think they got here!' He glares at me with disdain then turns his back.

A moment later he spins around and opens his arms, the bells on his costume jingling. 'Cheer up, tonight is Ragnarok! The circus is expecting me to bring a horde of the dead along and I hate to disappoint. If there's one thing I know how to do, it's put on a show!'

He vanishes and I swallow a sob, my chest heaving. When I look in the mirror I see only my normal reflection. Who was I to dream I could be a warrior, one of Odin's Valkyries? No. This is the real me: feeble and afraid, my eyes full of panic, mascara running down my face.

18

ONE LONG THREAD OF LIES

I stumble outside and the walkway is empty, the crowd of performers gone. The wolf sneers down at me and I breathe in a lungful of icy air and try to clear my head. I have to stop Loki. I have to win the wager or he will destroy the circus and everyone here. But how am I going to make Stig confess to killing Nina?

Part of me wants to go and confront him, but I need time to think. How do I even know that Loki is telling the truth? He's called the Trickster and the Sly One for a reason. Maybe there is no wager, or perhaps he *wants* me to make Stig confess and I'm walking into a trap. The only way to know for sure is to speak to Odin. If he really chose me as his player, then he should tell me the rules of the game.

I walk around the side of a tent and stop when I reach the costume trailer. I need a connection to Odin – perhaps something in Karl's notebook would help. A raven lands on the handle of the trailer door and twitches its head. It caws then flies away and I think about the last time I was in there. When I held Odin's mask to my face it tried to pull me closer. Hel was angry with me, and Sandrine said wearing her falcon mask gave her dreams that she could fly. What if the masks provide a link to the gods and creatures they portray?

I climb the steps to the trailer and open the door. The end wall is empty apart from a single golden face: Baldur. Of course, the actors will be getting ready for tonight's show, they will have the masks. Karl said that no one would play the part now that Nina has gone. That must be why it's still here. There is something desperately sad about the beautiful golden face shining alone in the darkness, and I have a sudden feeling it might be the key to everything.

I turn and jump down the steps. If I want to find the crooked mask, I need to find the man who plays Odin. The performers said Karl was dismantling the floodlights. If everyone is in the field trying to stop him, maybe that's where he'll be.

I make my way to the end of the walkway and scan the expanse of snow. Thick mist swirls over the ground and it takes a moment to see them. Around forty costumed performers are gathered around the circle of skull poles, just beyond the Viking ship. Those on stilts congregate at the back, including the three Norns, the ravens, and the frost giant I met on the first day. I walk over and there are more people I recognise: Sandrine in her feathered mask, the Chinese knife-throwers in their ballgowns, along with Oskar, Ruth and Ulva. I don't see Stig, or the actor who plays Odin. Most of the people are wearing masks so I can't see their expressions, but I can sense their anxiety. It rolls off them, heavy and cold like the fog.

I find a gap among the leather-clad Valkyries all wearing the same costume as me and push to the front. Karl stands alone in the middle of the circle, a look of cornered prey about him. He gives me a pleading look, as if hoping I've come to persuade the others, but there's nothing I can do. If they don't tell Loki's story, he's promised that no one's shall be heard.

A man wearing antlers addresses the crowd. 'Karl is right. There *have* been too many changes. We've always been family friendly, that's what we're about. This new fire show we're doing, not allowing children to enter and hiring security staff, it's a mistake. I say we call it off.'

A muffled voice croaks, 'We can't cancel, people have paid. The circus will go bust!' I look over my shoulder and a raven flaps his winged arms and twitches his head, his grey beak moving from side to side. There's something almost too bird-like about its movements and I have a feeling that I'm not looking at a man dressed up. Could it be that the figure standing next to me isn't entirely human? I glance over to the Norns. They crowd close to one another and whisper in hushed tones, their raspy voices alarmingly familiar. I stare at their crude masks, covered with clumps of earth and moss, a mass of twisted twigs stretched across the top. The cheek of one twitches and another frowns.

Even though I've seen their masks move before, it's still unnerving. I'm watching in wonder when an old woman touches my arm, startling me.

She wears tiny white antlers on her head, and beneath it a band of fringed leather so that I can't see her eyes. She pats my arm and speaks with a Russian accent. 'Don't worry, the circus has been going for a hundred years and it will go for a hundred more.' Her costume brushes me and I sense deep love tethering her to this place. The people here are her family, this is her home.

I do my best to smile but my chest is so tight I can hardly breathe. It's foretold that Loki will bring about Ragnarok, the end of the world, and tonight the circus is going to re-enact it. He killed Baldur, the most beloved of the gods, and he said himself that he doesn't care about humans. Loki is clever and scheming; the master manipulator. If there really is a wager, I'm going to need Odin's help. I don't know if the crooked mask will allow me to contact him, but right now it's my best hope.

Mumbles of disagreement turn to anger and suddenly everyone is arguing. I turn to the woman and shout over the noise, 'Have you seen the actor who plays Odin?' She shrugs and I ask the Valkyries behind me, but they haven't seen him. A group of antlered men look at me blankly, and then the guy with tattoos who was arguing with Stig comes over. He speaks loudly, as if he wants everyone to hear. 'That boy you're with, he's trouble.'

'Stig?'

He touches his finger first to his left cheek and then to the right one. 'He has two faces.'

'What do you mean?'

'His last girlfriend died. He has a temper, ask anyone here.'

Before I can say anything, he turns and walks away. I stare into the crowd of performers, my heart racing. Part of me was hoping I'd made a mistake when I read Nina's catsuit, but the evidence is undeniable. The reason he ignored my messages and then suddenly showed up, the reason people here don't trust him. I want to go after the boy and ask him what he knows, but there's no time. I have to find the crooked mask.

I call up to the raven performers behind me, 'The man who plays Odin, have you seen him?' The bird-men take a few steps one way and then the other, their feathers fluttering in the breeze. One of them twitches its head. 'Have you tried the costume-change in the big top?' The other nods, his beak moving up and down. 'Yes, try there.'

I thank them and hurry towards the tents. The walkways are busy now: performers are moving large wire structures, and crew in black jackets are carrying lengths of cable and unlit firebrands. Oskar shouts at someone and sends another member of the crew back the way they came. He looks determined and in control, despite the chaos around him.

I turn the corner and stop. Stig is there. For a moment I wonder if it's another trick, but something about the anxious look in his eyes tells me it's really him.

'Martha! I've been looking everywhere for you.' He glances at my costume. 'You look amazing. It suits you, being a Valkyrie.'

I wrap my arms around myself and stare at the ground.

'What is it, are you still sick?'

181

'I'm fine.'

'You don't look fine. You look like you've been crying. What's wrong? Maybe I can help?' When I don't say anything, he asks, 'Is it Loki? Or Nina – have you seen her again?'

He's trying to find out how much I know, wondering if I've figured out how she died. I lift my head and make myself look him in the eye. 'The guy you were arguing with – Nina's ex – did they get back together? Is that what happened? You found out and lost your temper?'

'No. Nina wasn't interested in him.' Stig gives me a strange look as if he's just realised what I said. 'What do you mean, *is that what happened?*'

'So what were you arguing about with him?' He doesn't answer and I keep talking. 'He thinks you had something to do with Nina's death, doesn't he?'

Stig drops his gaze.

I tighten my jaw, wishing he would tell me the truth. 'I touched the catsuit that Nina was wearing when she died. I saw her last memories. I know she was wearing a harness.'

Stig's face is a mask of confusion. 'I don't understand.'

'So you didn't climb the rigging and take it up to her?'

'No! I told you. We argued and then I left. What is this?'

He's so good at this – lying. I grab his arm and he frowns in surprise. The impressions from his jacket are weak and fleeting: apprehension, confusion and a residue of guilt. I search for a deeper emotion or memory stained into the material but there's nothing. Of course, that's why he bought new clothes. He knows how my gift works and that things have to be worn a while to absorb a person's memories. Why buy new things unless to deceive me?

182

Stig pulls away. '*Fy faen!* If you want to know something, you only have to ask.'

'OK. So why are you wearing new clothes?'

'What?'

'Answer the question.'

An injured look flashes in his eyes. 'They were in the sale and . . . if you must know, I wanted to put the past behind me. I've still got Dad's coat, but I decided it was time to stop wearing it.'

I think back to the leather trench coat he wore in the cabin. At the time I presumed the bitterness, jealousy and hate it contained came from his father. But maybe I was wrong, maybe it *was* all Stig. He said he'd left home because of family arguments, but now I know he broke into Mormor's cabin because he was on the run.

A cold rage rises inside me. 'Did you push her, thinking the harness would save her, or did you do it up wrong on purpose? Were you made to do it?'

Stig recoils as if I'd slapped him.

I search his eyes, desperately hoping that it was an accident or it wasn't really his fault. That he will admit what he did, but say he never meant for her to die.

Some of the crew walk in our direction and he waits for them to pass, then leans towards me. His pale blue eyes drill into me, but I refuse to back down or look away.

'Just admit it Stig. I know everyth—'

'How could you think that of me?' He speaks over me, his voice low and edged with danger. 'I don't know who you've been talking to, but I had nothing to do with Nina's death.'

I start to argue, but he turns and stalks away.

'Stig!'

He keeps walking and doesn't look back.

'You promised to tell me the truth!'

He shakes his head and keeps going, and I clench my fists. Even if he came back, he would only make up some story. How many more lies are there, I wonder? Like a magician's knotted handkerchief, I could pull and pull and more would come out; one long thread of lies, each more colourful than the last. I've been such a fool. When the *draugr* attacked him, I went into the rotting heart of the tree and begged Hel for his life. I couldn't bear him dying. I risked my life to save him – a murderer and a liar.

19

YOUR WORD AGAINST HIS

'Martha, wait!' Ruth appears behind me, her long auburn hair dancing wildly in the wind. She must have followed me up from the field. She watches Stig stride away then turns to me and frowns. 'What's going on with you two?'

I don't answer and she gives me a coy smile. 'You said you spent a few days together and then he left, so come on – spill. I'll find out one way or another, so you may as well tell me everything.' She gives me a playful nudge. 'I *am* psychic, you know.' I start to answer but then my eyes fill with tears. Ruth sees my face and her expression changes. 'Oh, sweetheart, whatever's wrong?' She wipes my cheek and whispers, 'I didn't do your makeup for you to cry it all off.'

I mutter, 'Sorry,' and she folds me into a hug. 'Come here, now.' She smells of fresh laundry and rosemary and suddenly I have an urge to tell her everything – about Stig and Loki and the wager. And then a feeling that isn't mine fills my heart: longing followed by choking guilt and shame. I've felt the same emotions in her shawl before. She desperately wants to go back to Ireland but she's afraid. It's so unfair. Why should she miss out on seeing her daughter grow up because of something that wasn't her fault?

She links her arm through mine. 'Come on, let's go to the canteen. You look like a girl who could use a tea with ten sugars.'

I glance at the big top. If I'm going to contact Odin and ask for his help, I have to find the crooked mask. 'Sorry, I can't. There's something I need to do.'

She pulls me close. 'Oh, shush. You can spare five minutes. Something tells me you didn't apply for the job here by chance. It's about time you were honest with me, don't you think?' I try to resist but she drags me away, past the costume trailer and then into the maze of caravans. We round a corner and the white canteen tent appears, its door flapping in the breeze like an invitation.

It's a relief to step into the warmth, and the smell of fresh coffee and frying bacon almost makes me feel hungry. Rows of trestle tables and benches fill the room and there's a glass serving-counter at the front. A group of elves sit to my right; behind them a man with antlers bites into a sausage and chats to a woman covered in tattoos. On the other side of the tent is the mime artist in makeup I saw before. He stares out of the large window panel

186

next to him and looks so sad I can't imagine his face ever changing.

Ruth walks over to a table sagging under the weight of a silver urn and a mountain of cups, while I take a seat. A moment later she hands me a drink and sits down opposite. 'They're still doing breakfast if you're hungry?' I shake my head and try to smile, but my mind is elsewhere. I can't stop thinking about Loki and the wager. It feels so surreal, like a nightmare I might wake up from at any minute. I can't sit here drinking tea. I need to find that mask.

Ruth sips her drink then lowers her cup. 'So are you going to tell me what's going on, or do I have to drag it out of you?'

I think back to our conversation in the psychic tent. She knows Stig took off before the police could question him a second time. Maybe I should tell her; she might be able to help. I lean forward. 'You know how Stig disappeared before?' Ruth arches an eyebrow and I continue. 'He was hiding in my grandma's cabin in Skjebne. He broke into the place and was there when I arrived.' She gives a disapproving tut and I keep talking. 'It was freezing and he had nowhere else to go, so I let him stay.' I glance at the people around me. No one is paying us any attention, but I lower my voice anyway. 'Stig lied to the police.'

Two women enter, both with masks around their necks. One wears her long blonde hair in plaits, her cheeks flushed pink, and the other is older and has cropped fair hair. She points at her shorn head and cries, 'How could he?' The other woman picks up a bowl of apples and murmurs, 'I don't know, I think it makes you look younger,' and her companion

187

yells and knocks the bowl away, sending the fruit bouncing across the floor.

Ruth twists in her seat. 'What is it with people here lately?' She rolls her eyes then turns back to me. 'Sorry, you were saying?'

More masked performers enter. One of them wears a grey cloak. Hope jumps inside me, but then he turns around and I let out a sigh. It's some other man, not the actor who plays Odin.

'You said Stig lied to the police. Martha?'

Ruth waves her hand in front of my face and my attention snaps back to her.

'Yes. He told them that Nina wasn't wearing a harness, but she was. He did it up for her. I think he did it up wrong and then pushed her.'

Her eyes grow wide. 'What? Did he tell you this?'

'Not exactly. I figured it out. I confronted him, and you should have seen his face. I think he killed her.'

Ruth frowns. 'If Nina was wearing a harness, why didn't the police find it?'

'Stig must have taken it. I'm guessing he was worried it might have his fingerprints and wanted to hide the evidence.'

'You're guessing? You can't accuse someone of murder on a *hunch*, Martha.'

My shoulders slump and I stare at the table. I thought Ruth would believe me, that she might even help, but I've been wasting my time. I start to stand but she pulls me back down. Her bright hazel eyes search my face. 'Don't get me wrong, there are plenty of people who don't trust that boy – God knows why he came back, he's about as welcome here as a wet shoe – but just because he took off doesn't mean he's guilty. You two were an item, weren't you? What makes you so sure?'

I should tell her the truth about my gift. She has some psychic ability herself, and if she believes in magic, surely she will understand. I take a breath, about to explain, but she speaks first.

'You know a verdict of accidental death is likely to be passed, and Stig, well, he's the type who never stays anywhere for long. He'll move on and . . .' She holds my gaze without blinking.

'And?' I ask.

'What's done is done.'

I stare at her in disbelief. 'I should just let it go, is that what you're saying? I should let him get away with it?' The words come out louder than I intended and a girl with pointed ears looks over.

I don't have time for this. I jump up and Ruth's eyes flick around the room and back to me. 'What choice do you have if it's your word against his?'

'That's it, isn't it? That's why you're afraid to go back to Ireland. You think people will believe your sister's husband and not you. I know it must be hard for you, but you can't let him get away with what he did.'

Ruth stares at me. 'What are you talking about?'

A cold thought slithers out from the back of my mind. Maybe there's another reason she wants to leave Nina's death in the past. There was some mistletoe on her altar; Loki fashioned a spear from mistletoe and gave it to the blind god to kill Baldur. Maybe *Ruth* is the one who invited him to the circus.

Ruth pushes her hair behind her ear with a trembling hand. 'I haven't told you about what happened in Ireland. Who have you been talking to?'

I stare at the table, a blush of shame creeping into my cheeks. Ruth has been through so much, I have no right to tell her how to feel or what to do.

'Martha? How do you –'

'The cloth figure in your caravan, the one wrapped in green thread. You did a spell to bind Nina. Did you put a spell on Stig too?'

A look of surprise flashes across her face. 'How do you know about that? Ulva is the only one I told.' She glances around the room and speaks quietly. 'Look, I don't see what my personal business has to do with any of this.' She sighs then adds, 'I will speak to Karl and tell him your suspicions about Stig. If he decides to inform the police, they're going to need evidence.'

A movement catches my attention and I turn my head and see a girl with short dark hair outside the window. Nina. There's something odd about the way she moves. She lifts one arm and holds it in the air and then her opposite leg hinges at the knee. She takes a clumsy step forward and I stare with cold fascination.

Ruth carries on speaking but I'm not listening. I bite my bottom lip, unease swirling within me as I walk over to the plastic window panel and look out. Nina lifts her other arm and I realise why she's walking oddly – there are strings attached to her hands and feet, leading straight up to the

190

sky. She takes several quick steps, her limbs bending awkwardly, and then her arms waver above her head and she tumbles down like a rag doll.

My heart bangs in my chest. I lean forward and check in both directions, the window billowing and touching my nose. Nina has gone. I glance over my shoulder and Ruth is looking at me, a bewildered expression on her face.

I turn back to the window and see a dark shape crouched on the ground, just outside the tent. Suddenly the jester stands up. His white face paint cracks and flakes as he grins at me, his red slash of a mouth pulled too wide and thin. He raises his arm, making the bells of his costume jingle. In his hand are two large wooden handles. He twists them and Nina's head jerks into view, her arms flopping on strings. Her eyes are no longer black, but glow pale.

I scream and press my hand against the window. 'What do you want with her? Leave her alone!'

The jester laughs and moves his fingers. This time her body sways from side to side like a pendulum. 'Tick tock, puppet girl.'

Ruth touches my arm. 'Martha, who are you talking to? Leave who alone?' I point outside but she doesn't see the jester or the ghost girl on strings. Ruth's face fills with worry and I realise how crazy I must seem. The elves stop chatting and suddenly the room is silent and everyone is staring at me. Masked faces tilt to one side and step closer and my head swims. I have to win the wager. Odin has to help me, there's no other way.

I turn to Ruth. 'What time will the last visitor leave tonight?'

She blinks in surprise.

I grab her shoulder, unable to keep the panic from my voice. 'What time will they leave? Ruth, what time?'

She touches her head. 'The closing parade is at seven so I suppose it will be an hour or two after that. Why?'

'Parade?'

'At the end of the night the performers parade down to the field for the fire show.'

An image comes into my head: the big top in flames and charred puppets crawling over the earth, and my stomach clenches so hard I think I might be sick.

'Why don't you sit down?' Ruth tries to lower me onto a bench but I pull away.

'There isn't time, I have to go.'

WILL YOU PAY THE PRICE?

I hurry to the rear of the big top and peer in through the door. A dozen or so people are getting changed and doing their hair and makeup. A few of the actors are there, some of them wearing masks. I see a man wearing a grey cloak and a hat, and almost cry with relief. If I'm going to understand what's happening and win the wager, I need Odin's help. Right now, the mask is my only hope of contacting him.

The actor is at the back of the room, talking to a man in a long green coat. No one gives me a passing glance as I hurry to a dressing table, then sit down and do my makeup. I'm just another Valkyrie getting ready for the show. Odin runs a hand over his beard and says, 'It always starts with me. I am Ofner, opener, the one who breathed life into the first humans, and Svafner, closer, the gatherer of lost souls.'

193

The other man yawns. 'Then maybe it's time for a change.'

I glance around and notice something white on the dressing table opposite: the crooked mask. I swivel in my seat, my pulse racing. No one is watching. I stand up and go over, then quickly check about me. I feel bad about taking it, but I can give it back afterwards.

Holding it close to my leg, I head for the door, just as a group of masked gods enters. Hel and Thor and Freya stand in my way. If I push past them or ask them to move, they might notice what's in my hand. I need another way. Behind me is the curved black screen that leads to the ring. Keeping my head down, I edge my way along it.

The tunnel is dark and I can barely see. I step through then blink and cover my eyes. A bright spotlight shines on the tree in the middle of the floor. Next to it is Odin's throne. I keep my gaze fixed ahead as I walk towards it, determined not to look at the rows of shadowy chairs. No one is here, but something tells me the auditorium isn't as empty as it should be.

I sit on the throne and study the mask, my fingers tracing the carved lines in the wood. It doesn't cover the whole face, but stops just below the nose. There's one eye-opening on the wearer's right-hand side; the other is solid and painted black. The eyes don't line up quite properly, making it seem crooked. I turn it over and touch the soft felt backing and the black ribbon tied to each edge. It's understated and plain, yet there is power in its simplicity.

I don't know what will happen if I wear it, but I have to try. A tingle of excitement runs through me. I can't believe Odin is just using me, like Loki says. If he chose me as his player, that has to mean something, surely? I lift the mask and its cheek twitches. I startle and drop it, then take a breath and get a hold of myself. The carved face is perfectly still but something doesn't feel right. I am too exposed here. I glance at the huge tree in the centre of the ring, and remembering how the Norns emerged from inside gives me an idea.

I pick up the mask then walk around the trunk. It looks like it's made of papier-mâché stretched over some kind of metal frame. Tiny glass light bulbs are embedded within a fine mesh of wire that stretches across the rough bark. At the rear is an entrance, so well hidden I would have missed it if I weren't looking closely.

I pull open the door and dots of lights flicker into life. Inside is surprisingly spacious. There are three large cushions on the floor and a pile of blankets, I suppose so that the Norns can be comfortable while they wait to go onstage. I close the door then sit on a cushion and rest my back against the trunk. It's easily as wide as the largest chamber of the tree in Mormor's garden but this one has much more headroom, stretching up into the trunk. Unlike the real thing, it doesn't smell of rotting leaves and damp earth. I pull a blanket over me then make a nest with the rest of the cushions. My shoulders drop and I take a deep breath. Maybe it's being enclosed, but I feel safe in here.

I hold the mask to my face and immediately feel its pull: a warm surge that draws me like a magnet. I tie the ribbon at the back of my head and it fits perfectly, the painted eye sitting over my blind side. I call his name softly, singing it under my breath. *Odin, Odin, Odin* . . . I say it over and over until I forget all other thoughts.

Odin, Odin, Odin . . .

My eyes close and a rush of energy flows over my body like hot air from a vent. And then I'm falling, plummeting into a black hole. I can't breathe. My feet kick and my body convulses. I need to . . . I can't . . . I tug at the mask, but it won't come off. My eyes roll back and everything goes black.

I'm standing at one side of the empty ring. It's dark and I can only just make out the scuffed white barrier. There's no tree, no throne. A sea of fog flows around my legs and I watch in wonder as shapes form in the mist before tumbling and dissolving back into swirling chaos. The lightest breeze touches my face and I lift my chin. The big top has gone, replaced by a vast black dome, clouds drifting across an endless sky.

Two ravens explode up from nowhere. Their wings beat furiously and a gust of wind blows back my hair. I raise my arm and then watch as they spiral upwards and disappear. The floor tilts and I don't know whether it's dropping away from me or I am rising. And then my feet lift and I'm floating. I'm actually levitating. I can feel myself expanding and drifting, the knots of my mind loosening and unravelling. What's happening to me? Fear and hope fight inside me as I drop to the ground with a thud.

A single spotlight comes on and I wince and shield my face. A man is standing in the middle of the ring with his back to me. He wears the tailcoat, trousers and top hat of a ringmaster, all of them white. But there's something strange about his head. It isn't there. I blink and look again, convinced it must be an optical illusion.

My heart thumps as I make my way towards him. He doesn't move or say a word. I step closer, wondering if I'm looking at a statue. Just a dozen paces away now.

'Hello?' The figure remains still. I walk around the side of him and my insides turn to ice. He's holding a long stick with a white mask fixed to the top. Behind it is nothing. His arms and legs are normal, his hands covered with gloves, yet his body ends just before the neck. Above the collar of his jacket is only air. I step back, unease turning to dread.

The mask on the stick has a single eye-opening. The other one is solid and painted black. Unlike the one from the costume trailer, the mask before me comes down to the chin and has a mouth. Deep wrinkles surround the lips and line the forehead. It's only a piece of wood, yet something about it terrifies me.

Suddenly the face moves. The forehead frowns and the lips pull back as a velvety voice intones, 'A gift for a gift. Will you pay the price?' The wood rearranges to form a new expression, the movements slow and clumsy like a clay model in an old stop-motion animation. I stare at the face, unable to believe what I'm seeing.

'Who are you?' I ask.

'Grimnir.'

The words of the Odin actor echo in my head. *A single name have I never had since first I walked among men. Wanderer, Wayfarer . . . Grimnir the Masked One am I.*

The face changes expression, the muscles under the wood shifting and rearranging to form a frown. I swallow and nod. If I'm going to win this wager, I will need his help.

The face softens to a smile and I look down to find that Nina's gold catsuit is in my hands. I blink at it, confused. The figure swings out its arm so that the mask looms closer. Seeing it move makes me feel queasy; the missing head is even more disturbing in profile.

The face speaks again. 'Each day my two ravens fly through the worlds. I fear for the return of Huginn, yet more do I fear for Muninn. Memory must come first and then thought.'

A flutter of panic beats in my chest. 'I don't understand.'

The mask comes closer and tilts forward, so that it's looking at the material in my hands. 'Let the impressions surface like a memory, don't pick and pull at them with thought. Only when your mind is empty can you remember what you know.'

Slowly I begin to understand. When I read the catsuit I grabbed the material, demanding it show me the truth. I pulled at the thread of Nina's memory so hard it snapped. The same thing happened when I touched Ruth's shawl in the psychic tent. Yet when I wasn't trying I was able to read it easily. The information came to me; it surfaced in my mind like a memory.

'I think I see.'

The mask chuckles and winks its one eye. 'You can *see* far more than you know.'

I glance at my hands and the catsuit has vanished. My right hand has become a fist. I turn it over and open it, and in my palm is a round metal pin. It's beautifully and intricately made, with a single rune in the centre. It's shaped like a Y, but with the central stick reaching to the top of the symbol, a tree with three branches.

'Algiz. The sign of the Valkyrie,' explains the mask. 'A gift for a gift and the price is danger.'

I open my mouth, a thousand questions on my lips, when a flash of white light obliterates everything.

Something I didn't see before

My eyes open and it takes me a moment to realise where I am. I tug the mask from my face then open my palm and gasp to see the pin. I have no idea why it was given to me, but I have a feeling I know why I was shown Nina's catsuit. It appeared just before the mask explained how to use my gift properly. There must be something else in the material I'm meant to read.

Taking a deep breath, I stand up and peer out from the tree. The ring is full of people, members of the crew dragging props across the floor and performers calling out instructions. I wait until no one is looking then walk through the tunnel and into the costume-change area. It's empty now: the clothes rails bare and the makeup and brushes tidied away as if no one was ever there.

I leave the carved face where I found it, then run my fingers over the smooth wood. Maybe Odin appeared to me like that because I contacted him through the mask. He has so many names; perhaps 'Grimnir the Masked One' refers to him being able to change his appearance. Although he can take any form, I know he most often appears wearing a grey cloak and hat and carrying a walking staff. That's how I pictured him: a wise old man with a beard, quick to laugh and with a twinkle in his eye.

My shoulders drop and I can't help feeling cheated. That's the Odin I wanted to meet. I desperately hoped for some sense of connection. I wanted comfort and reassurance, a kindly figure to guide me. Not this *Grimnir*. I think back to my ancestors' journals. I'm sure they mentioned something about our path being one of growth through hardship. Perhaps I need to prove myself and win the wager before I get to meet him properly.

I glance at my face in the mirror and sigh. There's so much I don't understand. Is Odin using me, or did he choose me as his player because he believes in me? Deciding he must have given me the pin for a reason, I fasten it to the front of my cloak and step outside.

The walkway is heaving with visitors, wrapped up in coats and scarves, eating waffles and talking excitedly. Being around other people is a relief; I can feel my sense of reality rushing back like blood returning to my body. A gang of teenage boys laugh and push one another. One of them points and for a moment I think they're making fun of my disfigured eye, but then I see the awe in their faces. I hold my head high and smile. To them I'm part

201

of the show, a Valkyrie with some seriously badass makeup.

I wait for them to pass then pick my way through the crowd. A man in front is pushing a wheelchair with an elderly lady inside. He stops abruptly and I avoid bumping into him, only for a woman coming the other way to brush past me. Her duffel coat is dripping with grief. It happened months ago, but it feels like yesterday. When she went in to him that morning his little face was blue. Cot death, the doctors said. Nothing she could have done.

Tears sting my eyes and I step away, straight into the path of a man holding hands with a woman. His leather jacket speaks of lust. He spies on his neighbour through the wall. He watches him in the shower. I grit my teeth and hurry on. An old lady is addicted to shoplifting, a teenage girl cuts her thighs with a razor, a man will never forgive himself for tying up a dog and beating it. Images, emotions and memories wash over me; snatches of people's lives, their hurts, longings, and regrets.

I stop and rub my temples, hoping it might dislodge the debris of their secrets from my head. No matter how I try, I can't seem to control my gift. The impressions come to me when I don't want them, yet evade me if I try too hard. I think about Grimnir's advice and feel sure that I'm right. Nina's catsuit must have something more to show me.

I step down from the path and trudge through the snow to Ulva's caravan. I knock on the door. When no one answers, I try opening it but it's locked. I walk around to the back and survey the rectangular window. If I want to read the catsuit again, I have to get inside.

A flash of movement makes me glance up. A man on ridiculously high stilts is striding towards me. His legs, torso and arms are encased in willow, his face covered by a wooden mask, cut out to look like flames and painted red. He stalks past, taking massive yet incredibly slow strides. Spindly twig fingers a metre long dangle from the ends of his arms and his hair hangs in ropes down his back, swaying as he walks. He looks like something fashioned from the forest and brought to life by dark magic. A creature stepped out of a nightmare.

I watch him head towards the big top, relieved that young children aren't permitted tonight, and then check no one is coming before tugging at the window. The rusty catch rattles inside but doesn't open. Looking for something to use, I spot a pile of bricks under a nearby caravan. I take one and bring it down on the window frame, hoping not to break the glass, and wincing at each loud bang.

Eventually the catch springs open. Leaning over with my stomach across the metal frame, I turn my body sideways then throw one leg inside. There's only a flimsy curtain and I roll onto the bed. The catsuit is where I left it. Fighting the urge to grab the material, I pull out the shoebox and place it on the bed. Grimnir said to let the impressions surface in my mind and not pull at the threads with thought. I sit and take several deep breaths then close my eyes and centre myself. When I feel ready, I reach out my hand. I don't demand anything from the material. I don't search for answers. I wait.

Nothing happens at first and then a familiar memory plays. Nina is climbing the rigging of the big top. She calls down, 'It's over, Stig! I mean it this time. I'm seeing someone else.' She grabs the trapeze and sways outwards, twisting and turning her body before snatching the bar with her other hand. She knows she's being reckless but she doesn't care. She wants Stig to worry. She wants him to come up to her.

And then the fabric shows me something I didn't see before.

Stig, standing in the ring, shouts, 'Come down if you're not going to wear your harness!' He waits a moment then flaps his arms. 'I'm not playing your crazy games!' Nina watches him walk away and her heart falters. Surely he must know there's no one else? She loves him. He disappears out of the big top and she climbs to a nearby metal platform and stares at the door. He'll come back, he always does.

Someone steps into the ring and Nina grins with satisfaction. A moment later the smile drops off her face. It's not him.

22

A FEROCIOUS RAGE OVERTAKES HER

Of all people, it would be *her*. Nina sighs and decides to carry on training. It's the only thing that calms her when she's upset. She calls down. 'Hey, Ulva, can you bring my harness up, please?' If Ulva's come to pick another fight, she may as well make herself useful.

Nina folds her arms and waits. She knows Ulva is angry, but she couldn't bear to let her mum take her away simply to abandon her again. For all her talk of change, the woman had alcohol on her breath. Taking the letter was wrong, but Nina had to do *something* to make her best friend stay.

Nina sighs sadly, her self-justification crumbling. She should never have promised her the part of Baldur either, but playing the lead was Ulva's dream. Even though Nina was willing to give up the part, deep down she knew Karl would never agree to it. She runs her hands over her gold catsuit and pride radiates through her chest. Like he said, she is the star. People come to the circus just to see her.

Nina watches Ulva pull herself up to the platform. She's wearing her fluffy pink sweatshirt, even though it's far too small for her now. Nina remembers the day they bought it. Karl told them to buy essentials but they spent half the money on cinema tickets and ice cream. Remembering makes her smile. Once the circus moves to a town, Nina will take her shopping again. It's been too long since they got away and had fun.

Her gaze drops to the mask around Ulva's neck. The thing is so huge and hairy and horrible. Why does she always have to be Fenrir? So what if her name means wolf; she should be allowed to play something else. As soon as she finishes training she's going to speak to Karl. If he won't let Ulva wear a different mask then Nina will refuse to perform.

She steals a glance at Ulva, unsure what kind of mood she's in. Ever since they started practising for this new performance, she's been strange, happy one minute and flying into a rage the next. Nina gestures to the harness and says, 'Thanks for helping.' Ulva smiles in reply.

Nina steps into the harness then turns her back as she's done a hundred times before. They've spent so many hours training together. Ulva is improving all the time, and one day she'll be good enough to take the lead. Nina smiles with relief, grateful that they're talking. She hates it when they fall out. She'll find a way to make things right between them, she always does. Stig too. She imagines him standing behind her. If he were here now, she'd throw her arms around him and kiss him.

Nina yelps. The harness is so tight it hurts. She tries to turn around, but the hands tugging the straps won't let her move.

Ulva growls, her voice full of spite. 'Admit it. You can't let me be happy, can you?'

Nina drops her head. She knows what's coming; they've been over it so many times.

'If it weren't for you, I'd be with Mum now. You think you can keep me chained here forever, but you can't.'

Nina blows out a sigh. *Chained?* What is she talking about? 'I've told you already. I didn't mean to hurt you. I was trying to protect you!'

Nina catches her breath, then spins around and gasps. Ulva is wearing the mask. What's she trying to do, scare her or something? The snout of the wolf wrinkles into a snarl and Ulva's eyes glow pale. Nina takes a shaky step back. She must be imagining it.

'Ulva, please! You're scaring me!' Nina swallows, her mouth parched. She glances down at the ring, desperate for help, but there's no one. The ground has never looked so far away, the drop so terrifying. She sees the end of the platform behind her and her stomach turns.

Nina steps forward and holds out her arms, gabbling now. 'I'll help you find your mum. We'll track her down together. If you want to leave, I'll help you. I promise.' Even as she speaks, she knows it's no use. It's not her friend in there. It's something else.

Ulva shoves her.

For one sickening moment she teeters on the edge of the platform, her hands grasping at empty air. Her heart stops and then she's falling. Panic explodes inside her. The harness . . . the cable will pull taut and save her.

But it doesn't. Her body slips through the straps and her neck jolts, excruciating pain radiating into her shoulder and arm. She dangles, gasping for breath. Choking. She grabs at her throat. Her head pounds with impossible pressure. She's going to pass out. She's going to . . . The strap gives and she plummets, hitting the ground with a thud. A flash of white-hot pain, and then nothing.

I drop the catsuit and tears are flowing down my face. Poor Nina. The panic and fear she felt, the pain. I saw and felt every detail so clearly it was like reliving my own memory. My shoulders slump and I bite my lip. How could I have got it so wrong before? Nina only *wished* that it was Stig behind her, doing up her harness. And I thought . . . I bury my face in my hands. He was telling the truth.

Ulva pushed Nina. She didn't mean to kill her, but she did.

How am I going to make her confess? And then I remember the harness. If I confront her with the evidence, perhaps she will admit everything. I need to find the sweatshirt she was wearing when she took it. I open the wardrobe and scan the rail. It's not there.

I drag her clothes from the shelves, dropping them into a heap on the floor. There's something pink and fleecy. I reach out to grab it, hungry for answers, and then force myself to be patient. Closing my eyes, I sit down and draw a deep breath. It takes me longer this time, there are so many thoughts and emotions racing inside me, but eventually my head clears.

Feeling calmer, I pick up the sweatshirt. I don't ask the material for anything, I don't search for answers. I wait. Eventually an image forms and I see the world through Ulva's eyes. She lifts the wolf mask to her face, acting more from instinct than thought. As soon as she looks through it, a green haze obscures her vision and a ferocious rage overtakes her. She sees Nina's mouth is moving but her words are a murmur.

Ulva's throat aches with bitter tears. All she knows is that the person she loved best in the world tricked her. The person she trusted most betrayed her. It hurts so much, it's like someone has driven a knife into her heart. She clenches her fists and her whole body shakes. She tries to fight it, but the urge for violence is so strong it blocks out all thought.

Nina steps closer, her arms outstretched, and Ulva shoves her.

A swish, a snap and a thud.

Ulva hears the noise then lifts her head and sniffs. At first she doesn't understand where Nina has gone. She peers over the edge of the platform, unable to grasp what she's seeing. Nina's body is caught in her harness, swinging from side to side. She summons every ounce of human reasoning she has left and pulls off the mask. The green fog lifts and her mind spins with sickening realisation.

Ulva climbs down the rigging and Nina drops past her, landing on the floor with a bang. One of her legs is at an awkward angle, her face clammy and white. 'Nina!' Ulva races over, her mind shattering into a million pieces. There's no blood, so maybe she's still alive. Ulva takes a hasty step back, all the energy draining from her, and stares at her trembling hands as if they don't belong to her. She didn't do this. She can't have.

Nina's harness is lying next to her on the ground. It should have saved her. Why didn't it save her? Ulva tries to remember doing it up. She was so angry and distracted; she must have fastened it wrong. Ulva covers her mouth with her hand and rocks back and forth. This can't be happening. She loves Nina! She didn't do this, she can't have, but who's going to believe her? They'll think she did it on purpose; everyone will hate her. Ulva picks up the harness. If no one finds it then it will seem like Nina was training without one. She shoves the harness under her sweatshirt and runs out to find help.

Karl is limping along the path, his head down. Ulva ducks into the hall of mirrors and watches him. He hasn't seen her. He wanders into the big top and she sobs with relief. He'll find Nina and call an ambulance. Maybe she will be OK. Please, please, let her be OK.

Ulva hurries to her caravan, her head pounding. Karl is probably calling the police right now. What if they can tell Nina was wearing a harness? She can't keep it in her caravan; they might do a search. She could throw it away, but what if they go through the bins? The forest . . . but someone will see if she starts a fire, and the ground is too hard to dig. She'll hide it in the undergrowth. Yes, she'll put it somewhere no one will think to look.

Ulva enters her caravan and stashes the harness in a green carrier bag, then heads to the woods. She follows the trail for a while then turns off, going one way and then the other. There's a broken tree that looks like it's been hit by lightning. She stops next to it and pushes the carrier bag inside, shoving it down into the depths of the rotting trunk.

23

EVERYTHING IS ABOUT TO FALL APART

I drop the sweatshirt and glance around the room. The bed is covered with purple cushions, the once-matching duvet cover now faded and thin. A stale sadness hangs on the air and I can almost taste the tears that have been wept here. There are no pictures or family photos in frames. The only decorations are the childish stickers that cover the wardrobe, half of them picked off to leave a sticky mess behind.

I might have a difficult relationship with Mum, but she's always been there for me. I know she loves me and wants to protect me. It must have been so hard for Ulva when her mother left her, but it can't have been easy when she came back either. The people here raised her; the circus is her home. Perhaps deep down she knew she was better off

212

staying, even though it was wrong of Nina to make the decision for her.

I sigh and my breath hangs before me. It's all such a waste. Nina thought she was doing the right thing, but she couldn't have known that Ulva's mum was going to let her down. One thing's for sure though. If it weren't for the mask, Nina would still be alive.

Ulva is out there now wearing it. She doesn't know the power it has over her. I can't let her hurt anyone else . . . I have to warn Stig.

I stand and then slump back down. What have I done? If Ruth tells Karl and he informs the police, then Stig might get arrested. How can I face him after the things I said, after the terrible things I thought? I wouldn't be surprised if he never talks to me again. I chew my thumbnail as a single thought gnaws at me. How did I get it so wrong?

I get up and reach for the light switch. The room brightens and just like that it becomes clear. I've been using my gift to search for answers, picking and pulling at the threads, demanding to be shown what I expected to see. Grimnir's gift is so simple that I didn't appreciate its magnitude until now. For the cloth to reveal its truth I must empty my mind. I need to put my preconceptions aside.

I know Stig didn't tell me the truth about things, but maybe I was too quick to judge his character. I was so fixated on the idea that he must be either good or bad that I didn't stop to consider any in-between. He should have texted me back, but I can't blame him for being scared after everything that happened. He hides from his problems but that doesn't make him a bad person. He lies to protect

213

himself, but he doesn't deliberately set out to deceive people. Stig was right when he said, *I know you want things to be black and white but sometimes they're not.* People are complicated, and so are the gods.

Even Tyr, the god of truth and justice, is capable of lying. He tricked Fenrir into wearing the magical chain in order to keep the gods safe. Tyr's was a noble lie; he deceived the wolf to protect those he loved, just like Nina did with Ulva. Loki tricks others for his own twisted amusement. What about Odin? He's driven by an insatiable desire for knowledge and will stop at nothing to get it, hanging himself until almost dead to discover the runes. If a few mortals are hurt in the pursuit of his ambitions, maybe it doesn't matter that much to him.

You think you have it all worked out, don't you? Everything black and white. Odin is good and I am bad. Loki's right. I have been looking for easy answers. Perhaps Odin has been using my ancestors and is using me. Or maybe it's more complicated than that. There could be reasons I don't know, things I don't understand. Loki wants to turn me against him, but I'm not going to fall into that trap. If I forget my idea of what Odin *should* be – a kindly old figure in a cloak and hat – then I won't be disappointed.

I turn off the light then go through the living room and open the outside door. The navy-blue sky is pierced with early evening stars and I shiver to realise it will be dark soon. Loud drumming drifts on the frosty air. It's not the music they usually play, this is wild and raucous, and then I remember the warrior women in the same costume as me – the Valkyries.

I jump down the steps and head into the site. If I'm going to save the circus and everyone in it, I have to make Ulva confess. But she's not going to do that, not unless she sees that I have evidence. I need the harness. I know Ulva turned off the trail, but I don't know which way she went. How am I going to find a single tree in a whole forest?

The walkways are empty apart from two security men patrolling the site. Music is coming from the big top, and I can hear the voiceover they play at the start of each performance. I have to hurry. I head to the rear door, hoping Ulva will be in the costume-change area. Maybe I can touch her clothes. The material might show me a flash of memory; some clue to reveal the direction she went. Even as the idea forms in my head, I know it's no use. I need to see the exact route she took through the trees. I need her to take me there.

I step inside and the room is packed with performers, some putting the finishing touches to their hair and makeup and others getting dressed or lining up by the curved screen. The atmosphere is hushed but charged. It feels different to the other times I've been here, the anticipation fraught with worry as well as excitement.

A woman with long blonde hair is admiring herself in a floor-length mirror. She wears a short cape of brown feathers over her gown, a stunning amber necklace at her throat. I watch, transfixed by her beauty, as the man who plays Loki approaches her. He wears a long green coat and a headdress with two horns at the front, reminding me of the jester's cap, but these are curved upwards rather than hanging down. A simple dark-green mask covers his eyes. He fingers the woman's cape then looks at her reflection and smirks. 'Tell me, who did you seduce to get the part of Freya?'

She smiles sweetly. 'Why, are you jealous?' He whispers something in her ear and she glares at him, and he laughs and walks away.

Ulva must be here somewhere. I edge around a group of dwarves and push further into the room. The seamstress adjusts the pointed ear of an elf then kneels and pins up the back of her cloak. I turn to avoid them and bump into a dressing table.

'Look where you're going!' Hel is seated at a mirror, one half of her mask carved and painted white to look like a skeleton. The wooden mouth grimaces and I startle and step back, reminded of the way it howled at me in the costume trailer. Ignoring my apologies, Hel leans forward and adjusts her wig. She wears a bald cap above the dead half of her face, a cascade of black hair on the other. The wooden mask moves again, the eyebrows furrowed in concentration, and I glance around me, convinced I can't be the only one to see it move.

The man who plays Odin walks by and Grimnir's words echo in my head. *You can see far more than you know.* I cover my blind eye and Hel's wooden face is inanimate. When I remove my hand the mask moves again. Before I can think about what this means, a shout sounds on the opposite side of the room.

The Loki actor is arguing with a performer holding a sword. Tyr steps between the two men, the model of a severed arm in his grasp. He raises it as if to keep the peace. 'What does it matter if he hasn't played Freyr before? As for him always turning up late, you're mistaken.'

Loki huffs. 'And who asked you? You're at the centre of every disagreement in this place, telling people to calm down and stirring up a fight. Where are you when the first punch is thrown? Not lending a *hand* then, are you?'

A huge man dips his head through the door, his face like thunder.

'Talking of being late,' scoffs Loki.

The man grunts. 'I may be late, but *I* am not afraid of a fight.' He fixes the Thor mask to his face and its wooden forehead furrows into a frown. 'Now shut your mouth or I'll shut it for you.' Loki shrinks back then regains his composure and spits, 'You haven't heard the last of this!' He turns and walks off, shoving people out of his way as he goes.

I glance around me and people shake their heads and talk in hushed tones. The atmosphere feels sour suddenly, as if everything is about to fall apart. In Karl's book of myths, I'm sure it mentioned the Trickster forcing his way into the hall of the gods and insulting each of them in turn. Maybe it's just a coincidence, but it's odd that the man who plays him seems out to cause trouble.

A group of performers comes in from the ring and my breath catches when I see Ulva, the wolf mask around her neck. I could tell her everything that's been happening but even if she believes me, she isn't going to hand me the evidence.

Suddenly an idea comes to me. I don't like tricking her, but if I'm going to win this wager I need to be clever. I walk over and look her in the eye. 'I know what you've done. I know where you've hidden the harness.'

24

THE DEAD SURROUND ME

Ulva's eyes flash dark. 'I don't know what you're talking about.'

She moves to walk past me and I block her way. 'I know you didn't mean to do it, but you have to tell the truth. You can come with me and tell Karl what you've done, or I will take the harness to him and call the police.'

'You're lying. You don't have it!'

The wolf mask glares at me with empty eyes, the fur on its snout bristling. Ignoring it, I lift my gaze to Ulva's face.

'After you pushed Nina, you took the harness and went to your caravan. You put it in a green carrier bag then went into the forest.'

'How did you . . . ?'

'I'm psychic, remember.'

She shoves me aside and goes out, just as I hoped she would. I stand inside the doorway, careful to stay out of view. After a couple of minutes I hurry along the walkway, the icy wind whipping my hair into my face. I know where she entered the forest from touching her sweatshirt. She followed the trail I walked with Stig.

At the end of the path, I step into the snow and dash from one caravan to the next, making sure to keep out of sight. When I reach the edge of the clearing, I stop and shiver. It's darker among the trees, dark enough for the dead to form. I push away a heavy spruce branch and a raven caws in warning. The forest is thick with gloom; tall grey trunks creaking and groaning in the wind. I can't see her. Panic rises inside me. Where is she?

A flash of blonde hair moves up ahead and I let out a sigh. Stillness hangs in the air, as if the forest is holding its breath. I follow in her footsteps, a thick carpet of snow and pine needles crunching beneath my boots. A pale face looms out from behind a trunk, and I spin to my left. Another face appears, and another, sprouting like mushrooms in the darkness.

I press my back against a tree and try to steady my breathing. When I look again there are more shadowy figures. A woman holding a baby is slumped against a tree trunk, her long hair hanging down, half her body dissolved into the bark. A raven lands on a branch then hops clean through her shoulder. I turn around and an old man stumbles aimlessly. They aren't *doing* anything. They're lost. Desperate souls doomed to wander the earth because I didn't get them back into Yggdrasil, because I didn't return them to the underworld.

Loki has rounded them up and brought them here, the same way he brought the dead to fight at Ragnarok. To spite me, but also to make me face up to what I've done. He said I'm no better than anyone else, I think only of myself, and he's right. My throat tightens and I fight a tear. I can't blame the dead if they want to hurt me, but I can't stand here feeling sorry for myself either. Whatever happens, I need to follow Ulva. I have to win this wager.

I step out from my hiding place and shadowy shapes flit through the undergrowth: men, women and children, all with empty black eyes. None of them seem to be aware of one another or their surroundings. I think about the dead in the big top and a shudder runs through me. I felt so cold and weak when one of them swiped its hand through me, and I don't have the light of the caravan to run to now. Before, it took just one of them to notice me, and then they all turned and stared. When the woman on the steps saw me, it was after I'd looked into her eyes. Maybe if I keep my gaze down, the dead won't pay me any attention.

The moon glints from behind a cloud and I catch a glimpse of Ulva hurrying below. She must have taken a turning off the path. I trudge along the trail and spot a gap in the trees. The ground is steep and twisted with roots. I grab a branch for support then stumble and slide down, stopping myself before I reach the bottom of a hollow.

Ulva stands in the middle of it, a shaft of silver falling on her like a spotlight. Shadowy figures writhe and weave around her. Massed together, the dead look like wisps of mist in the moonlight. Ulva glances in my direction and I crouch behind a trunk and watch as she pushes away a clump of hanging vines and approaches a decaying tree stump. She plunges her hand inside and pulls out a bag. After checking it, she shoves it back, perhaps thinking it's safest to leave it where it is. After all, if I knew where the harness was, I would have taken it.

I need to get off the path; she's going to come back this way at any moment. I stand up to go when a shadowy woman crawls towards me. She rushes forward on her knees and I turn my head and dive into the undergrowth, brambles scratching my face. The woman creeps away and I let out a sigh.

'Who's there?' calls Ulva.

I hold still, barely daring to breathe.

I wait until I hear her walk past me, then risk a glance her way. She clambers up the bank and heads along the trail. Once the forest has swallowed her up, I go to the tree and reach inside.

I hurry through the forest, keeping my gaze down and side-stepping the dead, and emerge into the clearing with the carrier bag in my hand. The floodlights are on and the tents and walkways are bathed in bright light. My shoulders drop with relief. If I can make it through the caravan field, I'll be safe.

Karl knows there's something strange happening at the circus. If I give him the harness, there's a chance he will believe me. When Ulva is faced with the evidence, hopefully she will confess. Karl will know what to do;

I'll make him understand it was the mask and not her fault.

The black-and-gold big top shines like a beacon under the floodlights. I want to run to it, but there's no way to know how many of the dead are out there and I don't want to draw their attention. I could go to my caravan but there's no point. I can't hide until morning; I need to unmask Nina's killer before the last visitor leaves tonight.

My nose and ears tingle from the cold as I scan the maze of vehicles. It's only been thirty minutes since I came this way, yet it seems so much darker now; the velvet-black sky studded with stars. Gathering my courage, I tighten my grip around the handle of the carrier bag. The dead didn't see me in the forest. If there are more, I will just move past them.

A cold gloomy mist hangs over the field. All the performers and crew are on the main site. There's not a single light from any of the caravan windows, no sound of a radio or flickering TV. The canteen tent is dark and closed up, its white canvas walls billowing like a monster wheezing its last breath.

I make my way between the vehicles, walking quickly, then glance down and gasp. An arm is sticking out from under a caravan, its fingers opening and closing. I hurry past it and a young boy, no older than eight, appears before me. He's wearing shorts and I can see that one of his legs is mangled, a shard of white bone sticking out. His face is convulsed in pain and there are tear tracks on his cheeks. I look down as he hops forward, then falls over, just missing me.

I cover my mouth, knowing there's nothing I can do to help, then turn and go a different way. The shadows are empty and I breathe a sigh of relief. A few more minutes and I will be under the floodlights. I walk a little further, and an old lady steps through the side of a caravan. She's naked and has long white hair down to her waist, covering her pot belly. I watch as she sinks into the ground, just as a man appears, his spine curved so badly he's almost bent double.

I edge past him and rush on. I'm halfway there now. Only a little further and I'll reach the trailers. Something flickers in the corner of my eye and I spin around. A swirl of black mist rises from the ground and forms into the shape of a man. He has a thick hairy chest and wears a woman's dress and ripped tights. His face is smeared with lipstick and he sucks the thumb of one hand. A plastic doll hangs from the other. I swallow hard and step back, desperately hoping he doesn't see me.

I turn and nearly bump into an overweight man in a hospital gown, standing with his back to me. Another figure appears and I force myself to lower my gaze. I just need to move slowly. I edge my way around them and a toddler with long tangled hair races around the side of a caravan. Our eyes lock and we stare at one another. She reaches out as if she wants me to pick her up, her dark eyes huge in her head, and a chill runs through me. I put a finger to my lips, my heart thudding in my ears, desperately hoping the others won't notice me.

The man in the hospital gown turns around. He lunges to grab me and I duck away. More figures approach from my left but I don't stop to look. I move fast, running now, past the last few caravans. I get to the costume trailer then stop and cry out. Dozens of dead are between me and the walkway. Shadowy shapes race across the field from every direction, swarming in a great rolling fog. There are too many. I'm not going to make it.

The glow of a lamp post flickers in the distance, not bright but better than nothing. I race to it then bend over and gasp for breath. The dead surround me on every side, the light keeping them from reaching me. An unnatural cold emanates from them; even from ten paces away I can feel the icy chill on my skin. Some open their mouth in a scream, others shout or sob. I can't hear their words but the wind roars with sorrow.

The way they jump and snatch reminds me of the restless souls I saw at the tree. I scan their black eyes and something shrinks inside me. It's not hate or rage I see in their faces but desperation. It's like they're drowning and I am the rope. I slump against the post and my eyes fill with tears. Why didn't I do as Hel asked? I should have made sure all the dead got back. I should have given my life rather than abandon them.

Even if I can't help the dead, maybe I can save the circus from Loki. The floodlights aren't far away; it wouldn't take long to run. I glance over my shoulder and there are even more figures than before, all grabbing at me. There's no way I can get through.

Long minutes pass and I feel myself growing weaker, the cold leeching the life out of me. Everyone is in the big top watching the performance; it could be ages before someone comes this way. I don't know how long I can last.

I need to call Mum. The last time we spoke she was afraid something was watching her at the tree – but she has to water it, the dead can't be allowed to escape again. My teeth are chattering and my hands tremble as I pull out my phone. I expect to hear a recording telling me to leave a message, but she answers and her voice brings a sob to my throat.

'Martha? What's wrong?'

Pitiful faces crowd closer. The boy with the mangled leg crawls over the snow and reaches out his arm pleadingly. 'Oh, Mum, I've done something terrible. I told you I'd got all the dead back before, but I didn't. I dropped the rope too soon and they didn't all make it into the tree . . . and now they're here at the circus.'

Her voice is sharp with fear. 'Slow down, I don't understand. Are you in danger?'

'I don't know. I think . . . I think they want me to save them. I wish I could, but I can't, Mum. I can't.'

'Is there somewhere safe you can go? Someone who can help you?'

'No, I'm on my own. The light is keeping them away, but I'm so cold my feet are starting to go numb. I don't know how long I have.'

'Oh, Martha!' Mum stifles a sob and then shushes me softly like she did when I was a child. I would give anything for her to hold me close and tell me everything will be all right.

'You have to promise me you'll water the tree, Mum. The next time you go there, try to listen. Don't be afraid. If you meet the Norns, you'll understand everything.'

She sniffs. 'I promise I'll try.'

226

My body sags against the pole. Mum is saying something but my thoughts are unravelling and I can't follow the thread of her words.

'Martha? Listen to me. You need to keep talking. You might feel sleepy but you have to stay awake. Tell me, why did you drop the rope?'

I hang my head. 'Mormor. She was trying to protect me from the *draugr*. I knew she'd never leave me. I had to make sure she went to the underworld.'

'You let go of the rope to make sure Mormor would be safe?'

'Yes.'

'Martha, my darling, you didn't have time to think! You did what you did out of love. You did your best; you have to trust what was in your heart.'

Compassion spreads in my chest. I realise Mum only hid the truth about my gift and Mormor dying because she wanted to protect me. I've tried to understand, and now I do. I know how easy it is to make the wrong decision out of love, because I did it too.

A noise sounds behind me: footsteps on the walkway.

'Someone's coming, Mum. I have to go.'

'I love you, Martha. Phone me when you can.'

'I love you too.'

I pocket my phone and wipe the ice from my lashes, almost too afraid to hope.

Stig strides through the crowd of dead and I rush forward, shaky with relief. At the same time, a shadowy figure breaks ranks and lunges for me. I drop to the ground and it dissolves in a swirl of black smoke where the light touches it.

Stig's face is ashen, and his voice wavers with disbelief. 'You're afraid of me? I know what you think, but you're wrong. I didn't hurt Nina.'

His words unpick a stitch in me and a sudden rush of affection fills my heart. I've been afraid to have feelings for him because I didn't want to get hurt, and then when I thought he killed Nina . . . I shake my head, unable to form the words I need to say. How could I have thought such a thing? How could I have hurt him like that?

'I'm sorry, Stig. I know.'

He hesitates and I hold out my hand. 'Please?'

He pulls me to my feet and I catch my breath. 'It was Ulva. She pushed Nina.'

'What? No, Ulva wouldn't do that.' He shakes his head and takes several steps back, and I have a sudden urge to throw my arms around him, afraid he might leave me.

'It wasn't her fault. It was the wolf mask.'

'What do you mean?'

'The mask did something to her. She wasn't herself.'

The wind whips Stig's hair around his face and he pushes it behind his ears. 'How do you know this?'

'I touched the catsuit Nina was wearing when she fell. I saw her last memory. I'm so sorry for what I said. I was wrong about you.'

'You were wrong about me and you're wrong about Ulva! She loved Nina!'

I look at the dead and a wave of coldness crashes over me. 'Please, you have to take this to Karl.' I hold out the carrier bag, which flutters in the wind. Stig raises his eyebrows. 'What is it?'

'Nina's harness. The police were right; she was wearing one. Ulva helped her into it after you left. You need to take it to Karl. It's evidence.'

'Evidence? But you said it wasn't her fault!'

Another shadowy figure lunges at me and I cry out.

Stig spins around. 'What is it? What's there?'

I swallow a sob. 'The dead. They're all around us.'

He turns and peers into the darkness, his Adam's apple bobbing as he swallows. 'Why can't I see them? I saw Nina in the cabin. If I saw her, then why can't –'

'Please, Stig, help me get into the light!'

He stares, panic written on his face, and then he takes the bag and nods. I tighten my grip on his arm and his coat buzzes with determination. He gives me a tiny smile and a flicker of warmth catches inside me. 'Ready?' he asks.

Before I can answer, he ploughs into the shadowy figures. Cold hands snatch at my coat and tug at my hair, pulling me on every side. I gulp and struggle to breathe. I want to tell him to turn back but I can't speak. Shadows dart before me, appearing and disappearing. A woman howls in my face, a young boy screams, men shout. I flail with my arms, trying to knock them away, but there's nothing there.

Something slashes my face and I scream. Stig pulls me onwards and I try to run, but my legs are shaking so much I trip over.

Dozens of icy fingers grab me, their grip stronger than ever, as if they can sense I'm weakening. They're pulling me down, dragging me to the ground. The dead are swarming all over me. I can feel them on my arms, my legs, my face, ripping my clothes, tearing my hair.

'Stig!'

A thousand voices cry out, just like when the dead followed the rope into the tree. Dark shadows swirl around Stig's face. He's saying something but I can't hear what.

'Get me to the light, please!'

A solid hand hauls me up. We run a little way but something tugs at my ankles and I go down. Icy hooks claw and dig at my face. I writhe on the ground and try to pull them off. I open my mouth to scream and cold fingers force their way into my throat. The air freezes in my lungs, my chest so full of ice I can barely breathe. The cold plunges deeper, razor-sharp teeth biting into the flesh of my stomach. They're *inside* me.

Wails and moans build to a shriek and I wince and cover my ears.

Pain rinses my mind of thought. I try to shout but my voice has gone.

'Martha! We're nearly there!'

He sounds terrified. I want to tell him it's too late. I don't have the strength to fight. I don't even feel cold any more. I feel nothing.

A strong hand reaches under my arm and pulls me upright. I grit my teeth and Stig drags me along, my feet pounding on the wooden walkway.

He stops and rubs my arms. 'You're safe now. You're safe.'

I blink through blurry lashes and see bright white light. A sob escapes me and I wrap my arms around his neck.

He holds me tight. 'It's OK. You're OK.' His coat is overflowing with love and worry. I wish I could stay wrapped in his arms. He's so solid and warm. I pull away and try to

230

speak but my teeth are chattering and it takes a while to get the words out. 'Please, take the harness to Karl. Tell him to come quickly. Tell him he's right, the circus is in danger.'

'No, I'm not leaving you.'

'I need to find Ulva and make her confess. There isn't much time.'

'But you can hardly stand.'

'I'll be OK. Please, Stig, I wouldn't ask if it wasn't important. You need to get Karl. Tell him to come. Now!'

25

FETTERS WILL BURST AND THE WOLF RUN FREE

Stig races away and I wrap my arms around my sides. I take a few shaky steps and my body slowly begins to thaw, the numbness in my limbs replaced by aching stiffness. I text Mum to say I'm OK, then search for Ulva. Karl will be here soon; I just have to keep her talking until he arrives.

I move to one side as a gaggle of visitors approaches me, bundled up in coats and hats. They're chattering excitedly, their breath forming tiny white clouds on the night air. Dozens more people spill out from the big top and then head into the smaller tents, or they turn right and congregate around the food vans, where they hand over notes in exchange for steaming trays of noodles and crêpes wrapped in serviettes.

A costumed performer stands outside each tent promising 'wondrous feats' and 'amazing sights'. I glance towards the psychic tent and see Sandrine in her feathered mask, shrilling and flapping her arms. Not that she needs to drum up business; there's already a long queue. Thinking about Ruth makes me feel bad. I hate letting her down, especially after our conversation in the canteen tent. I shouldn't have brought up her past like that; it wasn't fair of me. For a moment I consider going to apologise, but there isn't time.

A muffled shriek sounds behind me. I turn and see a woman pointing at the sky, her eyes wide. The impossibly tall creature I saw earlier is striding down the path, sending visitors scattering in all directions. More than twice the height of the other performers on stilts, it glows bright red, long tubes of neon snaking around its wicker torso and limbs.

I enter the nearest tent, where dozens of people sit on benches watching a magician. He whips away a cloth to reveal a birdcage with a woman squashed inside, and the audience claps as she climbs out, then flips onto her back and arches her body. She crawls across the stage on her hands and feet with her head hanging down at a disturbing angle, and there is something repulsive about the spider-like way she moves. The crowd cheer her on, their hunger for the weird and extreme almost distasteful. I scan the room, desperately searching, but there's no sign of Ulva or anyone in a wolf mask.

Outside a crowd is gathered around a tattooed man juggling human skulls. He balances one on top of his bald head and onlookers cheer as he tosses three more into the sky. Further along the walkway a masked Thor brandishes his hammer and flexes his muscles while men slap him on the back and women feel his biceps and pose for a selfie.

A teenage girl screams behind me and my heart pounds as a gang of boys rushes past, the impressions from their clothes exploding in my mind. Everything is colour and noise, a surreal, overwhelming mix of imagery and emotion.

A whoop sounds from the tent opposite. Keen to get off the crowded path, I step inside the doorway and scan the audience for Ulva. Inside are the Chinese girls in ballgowns. The one in the top hat is throwing daggers at the other, who is strapped to a round board. Knives land inches from the girl's limbs, the final one pinning the roses in her hair. The thrower spins the board and it creaks and clunks as her partner rotates. She walks away and then whips the white-handled knife from her top hat. The audience gasps as she runs the blade across her tongue and then turns around. She's going to throw it without looking.

A guy in the back row buries his face into the shoulder of the man next to him. One or two others cover their eyes, but most lean forward with an expression of ghoulish curiosity. That's the thing about the circus: people are excited by the prospect of danger – the thought that the trapeze artist will lose their grip; the knife find its fleshy target. Tonight, joy could turn to tragedy for everyone here. The thought makes me queasy and I step outside and gulp down the icy air.

The site is quieter now that most people have filed into the smaller tents. I head towards the big top hoping to see

Stig and Karl, but there's no sign of them. Two performers wearing furry cat masks rummage through the bins by the food vans. They lick their paws and then bound off and twirl against a man waiting outside a Portaloo, much to the amusement of his beer-sipping friends. Freya whistles for the cats and suddenly the men only have eyes for her. A moment later she has her arm draped over them and is laughing loudly.

Something moves at the edge of my vision and I turn to my left. Dozens of shadowy dead are wandering through the dark caravan field. The thought of their cold grasping hands makes me shudder and I move away – straight into the Norns. They loom over me, taking tiny steps this way and that, and I shrink back.

'Have you seen Karl? Or Ulva, the girl who plays Fenrir?' I ask.

The women shuffle closer and peer into my face, their eyes glittering behind their masks. They speak at the same time, their voice like wind through the dead leaves of a tree. 'The fetters will burst and the wolf run free. Much do I know and more can I see.'

The one with the shears grabs my wrist and I yelp at her icy touch. Her wooden mask frowns and clumps of earth and twig fall away as she points into the distance. 'O'er the sea from the north there sails a ship with the people of Hel. At the helm stands Loki.' Her eyes flash pale and bore into me and I pull away. It's not an actor behind the mask.

'I don't understand.' I shake my head and they mimic my movements in parody. The Norns decide the fate of

235

every being; they know the future. 'What's Loki going to do? If you know, you have to tell me. Please.' One of them cradles her chin in her hands as if she's weeping. Another raises her arms, palms pushed flat as if to hold up a falling roof. The middle figure opens her arms and the other two women step behind her. Suddenly they scurry off, their stilts tip-tapping on the walkway.

'Wait, please!'

Drumming sounds to my right and I spin around. Valkyries in the same costume as me march forward brandishing swords and beating animal-skin drums, and my heart thuds with each loud bang. With their fierce makeup and wild hair they make a formidable sight. They yell an ululation and the cold night air shivers. They mean war.

Members of the crew appear and jog in front of them, unravelling long coils of rope and gesturing for visitors to move aside. A few moments later, costumed performers arrive and assemble on the path, their cloaks and costumes flapping wildly in the wind.

I scan their masked faces and see Odin, Tyr and Freya along with a host of other gods, elves and dwarves. Sandrine in her falcon costume is there and so are the ravens, two cats, a boar and two wolves, plus the skeletal horse with eight legs from the hall of mirrors. The jaws of its skull snap open and closed, the person working it presumably hidden beneath its black blanket. There's no sign of the wolf Fenrir. Where is she?

The drumming continues and more performers join the parade. Thor storms up the path, yelling and waving his hammer, and excited visitors leap out of the way. Loki saunters over wearing a long green coat and a helmet with two upturned horns, a simple green mask over his eyes. He bows and waves to the crowds, who go wild to see him.

The horde of dead follows close behind, shaking their skull poles. Dwarves leapfrog one another and an elf girl whirls her way into the middle of the line and then shimmies under the rope. Hel strides over with her head down and takes up her position near the back, looking none too happy about it.

A whining and crackling noise cuts through the air and I look up and see speakers attached to the floodlights. The ringmaster's amplified voice booms out: 'Welcome to Ragnarok, the end of the world and the destruction of the gods!'

I can't tell where he is at first, and then I see a tiny figure spotlighted on a high metal platform in the field. At his words, the line of performers starts moving. Ruth said there would be a fire show after the parade. If Ulva is part of the procession, that's where she'll be headed. The path is heaving with visitors. I grit my teeth and make my way down, trying to ignore the impressions from people's clothes as I battle through the crowd.

The ringmaster continues, 'There shall come a winter unlike any the world has seen. Mankind will struggle to survive. It will be a time of axe and blood. Brother will slay brother, father will slay son, and son will slay father. The sons of the monstrous wolf Fenrir will swallow the sun and the moon, plunging the world into darkness and chaos. Yggdrasil, the great tree that holds together the cosmos, will tremble and the world's mountains collapse!'

I get to the end of the walkway and stop to catch my breath. Floodlights stand around the edges of the field, highlighting the ringmaster's platform to my left and the Viking ship and ring of skull poles, which now has a bonfire burning at its centre.

Oskar is there in a fluorescent yellow jacket, giving orders to the crew who rush about lighting firebrands. When no one's looking I hurry down the sloped entrance and duck under the rope, then wedge myself between two big barrels containing water. Before me is a large rectangular area with low fencing to keep back the crowd. I'm guessing that's where the fire show will be. If I wait here, I should be able to grab Ulva when she appears.

The cheers of the crowd intensify. Oskar unhooks the rope and the performers troop down in single file. When they get to the bottom of the slope, a crewmember hands them a flaming firebrand and they go through a gap in the fence.

The ringmaster's voice booms through the speakers. 'At Ragnarok, all chains will be loosened. The monstrous wolf Fenrir will escape his shackles and Loki will be free of his bonds. Jormungand, the giant serpent that dwells at the bottom of the ocean, will rise from the depths, spilling the seas over the earth. The convulsions will shake Naglfar – a ship made of the fingernails and toenails of the dead – from its moorings in the underworld. It will sail over the flooded earth bringing an army of the dead to the fight, helmed by Loki himself!'

The man who plays Loki turns right and jogs over to the Viking ship, and cheers and whoops go up from the crowd. Following him are men and women in antlers. Odin and most of the gods turn left and assemble opposite, along with the Valkyries, dwarves and elves.

A member of the crew sees me. He signals for me to leave but I shake my head and point at my costume. 'I'm part of the show!' He strides over and takes my arm. 'Then you need to come down the walkway. Sorry, it's for safety.' I glance around for Karl and Stig, but there's no sign of them. 'No, you don't understand. I have to stay here!'

He leads me to the walkway and I glance back and see the ringmaster waving his arms, an anxious look on his face. He calls down to a member of the crew, who shouts into her walkie-talkie. The ringmaster gestures towards the field and then I see it too. A scuffle has broken out amidst the masked performers. Thor shoves one actor and punches another.

The man escorts me through the rope and onto the path, and suddenly I'm four or five people away from the front of the spectators. Even if I see Ulva, I'm not going to be able to grab her. I scan the faces in the procession and spot her wolf mask. 'Ulva! Ulva!' I wave but she doesn't see me. A man hands her a flaming torch and she strides towards the Viking ship.

Once all the performers have entered, the crew beckon the public down. The crowd surges in behind me, everyone keen to get a good view. I squeeze past a woman then push past a man, elbowing my way forward. 'Sorry, I need to get through!' The gap in the fence is now closed. I throw my leg up and clumsily jump over, then run towards the Viking ship. Smoke stings my eyes and I wipe my face. A member of the crew shouts at me but I keep running.

Eventually I catch up with Ulva and grab her shoulder. She spins around and the mask wrinkles into a snarl. She growls and I step back. Whatever stares out from her eyes, it's not human.

26

SMOKE AND CHAOS

Ulva shoves me and I stumble and fall to the ground, shocked by her strength. She tugs off the mask, her chest heaving, and stares down at me. Her eyes blaze with hate but there's a flicker of something else there too: a girl who's alone and desperately afraid.

'Please, I want to help you. I know you killed Nina but it wasn't your fault.'

She turns to leave and I push myself to my feet and charge at her. I snatch the wolf's head with one hand and grab her cloak with the other and a jolt of energy surges through me. My eyes roll back and green mist fills my mind, and then I see a man. He has his back to me and is standing before a crowd of people without eyes. He sweeps his hand through the air in front of him, bathing them in green light, and suddenly I realise what I'm seeing. The faces aren't people. They're masks! The man is clutching the head of a wolf, and the creature howls as if it's coming to life.

I saw the same image when I touched Loki's sleeve in the psychic tent. He did something to the masks in the costume trailer; he brought them to life somehow. And whatever he did, he gave extra to the wolf Fenrir. Why choose that mask? And then I realise. In one of the performances, the ringmaster told how Loki fathered three monstrous children who were foretold to bring about the end of the world. It's Fenrir that devours Odin. The wolf is the most dangerous being, the ultimate force of destruction.

Ulva snatches the mask from me and runs for the Viking ship. I'm following her when the Valkyries yell a war cry. They stand in a semicircle, their long hair blowing wildly. The ones at the front spin burning shields, sending sparks shooting into the sky, while those at the back pound drums, their powerful arms moving in unison.

The ringmaster's voice shouts out, 'Heimdall, the watchman of the gods, blows the Gjallarhorn, signalling the battle has commenced, and the fire giant Surt begins the destruction!' A horn blares and loud battle music plays from the speakers, complete with clanging swords and trampling hooves. The crowd cheers as the enormous glowing red giant stalks across the field. He wears a mask painted to look like flames, and carries a flaming sword. The ringmaster adds, 'It is Surt who razes the world and turns it to fire!'

The Valkyries pound twice on their drums then lift their arms. At their signal, the dwarves run forward, holding long black poles ablaze with fire at either end. The drumming starts again and the dwarves spin the poles low to the ground while their partners jump over them, flames flickering around their ankles.

I look for Ulva but she's vanished into a wall of smoke and chaos. I whirl around and then bite my lip, tasting blood. I have to find her. I need to make her confess if I'm going to win the wager. If I fail, Loki will destroy the circus and everyone here – including me. A gust of wind blows embers into my face and I wipe my eyes then blink in disbelief. Horned figures are rising from the smog, the sky behind them blood red from the artificial glow of the giant. I gasp with recognition – it's a scene from one of Mum's drawings.

The ringmaster continues, 'Despite the Norns foretelling their doom, the gods bravely go into battle. Spinning his mighty spear, Gungnir, above his head, Odin charges at the monstrous wolf Fenrir!' Two men run at me, carrying a huge papier-mâché wolf-head. I jump back and they bend and weave, making the wolf leap.

Coughing on the smoke, I push my way further into the crowd of antlered performers. A man with long straw hair stomps across my path. He wears dirty sackcloth, a loose bag of hessian on his head with holes ripped out for eyes and a mouth. Someone jolts me and I lurch forward. A figure with a skull covering its face pushes me back.

I take a deep breath, determined to steady my nerves. Ulva must be here somewhere. I search the gloom and a shadowy arm tries to grab me. I spin around, my heart pounding, as more hands reach for me. The dead are forming in the smoke. I rush out of the melee, gasping and coughing.

Bang. Bang.

The Valkyries beat their drums as a trio of elves dances forward. They whirl hoops of fire around their bodies, gyrating faster and faster until the flames blur into a single stream of light. A woman's grey face looms out from the smoke, her mouth twisted in a scream. An arm on the ground tries to clutch my ankle. The dead are all around me.

I race for the floodlight at the entrance to the field, not caring that I'm running through the middle of the show. Members of the public hold up their phones, their faces lit by the glow of screens. A loud whoosh sounds behind me and I glance back and see flames burst from the wolf's mouth. Cheers go up and another stream of fire gushes into the night sky. Ash catches in the back of my throat and I spit out the taste.

Stig is at the front of the crowd, waving his arms and yelling. I see the tiny white-haired figure of Karl next to him and cry out with relief. I run and clamber over the fence and Stig pulls me to him. The ringmaster's voice blares out above us and I gesture towards the walkway. We need to get to somewhere we can talk.

We fight our way through the crowd and onto the walkway, and Karl turns on me. 'What is this nonsense about Ulva killing Nina? According to Ruth, you were accusing Stig just now.' He shakes the carrier bag like I have some explaining to do.

I glance at Stig and give him a pained, apologetic look, then lick my lips and swallow. 'It's true. Ulva did do up Nina's harness when she was training that day, but she didn't fasten it properly. They argued and Ulva pushed her. Afterwards, she hid the harness so it looked like Nina was training without one. She didn't want people to think she'd fastened it wrong on purpose. Ulva didn't mean to do it. It was the mask.'

Karl's eyebrows jump in surprise. 'The mask?'

I take a deep breath. 'I told you that Loki is at the circus. He did something to the masks in the costume trailer; he brought them to life somehow.'

Karl chuckles and I feel the blood drain from my face. Disbelief hardens to dismay. He's the one person I was sure would believe me; I don't understand. The old circus manager looks at Stig and back to me. 'Very amusing, but I don't have time for this.'

'But you *know* there's something bad at the circus. You agreed that the performers have been acting differently, that their personalities have changed.' Karl laughs to himself but I refuse to give up. 'When did it start? People changing, I mean?'

'I'll tell you when things went wrong . . . the day the owners started making changes!'

He starts to walk away and I grab his arm. 'When you did the myth of Baldur, that was the first time the circus had performed one of the Trickster's stories in, what, ninety years?' He doesn't say anything and I continue. 'After the fire that nearly destroyed the place, your father decided to never perform his stories again.' Karl shrugs and I think

245

back to what Loki said in the hall of mirrors. *So when the circus finally performed one of my myths . . . Well, let's just say I got a little excited.*

'After Loki caused the death of Nina, Odin came up with the wager to make him leave, knowing that a game would appeal to his twisted sense of fun.'

Karl sighs impatiently and I talk quickly. 'I know it's hard to believe, but the Trickster is real. He hates being kept out – that's why he lost his temper when he wasn't allowed into the hall of the gods. Excluding him from the circus made him angry. When you finally did one of his stories he got revenge by enchanting the masks.'

Stig steps forward. He glances at me with concern, but there's not a trace of doubt in his eyes. 'You have to listen to her, Karl. Martha knows about these things. If she says it's true, you need to believe her.'

Karl scoffs. 'Then you two are well matched, both as crazy as each other.' He stuffs the carrier bag into the large pocket of his duffle coat and walks away.

'Loki is going to destroy the circus. You have to listen to me!' When he doesn't stop, I shout, 'What about the runes in the trees?'

He turns around and flaps his arm. 'I did that.'

'What?'

'I hoped it would make them cancel tonight's show.'

I stare at him, not wanting to believe it. 'But how? There were hundreds of them.'

'I carved the trees on the trail last, the rest I did in the night. There weren't hundreds. People see what they want to see.'

'But you told me –'

'Look, I'm sorry if my little prank has put ideas in your head. There *is* something bad at the circus, and it's Oskar!'

I grab Karl's arm and he frowns at me, but I don't let go. I hold his sleeve and clear my mind, letting the material show me what it wants. Stig must realise what I'm doing as he tries to distract him. 'We don't want Oskar to ruin things either. Maybe there's something we can do to help?' Karl looks at him confused and then stares down at my hand on his arm.

His jacket speaks of guilt, but this time the material shows me something else. He doesn't feel bad because he introduced one of Loki's stories. He's not superstitious, he just hates change. He can't forgive himself for agreeing to the owners' demands to update the routines. In the end they brought in new management anyway. Karl couldn't argue; after all, he was in charge when Nina had the accident. Everyone told him to retire, but to what? He had nowhere to go. So he stayed and grew bitter.

Karl pulls away from me and limps back down to the field. He's given his entire life to the circus. The myths *are* more than just stories to him – they're his childhood memories, his life's work. He can't bear to stand by while some upstart ruins everything. He'd rather see the place shut down. Karl carved Loki's name on the trees, he *invited chaos* by trying to make them call off the show. He wanted to make the circus lose money, hoping the owners would hand its management back to him.

'Ruth was right, his superstitious thing was an act,' I say. Stig looks confused and I go on, 'He wanted people to think

247

doing myths with Loki would bring bad luck, but he didn't believe any of it.'

'What about his book? Did he make it all up?' asks Stig.

'Karl doesn't believe in the gods in the way his father did, but he was happy for people to think something terrible would happen if they didn't stick to the routines they've always done. He knows circus people can be superstitious. It suited him to repeat his dad's warnings, but really he just didn't want Oskar to change things.'

Stig shakes his head as if he can't believe it. 'Karl took the harness, so maybe he's gone to speak to Ulva. Should I go and find her?' he asks. I shrug, not knowing if it would help. I hoped that if I confronted Ulva with the evidence, she would confess. But Karl is so closed-minded, I don't see how I'm ever going to convince him.

A dark shape is standing further along the path, half hidden in the shadow of a tent. I peer closer and see the outline of a person. The walkway is empty, so how did I not see them before?

The jester steps forward and my heart jumps to my throat. I cover my mouth and point, but Stig only frowns. 'I don't see anything. What is it? What's there?' he asks.

The jester taps his foot and the bells on his shoe jingle.

Stig's voice is taut with fear. 'Is it Nina? Why can't I see her?'

I shake my head, unable to look away. There's something sickening about the slow way the jester smiles, and then I see what he's grinning at.

Sandrine ambles around the corner in her bird mask, whistling to herself. The long feathers bounce as she walks, her cheeks rosy from the cold. She makes her way towards the psychic tent and then stops abruptly. I wait for her to turn around but she doesn't. She walks backwards, taking long stiff strides, never once turning her head or looking over her shoulder.

Stig tugs my arm and whispers, 'What's she doing? Martha?'

I swallow hard, a bitter taste in my mouth. 'I don't know.'

27

THE WHOLE PLACE IS BURNING

rack-crack-crack. Sandrine's body convulses and then goes rigid. She rises into the air, her toes barely touching the ground, and slowly rotates. Her chin rests on her chest, her long hair hanging down as she glides forward, her boots bumping and dragging along the walkway. She halts a few metres before us, and somewhere behind me Stig makes a whimpering sound.

Sandrine's head snaps up, revealing the long feathers of her mask. Her eyes dart in every direction, her breathing fast and shallow, her chest fluttering like a panicked bird. I look towards the jester but he's gone. My blood pounds in my ears as I turn and check around me, and then a gruff voice whispers from behind, 'Such a pretty falcon. Rather too fond of preening herself though; a bit like her owner.'

I spin around and grab Stig's arm. He glances in every direction, unable to see Loki, his face pale with fright.

The jester chuckles. 'And where *is* Freya? In the back of a tent with a gang of dwarves, I shouldn't wonder. I may not bring out the best in people, but you can be sure they always show their true colours when I'm around.'

Loki might have a problem with Freya, but why pick on Sandrine just because she plays the goddess's falcon? I don't know what he's going to do, but the cruel sound of his laughter sends a jolt of fear through me.

I take a deep breath, determined to stay calm. If I'm going to help Sandrine I need to think. In the hall of mirrors, Loki said something about how he exposes the gods for what they really are. He thinks he's justified in riling them up because only then do they reveal their true nature. That must be what he did to the masks – imbued them with the qualities of the gods and creatures they portray to amplify people's personalities, to bring out the worst in them. Sandrine is excitable and a little vain perhaps, but nothing that deserves punishment.

'Please! Whatever you think of her, she's only human. Let her go!'

The jester snorts. 'Come now, a beautiful bird *should* preen itself.'

Sandrine's neck strains to one side, exposing her white throat. She sees me and tries to speak but all that comes from her mouth is a pitiful squawk. Her eyes flash with panic and then glow pale behind the mask like she's possessed. I watch in horror as her right arm jerks up and her hand makes a claw shape. She drags her fingers down her face and blood gushes from her cheek. Her other hand does the same, long black nails ripping her skin.

She scrabbles at herself faster and faster and a stream of blood drips onto the frosty walkway, forming a puddle beneath her feet. She claws her head and clumps of hair and scalp drop to the ground. She's tearing herself to shreds.

I rush forward but an invisible force holds me back.

Her talon-tipped fingers reach into the holes of her mask and Sandrine jerks and twitches her head, trying to pull away. Her hands keep moving, jabbing again and again.

'Please! Stop this!' I scream.

The joker laughs and Sandrine's body thuds to the ground.

Another moment later Ruth appears in the doorway of the psychic tent and races towards us. 'What happened? Is that Sandrine? Martha, what is it?'

I step back and shake my head. 'I'm sorry, I couldn't stop her. I tried.'

'Stop her from what?' Ruth runs past me and throws herself on her knees. 'My God, her face!' She turns and shrieks, 'Help! Someone get help! Please!'

She sobs and rocks back and forth, gently patting Sandrine's body like she doesn't know what to do. 'It's OK, sweetheart, help is coming. It's OK.'

Stig is bent over as if he's trying not to throw up. I want to go to him, but my legs are so shaky I'm not sure I can move. Sandrine's body lies on the walkway, her feathered mask soaked red.

Stig points a trembling finger. 'Her eyes.'

I cover my mouth, not wanting it to be true. Behind the mask are two bloody pits.

A member of the crew and someone from security thump down the walkway and suddenly I'm pushed back. 'Call an ambulance!' 'Get a blanket, keep her warm!'

Another man in a security jacket heads over to us and Stig straightens and shakes his head. 'She did it to herself. She . . .' He bends over again and the world starts to spin. The man is speaking to me but his words are muffled and slow. My head feels woozy and I stumble to one side. The security man beckons me over but I don't have time to be questioned.

I turn and run, my boots pounding the walkway in time to the thud of my heart. I have to find Karl and Ulva, I have to make her confess. The jester appears before me and I skid to a stop. He holds out his finger and then brings his hand to his ear, gesturing for me to listen. I glance around but there is only the sound of drumming and the cheers of the crowd. And then a terrified scream cuts through the night, followed by shouting and a stampede of feet. This isn't battle music played over the speakers. This is raw and real life.

The joker grins. 'It looks like the last visitor will be leaving soon.' A torrent of people streams towards me. Panicked cries fill the air as bodies jostle and push. I jump off the walkway and they charge past me, yelling and shoving. A swirling tide of dread washes over me. I'm running out of time.

The enormous fire giant strides up the path and I blink, unable to believe my eyes. His long wooden arms are aflame.

He veers and stumbles, a towering inferno on legs, and people below scream and dash to avoid him. His burning arms flail like windmills, catching the string of lights that hang between the big top and other tents. He keeps walking, the lights tangled around him. Electric cables fizz and spark, writhing and jumping like snakes. Bulbs explode with a pop and shatter of glass. People shriek and cover their ears. Above them the lights go out one by one, leaving only the harsh glare of the floodlights.

A woman stops to catch her breath and I rush over. 'What's happening down there?' I ask. Her face is streaked with ash and it looks like she's been crying. She gasps and points to the bag on her shoulder. I open it for her and she pulls out a blue inhaler. She takes a few puffs then holds her breath a moment. 'The performers turned on each other. Fighting, and the fire giant . . .' She shakes her head and draws another desperate breath. 'He was setting fire to people. A man with sackcloth over his face, his head went up in flames!'

I start to ask more but she hurries back into the crowd. It's the masks, it has to be. Loki has gone too far. The masks aren't just bringing out the worst qualities of the gods in people, they're starting to possess them. The ringmaster said that Surt, the giant, started the battle at Ragnarok by setting fire to the world. The masks are making the performers act out the actual story. That's why the man who plays Thor was thumping someone in the field earlier, why the man who plays Loki was stirring up trouble in the costume-change area, why Hel was so angry when I bumped into her. The actors are turning into the gods they portray. Loki is using the masks to make the place destroy itself.

254

A whoosh and bang sounds to my right and I spin around. The giant lies sprawled across the walkway, the tent next to him ablaze. Flames jump and crackle along the canvas at frightening speed. Panicked visitors cough and cover their mouths. The Chinese knife-throwers lift up the rope that lines the walkway and people duck under it and run into the dark caravan field, where they shiver and huddle together in groups.

Oskar paces up and down in his fluorescent jacket, holding a megaphone. He coughs into it and then takes a moment before shouting, 'Do not run! I repeat, do not run! Make your way to the exit if safe to do so, or cross into the caravan field! Emergency services have been called. I repeat, do not run!' His voice falters over the last few words, and he shakes his head as if determined to compose himself. He lifts the megaphone and says a few lines in Norwegian before repeating the message in English.

I shiver and look all around. Lots of people have already left the site. How long will it be before the last visitor goes?

A lady pushing a disabled teenage boy struggles with his wheelchair. The fire giant's legs are blocking the path; she can't get the wheels over them. I run over and drag what remains of the half-burnt stilts to one side and she mutters a 'thank you' with tears in her eyes. Members of the crew yell at one another and someone points a fire extinguisher at the giant, dousing the man inside with white foam. He screams and writhes on the ground, and the smell of burning flesh and charcoal makes me feel sick. I cover my nose and someone grabs my arm.

A blast of hot air hits me like a wall.

'The tent is coming down!'

The man's voice yells again and I'm dragged backwards. Above me, a massive section of canvas flaps like the sail of a ship. Flames flicker at its edge, turning the night sky orange. The wind whips it away and it snaps and crackles before landing on another tent. Sparks instantly catch and turn to flames. The whole place is burning down.

Panic courses through me. I run in one direction and then stop, unsure which way to go. Maybe Karl is down in the field trying to stop whatever's happening. I turn and fight against the flow of people. Among the fleeing visitors are pale-faced Valkyries and bedraggled dwarves and elves. A huge man wearing antlers helps a heavily pregnant woman stagger down the path. An elf girl is crying hysterically and he wraps his other arm around her and sweeps her along too.

The ground is slick with mud and ice and my boots slide around beneath me. A man lies on the slope at the entrance to the field, receiving mouth-to-mouth from the Russian lady, who is wearing tiny antlers on her head and has fringing over her eyes. At first I can't believe what I'm seeing. The display area is shrouded with smoke and dotted with tiny bonfires from discarded firebrands. I can't see clearly, but it looks like dozens of figures are fighting one another. The ravens on stilts, the Norns and frost giants stand high above the rest, picking over the smoky earth like alien creatures. In the distance the sky glows orange: it's not just the bonfire in the ring of skulls, the Viking ship is ablaze too.

The speakers are pumping out music, only now they play eerie instrumental sounds suitable for the aftermath of an apocalypse – the end of Ragnarok. Abandoned handbags and phones stick out from the churned-up snow. There's even a boot. The sound of fighting drifts out from the field and somewhere nearby a man groans. I swallow a tear and wipe my nose on my sleeve. I thought I could do this. I thought I could save the circus and make Odin proud of me, but I couldn't. I've failed.

A figure limps towards me through the smog. Karl's head is bleeding, his face weary. He sees the flames and the thick plume of smoke behind me and makes a muffled choking sound. 'The tents . . . are they on fire?' I nod and tears fill his eyes. '*Nei!*' he mumbles in Norwegian, and then swallows before saying, 'Please, I am ready to listen to you.'

28

HE TRICKED ME

Karl nods without saying a word, his expression tight and anxious. His eyes flash with doubt when I tell him about the wager again, but the tremor in his voice makes me think he's not sure what he believes any more. 'So we need to make Ulva confess?'

'Yes. I know it sounds crazy, but –'

He waves away my concerns. 'I think I saw her by the ring of skulls.'

I peer into the smoky display area and hesitate, not sure I can face the dead. Karl coughs and wipes his mouth, then says, 'Not that way. It's not safe.' We turn right and trudge around the edge of the field. I'm grateful for the bright floodlights.

Karl doesn't try to make conversation, seemingly lost in his own dark thoughts, and I don't either. I don't want to think about what's happening out there in the smoke and chaos and I can't bear telling him about Sandrine. The image of her lying there like a broken bird brings a sob to my throat. I have to stop more people getting hurt, but how? How can human beings be anything but powerless against the gods? A hot, nauseous feeling comes over me and I glance towards the slope. The woman is still giving the man first aid, which means the last visitor hasn't left. I can't give up.

When we get to the Viking ship, Karl gestures at me to stay back. A dense wall of flame roars into the sky, the heat ferocious. A wooden shield crashes down in a hail of sparks and the head of the dragon looks like it will be next. I cough on black smoke, my eyes stinging, and hold my arm up in front of my face.

We walk a little further, then he points. 'There!'

Ulva is in her wolf mask, crouched over a cloaked figure on the ground. The bonfire in the ring of skulls blazes behind her, turning the sky crimson. She looks bigger, almost twice the normal size, the outline of her body dark and hazy. I wipe my eyes in disbelief. She's still human, but it's as if she's been overlaid with the image of a wolf.

We run towards her and she turns her head and growls, her eyes flashing pale behind the mask. Neither of us moves or says a word. Not wanting to make any sudden movements, I whisper to Karl, 'We need to get the mask off her.'

He steps forward and the wolf snarls viciously as Ulva springs at him, knocking him onto his back. She pins him down, her hands on his shoulders. I watch transfixed as she throws back her head and lets out a guttural howl.

'Martha!'

The sound of my name snaps me awake. Karl shouts again and I lunge and tear the mask from Ulva's face. At the same time he rolls over and she tumbles onto her back. She beats him with her fists, but somehow he manages to stand up, hoisting her with him. We each hold one of her arms behind her back. She thrashes and writhes and the mask falls from my hand. She's so strong; we won't be able to hold her for long.

'You need to tell us what happened to Nina!'

Ulva twists her head around and glares at me, her eyes bloodshot. Without the mask, the image of the wolf has gone, but there's still something ferocious about her.

Karl reaches into his pocket and pulls out the carrier bag with the harness inside it. Ulva sees it and goes limp, as if the fight has left her. Karl opens the bag. 'Can you explain this, Ulva?' She lowers her head and I'm not sure if she's about to cry or launch another attack.

Something moves at the edge of my vision and I glance at the ground. The snout of the wolf mask snarls and I want to kick the hideous thing. Instead I pick it up, run forward and hurl it onto the bonfire. It goes up instantly, its fur fizzing and crackling around the edges before the whole thing turns to flame. Thick green smoke snakes into the sky and the image of a giant wolf's head appears, howling and writhing as if held by invisible bonds.

Then it's gone.

Ulva blinks as if she doesn't know where she is. She mumbles something in Norwegian, then sees me and asks, 'What happened?'

Karl takes her hand. 'You don't remember anything?'

She touches her head. 'I remember being in the procession but . . .'

Karl picks up the bag and holds it out to her. 'Do you remember this? Do you remember what happened to Nina?'

Ulva wails, 'I didn't mean to do it. We were arguing and I . . .'

Karl glances at me and back to her. 'What did you do, Ulva?'

'I pushed her.' She says it as if she can barely believe it herself. 'I killed Nina.'

Karl wraps his arms around her and kisses the top of her head. 'Shush now, it wasn't your fault. Everything's going to be OK. It's over, I promise.'

I wipe away a tear of relief. Ulva confessed. I unmasked Nina's killer. Loki will leave the circus and no one else will get hurt.

The noise of fighting and shouting has stopped. Apart from the eerie music and the crackle of flames, the night is quiet. It's really over. I throw my arms around Karl and Ulva and tears of relief turn to joy. I hug them and grin, realising that I did it. I won.

Ulva stares at something behind me, her eyes wide, and Karl gasps. 'Martha, I thought that if Ulva confessed, then . . . ?'

261

I spin around and my body freezes. Twenty or more masked performers are standing there in a line. Their costumes are dirty and singed. Tyr's arm drips with blood. One of the ravens has lost his wings and another his stilts. They all step forward at the same time like automatons, their eyes glowing, and I know it's not actors behind the masks.

'No!' The scream comes from deep inside me. I stare at the sky and yell at the top of my voice, 'Ulva confessed. I won!'

Slow clapping sounds behind me and I turn and see the jester. '*Did* you?' he laughs.

I stare at him and hate twists inside me. All this is his fault.

And then I realise. Loki is the one I need to unmask. He caused Nina's death, just as surely as he caused the death of Odin and Frigg's son. He tricked the blind god Hodr into throwing a spear made from mistletoe, knowing it was the one thing that could kill Baldur. He manipulated things from behind the scenes. I was never going to win the wager, because that would mean getting Loki to confess.

'He tricked me.'

Karl glances at me. 'Who tricked you?'

I point but he doesn't see the jester. Loki must be invisible to him, just as he was to Stig. My body feels heavy, all my energy gone. Loki has won. He won't stop until everyone is dead and the whole place is destroyed. I shake my head, my voice barely a whisper. 'It's over.'

The performers snap their heads towards us and come closer, their masks a confusion of shades and hollows in the flickering light of the bonfire. I scan the faces of gods and animals, their eyes pale behind their masks, and know there's no use trying to reason with them. Karl grabs Ulva's hand and mine and we huddle close together. He pulls us into the circle of skull poles, the heat of the bonfire unbearable behind us. The performers stride forward until they're standing between the poles. The skeletal eye sockets of dogs, stags, and rams regard us with cool disinterest as the performers step closer.

My mind spins, desperate for a way out. Perhaps I can make a bargain with Loki, or offer him something, or trick him. But how? I shuffle closer to Karl and Ulva, afraid that everything will be lost if I don't come up with an idea soon.

The jester laughs to see us cower. 'You humans play-act at bringing our stories to life, but you are nothing to us. We make an army win here, another lose there.' He clicks his fingers and the performers hinge at the middle, their bodies flopping over like puppets whose strings have been cut. He waves his arm and they stand upright.

The jester walks along the line of masked actors and the heat of the bonfire makes the air shimmer around him. He stops when he comes to the man wearing a helmet and a green mask over his eyes. The bells on his cap jingle and then his appearance flickers and changes into the man with long red hair brushed back from his forehead.

He goes over to Karl and takes an elaborate bow, and the old circus manager gasps. 'Nei! My father was right!' He points with a trembling finger, as if he can't believe his eyes, and I realise that for him Loki must have materialised out of thin air.

263

Loki shakes his head at Karl, then rolls his eyes and points at the man who plays him. One of the horns is missing from his headdress and his cloak is ripped. 'It took you ninety years to find someone handsome enough to play me. You had all that time to come up with a decent costume and *this* is what you manage. And black hair . . . really?'

Karl looks at him blankly, his face frozen with fear.

'Nothing to say for yourself? No begging or pleading? I must admit, this is turning out to be rather boring. Well then, time to finish what I started.' Loki raises both arms and suddenly the wind picks up. The performers turn with a jerk to face one another and an image of Sandrine's mutilated face flashes into my mind. And then I feel my body twist, forced to turn towards Ulva. Panic surges through me. He's going to make us destroy one another. We'll be made to tear each other apart. I scan the smoky field, desperately hoping to see Odin. But there's no sign of him or anyone else. No one is coming to save us.

'Wait. I have something to say!' I shout.

Loki sighs. 'Please, save yourself the trouble of trying to outsmart me. Better minds have tried over the years, and all of them failed. I am the Trickster – the master manipulator!'

I look at his smug face, desperate to think of something. I need a way to make him admit that he enchanted the masks.

And then it comes to me. Loki takes such pride in his powers of manipulation; maybe I can use his vanity against him? I call to Karl in a loud voice, 'It wasn't Ulva who killed Nina. I know who was really behind her death.' Like mine, Karl's body is held in paralysis, but his eyes swivel towards me. Loki arches an eyebrow but I pretend not to notice and carry on talking. 'Odin. He's the real mastermind behind this, the one pulling the strings.'

Loki stares at me in surprise and his smile drops.

I focus my attention on Karl. 'Odin was the one who told Loki why the circus stopped performing his stories, about the fire that happened all those years ago and how your father thought he'd started it. Odin laughed and teased him, saying it's usually his fault when things go wrong. He manipulated Loki into causing mischief, knowing he wouldn't be able to resist. It was his idea. Loki is just a puppet, a player in his game.'

Loki strides over and my body becomes my own, released from his control. 'Odin?' he scoffs. 'It was me who thought to bring the masks to life. I saw to it that the human who played Baldur would die, knowing it would sting Odin. He didn't manipulate *me* into anything!'

A flash of understanding crosses Karl's face. He turns to Loki and asks, 'So you're the one who killed Nina. You have just confessed, if I understand correctly?'

Loki's face darkens and for a moment I think he's going to yell, but instead he laughs. It goes on and on. Just when I think he's about to stop, he laughs some more. He glances at Karl and then back to me, wagging his finger. 'Very clever. You know, for a pitiful human, I'm starting to like you.'

I take a deep breath. 'So it's over? You're going to leave?'

Loki shrugs. 'Yes, you won. I can't say I'm happy about it. But those were the terms.' I stare at him, waiting for some clever comeback or final bit of trickery, but he just sneers. 'I'm not one for long goodbyes, so I shall take my leave of you and this place.' He looks around with disdain, as if he didn't think much of it to begin with anyway, and then sighs dramatically. 'I just hope it was worth it. Though I'm sure you checked the terms before entering into a bargain with him. Only a fool wouldn't.'

'What do you mean?'

He looks at me as if I really am stupid. 'Odin doesn't care about this place or the humans here any more than I do. He set up the wager because he needed a way to make you ask for his help. *A gift for a gift.*' Loki sees my surprised face and snickers. 'He used those very words, didn't he? Oh dear, and you took his help without asking the price.'

I think back to the strange vision of the mask. I needed Grimnir's help, I had to say yes. I remember Mum's warning when I first came here – don't trust anyone – and cold dread trickles down my spine. Could I have got it wrong? No, I don't believe it. Loki is lying.

When I don't say anything, he checks his nails nonchalantly. 'Well, it's been a pleasure, as they say. You shall miss me, no doubt. But don't worry – I have a feeling our paths will cross again one day.' He bows, waving his arm with a flourish, and then vanishes.

I stare into space, my muscles tense and my nerves taut, not daring to believe he's really gone. Long seconds pass and I brace myself for him to return but he doesn't.

Relief comes over me, slowly at first and then all at once until I am weak with it. I look at the actors and their eyes are normal. Karl and Ulva hurry along the line, pulling off masks and throwing them on the fire. The faces of gods and animals appear in a swirl of green smoke. One by one the performers stare around, blinking like sleepwalkers waking from a nightmare.

I GO WITH HIM

When we get back to the main site, paramedics and firefighters are there along with the police. The walkways are covered with soot and littered with debris: broken glass, scraps of burnt canvas and people's dropped belongings. The night air reeks of smoke and is thick with falling ash, so that it looks as if it's snowing. Two of the smaller tents have completely burned down and the front of the hall of mirrors is charred black. Firefighters jog past, dragging lengths of hose, and first-aiders help the last few tearful visitors, some seemingly suffering from burns and twisted ankles and others with smoke inhalation and shock.

Karl speaks to a paramedic, who calls for assistance and then hurries down to the field. Some of the actors were able to walk up with us, but most of them are too badly injured. A lady attempts to check me over but I pull away, determined to keep walking even though I don't know where I'm going. I just know I have to find Stig.

Performers and visitors shuffle along the path, all with the same dazed look in their eyes. Like them, I stumble and stare around in bewilderment. My heart beats fast with worry but my mind is numb, my thoughts too slow to comprehend the speed of the destruction. An hour or so ago the circus was filled with expectant faces and laughter, and now it's reduced to a wasteland. I tell myself I should be happy it's over, but how can I feel joy surrounded by such devastation? And for what? For some twisted game of the gods.

I can't ignore the fact that Odin was a part of this. He got me here and then left me to fend for myself. Loki has appeared to me many times, so why couldn't he? All I had was a brief encounter in a vision. Loki's departing words replay in my head and I tell myself that it can't be true. Odin wouldn't have done all this just to trick me into entering into some kind of bargain with him. But then why isn't he explaining things? Is he even pleased that I won the wager? I don't expect gratitude, though it would be nice, but surely I deserve an explanation.

I head towards the entrance, hoping Stig will be there. Ahead of me, Oskar is standing outside the big top, talking to a policeman. He points towards the field and says something then pushes his glasses onto his head and rubs the bridge of his nose. His eyes look red and sore as if he hasn't slept for days. He shakes his head and his expression says what everyone is thinking: how could this have happened?

I turn the corner and circus workers wander by in a daze. Two men in crew jackets talk, their eyes wet with tears, and a group of Valkyries stand in a circle, singing softly with their arms wrapped around one another.

'Martha!' Ruth rushes towards me, her makeup smeared and her auburn hair covered with ash. 'Have you seen Karl?'

'Yes, he's OK. He's gone back to the field with the paramedics.'

'Are there many hurt down there?'

I bite my lip, not wanting to tell her.

Ruth sees my face and stifles a sob. 'I can't understand it. They say the fire giant deliberately set fire to performers and people in the crowd. I've known him for years, he was a lovely guy, it doesn't make sense. And Sandrine. She was such a happy person. Why would she do that to herself?'

I stare at the walkway, not trusting myself to speak. Maybe if I'd done things differently, if I'd figured out Loki's trickery sooner, no one would have got hurt.

Ruth puts a finger under my chin and lifts my head. 'You're OK though?'

I nod. 'I'm sorry about Sandrine. And I'm sorry for what I said about you in the canteen tent.'

She sniffs. 'It's OK. I've been meaning to go back to Ireland for years, and I've got nothing to stay here for now.' She embraces me and her shawl is sodden with anguish. But despite her fear, I can tell she's excited about seeing her daughter again.

'Are you sure you're all right?' she presses me. 'I was worried about you . . . That business with Stig?'

I shake my head. 'I was wrong about him.'

He wasn't the only one I was wrong about. Ruth felt uneasy about the binding spell she'd done, but it had nothing to do with Nina's death. I feel bad for suspecting her and think about apologising, but decide some things are best left unsaid.

Ruth smiles. 'I need to check on the others, but I'll see you soon, yes?' I nod and she hugs me again and whispers, 'I'm glad you're OK.'

She strides away and I turn and look around. Maybe Stig went with the police to give a statement, or perhaps he was injured in the crush. A hot, stifling feeling comes over me, despite the cold. After everything we've been through, I *have* to see him. I need to know he's OK. I need to hug him and tell him again that I'm sorry.

I'm heading for the exit of the circus, hoping to find someone to ask, when he rounds the corner, walking as if in a daze. Then he notices me and his eyes glisten. We stand a few paces from one another as ash drifts around us like snowflakes. He holds out his arms and I step into them, and his coat is heavy with fear and love. He's been wandering the site looking for me, afraid I'd been hurt or worse.

He holds me tight, then pulls away and gazes at me. A smile spreads across his face and I have a sudden urge to tell him how upset I was when he left and how much I've missed him. I think about all the people I read for in the psychic tent. It took courage for them to be vulnerable, to drop their masks and show their true feelings.

He lowers his head towards mine and our bodies press close. His coat tells me how much he wants me, how he wants to spend days and nights wrapped up with me and never let me go. More impressions surface in my mind, a rush of emotions and flashes of childhood memories, and I have the feeling he wants to give himself to me. He doesn't want to hold anything back; he wants me to know everything there is to know about him. I'm familiar with the emotion – it's how I felt at the cabin.

We kiss for a few wonderful moments, and then I pull away. 'I'm sorry for thinking the worst of you, Stig.'

He shakes his head as if it's forgotten. 'We all make mistakes. I'm sorry I didn't reply to your messages. If I could change things, I would.' He strokes my hair and whispers, 'Maybe I could come to the island with you.'

'I thought you were afraid to go back to the cabin.'

'I am, but I want to be with you, Martha.'

He holds my hand and his glove reveals it's true. Despite the horror of what happened to Sandrine and seeing the dead at the cabin, he wants to be with me. Something flickers in my chest, but it's not a buzz of elation. Stig has so much goodness in him, but now I can use my gift properly I can see other things about him too. He runs from his problems, going from one person and place to the next. That's why he's so upset with his mum for selling the house he grew up in – he doesn't feel that he belongs anywhere now. Inside he's lonely and lost and he thinks the best way to avoid feeling that way is to move on, like his dad always did. And like his dad, he has a romantic notion of riding off into the sunset. The idea of staying put and working things out isn't quite so appealing.

Stig squeezes my palm and looks at me hopefully, but I don't know what to say. He admitted himself that he goes into things too quickly, and something tells me a relation-ship would be a distraction from what he really needs to do: deal with his feelings about his parents' break-up and work things out with his mum. If I'm honest, a relationship wouldn't be right for me either. I have so much to think about with Mum and the tree and starting a new life. As much as it would be lovely to have his support, I need to focus on myself.

'I'm sorry, but I don't th—' A ball of sadness rises to my throat as I realise what I'm about to do.

Stig's expression darkens, hope replaced by disappoint-ment. He sees my face and gives me a tiny smile. 'Hey, it's OK to want something and not at the same time. Life is like that sometimes, complicated.' There's such kindness in his voice, I can tell he doesn't want me to feel bad.

My heart twists at the thought of losing him. Forcing myself to be strong, I take a deep breath and hold his gaze. 'I know I didn't answer you before, but I did miss you.' Stig arches an eyebrow and I continue. 'It's just . . . I need to focus on Mum and things, and I think it would be better if you went home and saw your family.'

He huffs and I hold his sleeve and pull at the material. 'It's what you need to do.'

Stig gives me a wary look. 'Is that your professional opinion?'

I nod and continue, 'You need to stop running, Stig. You need to work through whatever issues you have with your mum, and you need to make a life for yourself and put down roots.' He smiles at me wonderingly and dimples appear on his cheeks. 'If I'd known you were this good, I'd have insisted on my twenty-minute reading in the psychic tent.' When I don't answer, his shoulders slump and his voice becomes serious. 'I suppose you're right. I can't keep avoiding Mum forever.'

I fight back tears and try to smile. 'Maybe we can meet up as friends some time.'

'I'd like that. And I'm going to text every day.'

'And I might reply . . . if I'm not too busy.'

He laughs and then glances towards the exit. 'The police are organising transport and hotel rooms for people. Do you want me to get your bag from the caravan?'

I take the key from my pocket and hand it to him. 'Thanks. I'll meet you by the entrance in a bit.'

The thought of saying goodbye makes my throat ache with unshed tears. He looks at me and his eyes shine with emotion, as if he knows this could be the last time we'll be together.

'Back soon, then.'

I nod and his gaze lingers on me a moment longer, then he turns and walks away. I tell myself it's for the best, but my heart aches with regret. I know it's the right thing to do, but that doesn't make it hurt any less. I watch him go, and then my thoughts turn to Mum.

I phone her and she answers instantly. 'Martha!'

'Everything is fine. I'm coming home now.'

'Oh, thank goodness. I did as you asked and I went to the tree.' She sounds out of breath and for a moment I worry she's scared, but then I realise it's excitement I can hear in her voice. 'I met the Norns. They showed me a vision in the well and I understand now. I know why it's so important that I take care of the tree. You have such an important destiny to fulfil, Martha. You mustn't worry about me.'

'Really? You spoke to them? That's amazing. I want to hear all about it when I get back.'

'We'll see each other soon enough, don't worry. I love you, Martha, and I'm so proud of you and what you're about to do.'

I ask what she means but the line goes dead. I'll be home soon; she can tell me then.

Flashing blue and red lights flicker through the wall of trees in the distance. I pause by the ticket tent and gaze across the snowy field. The wooden archway is lit by a single spotlight. Surrounded by swirling smoke and falling ash it looks indestructible, as if it's been standing for a thousand years and will stand for a thousand more.

I know I won the wager, but I still can't believe it's all over. I glance behind me at the destroyed circus, relieved to finally leave this place, and then turn back and gasp. Nina is standing in front of the archway. She gazes at me with empty black eyes then nods. It feels like a farewell. I have so many questions; was she sent to haunt me against her will? Where will she go now?

I raise my arm, about to call out, when a figure emerges from the swirling smoke behind her: a man in a grey cloak and a wide-brimmed hat, holding a walking staff. He rests a hand on Nina's back and a smile spreads across her face. She looks at me one final time, then walks through the archway and vanishes.

The man touches the brim of his hat in acknowledgement, and I stare at his long grey beard and single eye in wonder. I know who he is, but I want him to tell me.

'Who are you?' I call.

He turns and speaks loudly, his voice rich and velvety. 'A single name have I never had. Grimnir the Masked One, Ofner and Svafner, Gatherer of Lost Souls am I.' He bangs his walking staff and shadows stream towards him from every direction. I step back as a rush of icy air chills my face. More and more of the dead come, sucked into the archway. They swirl and spin, just like the others did when they followed the rope into the tree, and I smile with relief. The dead won't be left to wander; he'll return them to where they belong.

I walk towards him and stop a few paces away. I can't let him leave without giving me answers. 'Why did you choose me? What was it all for? Please, I need to know.'

Odin holds out his right fist. 'You like things that are easy to understand, meanings so small and neat you can hold them in the palm of your hand. Win or lose, good or bad – everything black and white, as my friend Loki likes to say. But things are never that simple.' I study his face and his single blue eye sparkles. 'Sometimes the truth is grey, and sometimes there is none to be found.' He uncurls his fingers and his palm is empty.

The gesture reminds me of the vision when I opened my fist and found the metal pin. I reach my hand to my cloak and touch it now. Odin smiles kindly and his laughter lines deepen. 'The sign of the Valkyrie. A gift for a gift and the price is danger.'

276

Suddenly I understand what he meant in the vision. He wasn't trying to trick me into asking for his help, he was offering me a reward for winning the wager! If I accept and become a Valkyrie, I need to know it could be dangerous. Loki was twisting things and trying to fill my head with doubt, as usual.

Odin touches the brim of his hat and adds, 'My gift to you – now yours for the taking.'

'So the wager . . . it was to test me?'

Odin strokes his beard. 'Yes and no. The wager was the lesser of two evils – an exercise in damage limitation, if you will. Loki would not be deterred; I took the steps necessary to lessen the impact of his mischief.'

I nod, accepting his justification. Loki was set on destroying the entire circus and everyone here. People were hurt, but it could have been worse if I hadn't won the wager.

'As for testing you, I prefer to call it an opportunity for observation. Just because a person can see things others cannot, doesn't mean they're able to perceive the truth. That skill requires a certain wisdom. I had to know if you were ready.'

He looks at me expectantly and a thrill of trepidation sparks and catches fire inside me. Can I really do this, become one of Odin's chosen ones? I've already said goodbye to Stig, and Mum told me not to worry about her or the tree. She said she was proud of what I'm about to do, as if she knew this would happen.

I grip the pin and a profound sense of belonging radiates through me. Being at the circus has helped me discern truth from lies, but it's given me something else too. Learning how to use my gift properly has taught me to trust my intuition. I don't know what the future holds, but this feels right.

I step forward and ask, 'So where are we going?'

Odin chuckles and a universe of possibility twinkles in his eye. 'Somewhere we can see clearly. Come, I have much to show you.'

I pause, anxiety fluttering inside me. 'I will come back, though, to this world, I mean?'

'Of course.'

There are so many questions I want to ask, so much I want to know, and this is my chance. The women of my family have made countless sacrifices to fulfil their sacred duty to water the tree. Their journals are full of musings about their place with the gods, and I owe it to them to seize this opportunity. Taking a deep breath, I straighten my shoulders and go to his side. The archway glows with brilliant white light, whatever lies beyond it obscured by mist. Odin steps through and I go with him, my heart full of pride.

THE END

Acknowledgements

First and foremost, a heartfelt thank you to my writing mentor, Lee Weatherly. Incredibly generous with her time, Lee chatted over my various plot ideas (and was the one who came up with the circus setting!) as well as offering feedback on my early drafts. Thank you for always pushing me to go bigger and bolder.

I must also thank my dear friend Maddy Elruna, a gifted shaman and tarot reader who introduced me to the Norse gods. She has been a constant source of encouragement throughout my writing journey, as well as providing a valuable link to Odin.

A lot of people are involved in the making of a book and I've been blessed with a great team at Hot Key, especially my editor, Felicity Alexander, and Leo Nickolls, who did the stunning cover artwork. Not to mention one of the best agents in the business, the very wise and ever-patient Amber Caraveo of Skylark Literary.

I also owe a huge debt of gratitude to the many beta readers who read early versions of this story. Each one gave me amazingly useful feedback that helped to shape the book. There are too many to mention them all, but a particular thank you to Charlotte of Myth-Take Reads, and Gemma Scammell, tutor on the Young Adult Fiction course at Cardiff University, and student Emma Carr-Ferguson, for her impressively insightful comments.

I've also been lucky enough to have wonderful support from family and friends (a special shout-out to everyone in the village!), for which I'm endlessly grateful. No one has read more of my work than my mum, Leoni, who has the dubious honour of reading my very first drafts. Thank you for all your help over the years.

It genuinely means the world to me that readers enjoy my stories. I'm grateful to everyone who has taken the time to chat to me at events, contacted me via social media or left a kind review. Writing can be a frustrating and lonely business, and there have been times when your enthusiasm has given me the boost I needed to keep going – so thank you.

Last but not least, a big thank you to my son Alfie, for allowing me to share my love of Norse mythology with you and just for being you. I love you to infinity. I also don't know where I'd be without my partner, Andy. Thank you for your unwavering belief in me, endless cups of tea, and for always knowing the right thing to say.

ABOUT THE AUTHOR

Rachel Burge works as a freelance feature writer and
has written for a variety of websites, including
BBC Worldwide, Cosmo and MTV. She lives in
East Sussex with her partner, son and
black Labrador, Biff. She is fascinated by
Norse myth and swears she once saw a ghost.

🐦 @RachelABurge
📘 RachelBurge
📷 rachelburgewriter
📌 burge0709
www.rachelburge.co.uk

HOT KEY BOOKS

Thank you for choosing a Hot Key book.

If you want to know more about our authors and what we publish, you can find us online.

You can start at our website

www.hotkeybooks.com

And you can also find us on:

We hope to see you soon!